# The Wirral Gal

## In Speke

### Thomas Brant

# CHAPTER 1 – Welcome to Speke
## Monday 2nd September 2024

Penny Carmichael had to chuckle at the irony of what name she had chosen for her radio career. After all, being born on the Wirral and having a grandfather who was a John Lennon fanatic had left her no choice but to embrace the Beatles connection. Her grandfather had insisted that she was destined for greatness, though Penny Lane, as she planned to style herself on air, wasn't so sure.

Being a graduate of the Bauer Academy, Penny had cut her teeth in the highly competitive world of CHR (Contemporary Hit Radio). She'd spent countless hours refining her delivery, working on her banter, and perfecting the art of "hitting the post"—the timing skill of talking up to the second a song's vocals begin. But this wasn't Bauer anymore. Manic Radio Liverpool was a whole new world.

The irony was not lost on Penny, being a Wirral native stepping into the world of Scouse radio. The divide between the Wirral and Liverpool was more than just a stretch of water; it was cultural, linguistic, and, as she quickly learned, deeply ingrained in the listeners' expectations. But Penny Lane had chosen her name to bridge that divide—or at least, that's what she told herself.

Looking at the logos on the sign of the door, she had to chuckle, as she saw that the hub was home to Chester & The Wirral Vibes, the local station often mocked by Liverpudlians for being "posh radio", Western Ulster Vibes, a Londonderry and Derry station that seemed wildly out of place in Speke, North Wales Sound, which covered Wrexham, Mold, Rhyl and Llandudno, Cumbria Vibes, a Carlisle station whose quiet countryside tones felt almost alien to the hustle and bustle of Liverpool, Ulster Vibes, the pan-Ulster station that added a unique Northern Irish flavour to the eclectic mix, Manic Radio Lancashire, the Preston and Lancaster station that brought a touch of the Red Rose County's charm, and finally Manic Radio Liverpool, the flagship CHR station for the region.

Then there was Manic Radio UK, the national version of Manic Radio, whose logo proudly sat at the top of the signage, as if reminding everyone that while they might work for a local branch, the corporate mothership always loomed large. Penny couldn't help but feel a mix of awe and apprehension as she stepped into the Speke hub for the first time. It was a hive of activity, with the polished energy of a station that prided itself on being cutting-edge yet relatable.

"It's just like Bauer and the Hits Radio network, but with legacy brands instead of what Bauer did back in April and scrapping the legacy names," Penny muttered to herself as she pushed the heavy glass door open. "It's weird not hearing Radio City on the airwaves anymore, but I guess that's the way things are going."

Inside, the Speke hub was everything Penny had expected and more. Brightly lit studios with soundproof glass offered glimpses of Sue and Kyle, the network early afternoon presenters, on-air while the various local teams for Lancashire, Ulster, Liverpool and Cumbria were getting ready for their drive time shows. Penny knew that some Manic stations had a regional Breakfast and Drive show, while others merely had Breakfast only, thanks to OFCOM rules requiring a minimum of 4 hours a day of locally-produced content. In Liverpool, though, the rules were a little more flexible, as the city's long-standing reputation for vibrant radio meant Manic Radio Liverpool operated as a flagship station for the north-west, producing not just breakfast and drive, but most of the daytime Network content too. It was a testament to Liverpool's status as a radio powerhouse, even in an era where local identity was being increasingly swallowed by national brands.

"...Northern Ireland are dealing with anti-immigration protests in County Tyrone," Penny heard from a small 'broom closet' studio as she walked through the corridor. Looking at the door plate and she saw it was labelled 'News Presentation - North West'. Looking at her watch, she saw that it was quarter to two.

"Are they pre-recording the next news bulletin?" Penny wondered aloud. It wasn't uncommon in the CHR world, especially when juggling regional updates across multiple stations, but it still struck her as a bit surreal to see so much being run out of this single, sprawling hub in Speke.

Looking through the window, she saw a news presenter holding several scripts, each with a logo or logos relevant to which regional station the bulletin was destined for. The logos ranged from Manic Radio Liverpool to Chester & The Wirral Vibes and North Wales Sound. Penny recognised the juggling act; she'd learned at Bauer how CHR news teams balanced quickfire local updates with the broader regional and national context their stations demanded.

"Oi, you must be Penny Lane!" a voice called out from behind her, startling her out of her observations. She turned to see a woman with brown hair and a mischievous grin, holding a coffee cup in one hand and a clipboard in the other. "Toni Green. I do the network evening show. Nice tits."

Penny blinked, momentarily caught off guard by the audacious greeting. She laughed nervously, unsure whether to thank Toni or laugh along.

"Er, thanks, I guess?" Penny replied, adjusting her backpack on her shoulder.

Toni grinned wider, clearly enjoying Penny's awkwardness. "Relax, love. Here at Manic, we do coke like it's going out of fashion, and casual hook-ups are smiled upon. Especially on Big Weekenders. Let me guess... 40DD?"

Penny blushed fiercely, her mind scrambling for a response. Toni's unapologetically brazen attitude was like nothing she'd encountered in her relatively polished, professional upbringing at Bauer.

"38D, actually," Penny shot back before she could stop herself. The words hung in the air for a beat before Toni burst into laughter, her cackle echoing through the hallway.

"There you go!" Toni said, wiping a tear from her eye. "You'll fit in fine here, Lane. There are only two rules round here - no shagging on air, and no snorting coke while doing links. Orgies, group sex, threesomes... they're all practically encouraged off-air as long as you keep it quiet enough for the mics not to pick it up. Hell, if you get yourself knocked up, you get a £32k bonus in your pay, £2k a year until the baby's 18. It's not an official policy, and the menfolk aren't allowed to know about it, but most of us try and get ourselves up the duff as much as possible. I should know, gorgeous."

Penny's face went through a kaleidoscope of emotions—shock, amusement, and mild horror—all in the span of about three seconds. She had been warned that Manic Radio had a reputation for being a little wild, but this was something else entirely.

"Erm... good to know?" Penny stammered, unsure if Toni was being entirely serious or just pulling her leg. Judging by the twinkle in her eye, it was probably a mix of both.

Toni took a long sip of her coffee, clearly unfazed by Penny's awkwardness. "You'll get used to it, Lane. This place is nuts, but it's the good kind of nuts, most of the time. You've got to be a bit mad to survive CHR, especially here. And trust me, once you get your head round the chaos, it's the best gig in the business."

Penny tried to smile, but her nerves were starting to bubble up again. This was her first real chance to prove herself on a station with this much clout, and she couldn't afford to muck it up. "I'm sure I'll get the hang of it," she said, more to herself than to Toni. "So… do you have any advice for a newbie?"

Toni's grin softened slightly, and she leaned against the wall, crossing her arms. "Yeah. Rule number one: don't take yourself too seriously. The listeners don't want to hear a robot. They want you. Well, the you that's a bit polished and sparkly, but still human. Rule number two: hit the post, every time. Miss it, and they'll never let you live it down. And rule number three—most important of all—everyone's bisexual by time they've been here a month. You'll be snacking on cock, pussy and arse as much as you like. The cocaine is cheap, and the parties? Well, let's just say they make Glastonbury look tame. You'll learn quickly who's up for what, but don't let it distract you from the job. On air, you're a pro. Off air... well, it's Manic, innit?"

Penny blinked again, unsure whether to laugh, run, or call HR. Instead, she forced a smile. "Sounds… lively."

"Lively's one word for it," Toni said with a wink. "But don't worry, Lane. You're going to smash it. Just remember, it's all about the vibe. The music, the banter, the chaos—it's what keeps the listeners hooked. Oh, and don't be afraid to ruffle a few feathers. The bosses love a bit of drama, as long as it trends."

Penny nodded, though her heart was pounding. She wasn't sure what she'd expected when she signed her contract with Manic Radio Liverpool, but it certainly wasn't this. Still, she reminded herself why she was here: to make a name for herself, to bring her personality to the airwaves, and, if she played her cards right, to prove that Penny Lane could become a household name.

"Come here," Toni then said, gesturing to a broom closet with a grin on her face, and Penny was both curious and apprehensive as she followed. The broom closet turned out to be literally a broom closet, and as soon as Penny stepped in and turned, she felt Toni's lips against hers. Penny froze, her mind racing before she returned the kiss, her tongue darting out and tentatively meeting Toni's. Her heartbeat hammered in her chest as her thoughts scrambled to process what was happening. The kiss was fiery and impulsive, and as quickly as it had started, Toni started kissing her way down the younger presenter's body, the narrow space of the broom closet adding a sense of urgency and electricity to the moment.

Undoing her blouse as Toni started placing hickeys on her neck, Penny knew that she wanted this, that the last time she had been kissed like this was her ex-boyfriend, who had ran off with a Hits Radio Manchester producer and left her heartbroken and second-guessing her self-worth. But this—this was different. Toni's boldness was intoxicating, her hands confident and unapologetic as they slid along Penny's waist. Penny couldn't suppress a moan, her nerves momentarily drowned out by the rush of adrenaline and a desperate need to feel wanted.

Then she felt Toni unhook the back of her skirt, slowly and deliberately letting it slide to the floor. Penny gasped, the realisation of what was happening hitting her in a way that sent her heart racing even faster. This was wild, impulsive, and absolutely not in her original plan for her first day at Manic Radio Liverpool.

"Toni," Penny whispered, her voice a mix of hesitation and desire. "What if someone walks in?"

Toni smirked, her confidence unwavering. "Let 'em. If it's a bloke, then it's a cock we can share. If it's a lass, well, they might want a taste too." She winked and then paused, studying Penny's expression with a mix of mischief and concern. "Unless you're not into this, love. No pressure, honestly. We're all about consent here—chaos, sure, but it's gotta be the fun kind."

Penny hesitated, her pulse hammering in her ears as she processed the moment. Part of her wanted to dive headfirst into the madness, to let go of every inhibiting thought that had held her back. But another part, the part raised on professionalism and self-preservation, whispered caution.

But the madness side won out, and she pushed her panties down, allowing Toni easy access to finger her while she leaned back against the closet wall, letting the rush of adrenaline override her nerves. The small, confined space amplified every sensation, every touch, every whisper of fabric against skin. Penny knew this was reckless, unorthodox, and a far cry from the polished, professional radio world she'd envisioned herself joining. But maybe, just maybe, this was exactly what she needed to shake off the constraints of her past.

Toni's confidence was infectious, her touch electric as she navigated the boundaries of their mutual curiosity. Penny's breath hitched, her mind momentarily free from overthinking. In that fleeting, intense moment, she felt alive in a way she hadn't in years—raw, unscripted, and undeniably herself.

Suddenly the door opened, and Rory Carter, her soon to be colleague on the Manic Radio Liverpool drive show walked in, a grin on his face. Penny remembered that Toni had said that if a bloke walked in then it was a cock that they could share, and her cheeks flushed a deep crimson as she realised the sheer absurdity of the situation. Rory's grin widened, clearly enjoying Penny's expression of sheer shock.

"Well, this is a hell of a first impression," Rory quipped, leaning casually against the doorframe. "I was just coming to grab a mop, but this is way more entertaining. Mind if I joined in?"

Penny looked at Toni, who nodded, and Penny decided that if Toni was alright with it, then she might as well embrace the chaos fully. Penny nodded hesitantly, her cheeks still burning with embarrassment but also tinged with a strange thrill. This was not how she had imagined her first day at Manic Radio Liverpool, but then again, nothing about this station seemed to follow the rules.

Toni grinned wickedly, stepping back slightly to make room in the cramped closet. "Rory, you sly dog. Don't just stand there. Shut the door and prove you're not just here for a mop."

Rory chuckled and closed the door behind him, the small space now feeling even tighter with three people inside.

It was then that Penny noticed the bulge in his denim shorts and felt a sudden wave of nervous anticipation. This was uncharted territory—wild, impulsive, and completely off-script. She'd come to Manic Radio

Liverpool to carve out her professional identity, to prove she had what it took to make it in the cutthroat world of CHR radio. But here she was, in a literal broom closet, in a situation that felt more like the plot of a risqué comedy than the beginning of a serious career.

The next thing Penny knew, she noticed Toni had released her own skirt, and was wearing panties that had no crotch or, more accurately, were designed specifically for easy access during situations like this. Penny's mind raced as she considered what to do next. This was reckless, absurd, and not at all how she'd envisioned her first day on the job. But then again, this was Manic Radio—a world she'd been warned was unpredictable, unfiltered, and unapologetically chaotic.

"Toni," Penny said, her voice trembling slightly as she tried to inject some humour into the moment. "Does every new recruit get this kind of induction, or am I just special?"

Toni laughed, the sound throaty and carefree. "Oh, love, you're special, alright. Welcome to Manic. Hope you can keep up."

Penny couldn't help but laugh nervously, caught between embarrassment and exhilaration. She glanced at Rory, whose mischievous grin showed no signs of discomfort or hesitation. If anything, he seemed entirely at home in this bizarre initiation ritual.

"You're not going to let this slip to management, are you?" Penny asked, half-joking, though there was a real edge of concern in her voice.

"Management?" Rory scoffed, unbuckling his belt. "They don't care if we shag our way through the building. As long as consent is clear and we hit our listener metrics, you could do it on the studio desk for all they care." His tone was playful, but there was an undeniable edge of truth to his words.

"You know, I remember my first day at Bee Manic," Toni said, grinning as Penny got down on her knees. "I walked into the building, and my colleagues, Emma Lang and Kyler Thompson, naked as the day they were born, shagging, in one of the offices, and you know, her tits were 42DD, smashed up against the glass, Kyler fucking her like a whore. Within a few weeks, I was all in on the Manic chaos. It's not for everyone, but once you embrace it, it's a hell of a ride." Toni's words hung in the air as she glanced at Penny, who was clearly caught between wanting to impress her colleagues and grappling with the surreal, unpredictable nature of her new workplace.

Penny chuckled as she crawled over to Rory, the tight broom closet making the three bodies have even less room than what it had had before. Seeing Rory's jeans having opened, she grinned, as she saw the opening in his boxers.

* _ * _ * _ *

"Hi, I'm Abby Blue, your producer," Penny heard later when she was sat in the production office, listening to the briefing that she was about to receive for her debut on Manic Radio Liverpool. She tried to focus on Abby's words, but her mind was still racing from the whirlwind of her induction earlier. The chaotic energy of Manic

Radio had already proven itself to be unlike anything she'd encountered before, and it was only her first day.

Abby was in her late twenties, with a sharp bob haircut and a clipboard that seemed permanently attached to her hand. Her expression was as though she had been thoroughly ravished by one of the staff in the building, and Penny noticed a slight baby bump on her abdomen. The bump was subtle, but it caught Penny's eye, triggering a fleeting thought about Toni's offhand comment regarding the station's "pregnancy bonus." Penny stifled a nervous laugh, forcing herself to refocus on Abby's words.

"Right, Penny, we're all set for your debut on the Drive show, one of two local slots that we have here at Manic for the Liverpool audience," Abby continued, her tone brisk but not unkind. "You'll be co-hosting with Rory Carter, as you know, and he's one of our best Drive presenters… top 3 across the Manic network."

"Who's the top slot for the Drive show?" Penny asked, eager to latch onto any shred of normalcy amidst the chaos of her first day.

Abby smirked knowingly, flipping through her clipboard. "That'd be Pete Smith, does the Midlands Drive. 52, has been in radio for 30 years, still at the same station that he had joined when he left Uni and became a presenter at 21. He's a legend, proper old school. Doesn't quite fit the Manic mould, but his listener figures are through the roof. Second is the Network Drive, one we have for areas that don't have their own localised slot—Danny O'Neil does that slot here from... Hey Danny!"

Danny O'Neil entered the room with a swagger that could only come from years of being a trusted voice on air.

Dressed in a Dua Lipa Radical Optimism t-shirt, a pair of ripped jeans and Louis Vuitton trainers which Penny knew were at least £800 and so pristine they looked like they had never touched a Liverpool pavement, Danny gave Penny a quick once-over and a broad, easy grin.

"Ah, you must be the new blood! Penny Lane, right? Gotta say, bold move going with that name around here. You're either gonna be a smash hit or the bane of every Scouser who hears you. Where ya from?"

"Hoylake," Penny replied, bracing for the inevitable reaction. "Born and bred on the Wirral."

She watched as Danny burst out laughing before his accent went from the kind of accent you would hear on a CHR station to a Wirral twang that sounded more like something out of Chester & The Wirral Vibes.

"Hoylake, eh? I'm a Heswall lad, born and raised," Danny said with a broad grin, his Wirral accent emerging in full force. "Abby here's a New Brighton gal, and Calvin, one of the Northern Ireland hosts, is, for his sins, not actually from Northern Ireland... he's a true paddy from the other side, a Dublin boy through and through." Danny's grin widened. "Rory's a Manc, so's Toni, Kyle and Sue are Brummies who came up here back in 2020 when Covid forced Manic to network everything bar Breakfast and Drive, and Big Lou, the mid-morning host, he's a Geordie who's pretending to be a Londoner. You see, here at Manic, you have to ditch the local accent and embrace the

CHR neutral voice," Danny explained, his tone shifting to a polished, generic accent that Penny recognised immediately. "Doesn't matter if you're from Liverpool, London, or Llandudno—on air, you're all about energy, clarity, and relatability. That's the Manic way."

Penny laughed at the tattooed swagger of Danny O'Neil as he effortlessly shifted accents like flipping a switch. She could already tell he was the kind of person whocould win over any room, a natural performer with a razor-sharp wit.

"Good to know I'm not the only Wirral escapee," Penny said, her own accent softening slightly as she subconsciously adjusted to the room's energy. "Though I'm guessing I'll have to tone it down for the listeners."

"Not tone it down, love," Danny said with a wink. "Just smooth it out. Manic doesn't do local quirks on air, unless it's for a bit. The bosses reckon a nice neutral CHR voice is what keeps the advertisers happy. Doesn't stop us from taking the piss off-air, though. There's only 4 on-air personalities allowed to keep their local accents in the whole Manic network."

Danny leaned casually against the desk, flashing his trademark grin as he counted off on his fingers. "First up, there's Pete Smith on the West Midlands Drive—he's too much of a legend to mess with. Proper Black Country accent, and his audience wouldn't have it any other way. Born and bred in Dudley, been in radio for 30 years, and has been on the mic for all sorts of major events, from when Princess Diana died all the way through to Lizzy carking it. Then there's Tim and Ellen on the East

Midlands Drive - Tim's a Derby bloke who's been on air for 23 years and has the sort of East Midlands twang that listeners love, and Ellen's a Walsall girl who worked with Pete for 27 years, so has the authority that comes with being a trusted voice in the region. She's got that warm, down-to-earth tone that makes you feel like you're chatting with your best mate. The fourth? The Scots, Paddy and Taffy hosts, as they have to present to audiences who feel more connected to those specific accents. It's part of the regional charm that they won't let go. But for the rest of us, we're all singing from the same CHR hymn sheet—bright, upbeat, and universal."

Danny's explanation was a reminder of how far Penny had ventured from the world of Bauer. She felt a mix of pride and nerves, knowing she'd have to navigate this tightly controlled yet wildly unpredictable environment.

"Anyway, I had to admit," Danny continued, "When the bosses played your tape and I was on your panel, I had to admit, you sounded like you were a Hattie Pearson clone. You trained with Bauer, didn't you?"

"Yeah, Bauer Academy," Penny admitted, nodding. "It was intense, but it gave me a solid foundation. Hattie Pearson was one of the guest trainers during the course. I guess I picked up some of her style."

Abby let out a low whistle. "Good. The bosses expect all the women here on air to sound like her and the blokes to sound like Capital's Roman Kemp or Hits Radio's Fleur East if they could bottle their energy and charisma. Manic wants stars, Penny, not just voices. If you're aiming to be a household name, you're on the right track. Just make sure you add your own twist. People don't want a clone; they want you, but with that Manic polish."

Penny nodded, her nerves settling slightly as the camaraderie in the room began to put her at ease. Despite the overwhelming chaos of her induction, she was reminded why she'd pursued this career. She loved radio—the music, the storytelling, the connection with listeners. Even amidst the whirlwind of eccentric personalities and unorthodox traditions, she was determined to make her mark.

"Right then," Abby said, tapping her clipboard with authority. "You and I are heading to Studio 2 for our show with Rory, Danny's next door in Studio 1 as his network drive show goes out, and you'll see some of the others in their studios as we pass them. Welcome to the jungle, Penny Carmichael."

****

# CHAPTER 2 – Settling In
## Tuesday 3rd September 2024

Penny noticed an email waiting for her in her inbox as she logged into one of the spare computers at the Speke hub on her second day. The subject line read: "Meet & Greet: Regional Head of Programming". She clicked it open, scanning the message quickly.

**From**: *alan.hamilton@manicradio.group*

**To**: *penny.charmichael@speke.maincradio.co.uk*

**Subject**: *Meet & Greet: Regional Head of Programming*

*Hi Penny,*

*Welcome to Manic Radio Liverpool! I hope your first day was... memorable.*

*Let's have a quick chat today to discuss your role, how you're settling in, and what to expect moving forward. Please pop into my office at 1:30. I'm on the second floor—look for the door with my name on it.*

*Cheers,*

*Alan Hamilton*

*Regional Head of Programming, North West*

Penny sighed, feeling a mix of curiosity and apprehension. She wasn't sure what Alan's tone implied—was he joking about her induction, or had word spread already about her whirlwind first day? Shaking her head, she made a mental note to be on her best behaviour during the meeting.

"Looks like you're about to get the corporate induction," Mags O'Leary, one of the Ulster Vibes presenters said, chuckling as she passed behind Penny. "Alan's cool. He's 31, an Oxford grad and is like the rest of us, always open to a shag if it's consensual. Don't let the suit and title fool you. But if he offers you a coffee, make sure you say yes—his personal stash is miles better than the office swill." Mags winked and continued, leaving Penny more perplexed than ever about the peculiar culture at Manic Radio.

Penny glanced at her watch. She had a couple of hours before her meeting, so she decided to familiarise herself with the newsroom and production areas. The Speke hub was a labyrinth of sleek, glass-panelled offices and buzzing studios. The air was charged with the hum of activity—presenters recording links, producers running last-minute edits, and techies troubleshooting what sounded like a particularly stubborn soundboard issue in Studio 3.

Her steps led her past Studio 1, where the mid-morning show, led by Big Lou, or Louis Cole as he was known, a heavyset man in his 30s who had previously been with Tyne & Wear Tune, a station that had joined the Manic network in 2022 when Manic and Lite merged. Lou was in full flow, delivering links with charm and energy, as though he was 18 and fresh out of university. Penny paused for a moment to watch him through the glass. Lou exuded a natural charisma that made every word he said seem effortless. His booming laugh filled the studio, and Penny could see why he was a favourite among listeners.

Suddenly she saw that he noticed her and motioned for her to come into the studio. Penny was unsure of the invitation but decided to take a deep breath and go for it. As she stepped into Studio 1, Lou waved her over with a broad grin.

"Ah, the Wirral gal herself!" Lou's voice was as rich and warm in person as it was on air. "Penny Lane, isn't it? I've been hearing whispers about you already. Don't worry, all good things—mostly."

Penny laughed nervously, still trying to adjust to the high-energy environment. "Thanks, I think. I didn't mean to interrupt, I was just passing by and—"

"Nonsense!" Lou interrupted, gesturing to the spare chair near his desk. "You're not interrupting. This is Manic Radio—we thrive on spontaneity. Sit down, let me introduce you to our lovely listeners as we're live on the various Manic stations across the UK."

Before she could protest, Lou hit the button for the mic, his voice shifting effortlessly into his on-air persona as the advert for McDonalds faded out.

"Alright," and then he stopped, as the split links said the stations name in his voice, depending on which region or local station the listener was tuned into, before restarting his sentence. "Listeners, we've got a special surprise for you today! Joining me in the studio is our newest recruit, straight out of the Wirral and ready to bring her sparkle to the airwaves—say hello to Penny Lane!"

Penny blinked, startled by how quickly she was being thrown into the spotlight. She hesitated for only a moment before leaning into the mic, her instincts kicking in.

"Hi, everyone! It's great to be here," she said, her voice bright and confident. "Thanks for having me, Lou—and for the, um, spontaneous introduction!"

Lou grinned, clearly pleased with her quick recovery. "Ah, spontaneity is what we do best here, Penny. So, tell us—what's it like making the leap from the Wirral to the wonderful world of," another pause for the split links to insert the station names before continuing. Penny noticed that he was pressing a button every time he paused so it would insert the split link in the broadcast.

"Well, Lou, if I'm honest, it's a bit nerve-racking. I did my first drivetime show with Rory-"

"Which can be found on the Manic Prime app, available on your app store," Lou interjected, and Penny could see from the script that was printed out that he had to promote certain items during his show, unlike her yesterday, when the entire show between her and Rory was fully scripted, down to the banter that they had between links.

Penny was a bit confused why, unlike her and Rory, Lou was permitted to have bullet points and bare bones talking points rather than a fully scripted show, but she decided to ask him when he was off air and not broadcasting live. She nodded to herself as Lou finished his promotional line, flashing her a quick smile as he queued her up to continue.

"Right, so as I was saying, I did my first drivetime show with Rory yesterday," Penny said, her voice steady despite the on-air nerves. "Let's just say it was... a crash course in the Manic way of doing things! But I'm loving the energy here—there's never a dull moment, that's for sure."

Lou chuckled, his laughter rolling through the studio like a wave. "That's the spirit, Penny! And don't worry, Rory's a bit of a whirlwind, but you'll get used to him. Anyway, would you like to introduce the next song?"

Penny looked at the PlayoutONE Pro software that Manic used and saw that the next track scheduled to play was a throwback to October 2006, and the UK number 1 for 2 weeks: "Welcome to the Black Parade" by My Chemical Romance.

Penny couldn't help but grin. "Oh, Lou, you've set me up perfectly here," she said, leaning into the mic with growing confidence. "This is a perfect throwback to when emos were taking over MySpace and eyeliner sales were through the roof. Get ready to scream along, because here's Welcome to the Black Parade, here on Manic Radio, across the UK."

As soon as Penny said that, the familiar notes automatically played as the system played out the iconic piano intro to "Welcome to the Black Parade." Lou gave Penny a thumbs-up, his grin widening as he muted the mic and leaned back in his chair.

"Not bad at all, Penny," Lou said, his tone genuine. "Quick on your feet, confident delivery... and you actually know your music history. You'll go far if you keep that up."

Penny smiled, her nerves settling slightly. "Thanks, Lou. I was a bit nervous jumping in like that, but it's nice to know I didn't completely mess it up."

Lou waved off her modesty with a casual gesture. "Nerves are good—they keep you sharp. Just remember, listeners can hear everything. Confidence and authenticity are key, even when you're winging it. And, trust me, here at Manic, there's a lot of winging it."

As the track continued to play, Penny glanced at the schedule in the PlayoutONE software. The system displayed the next few songs, an ad break, and a quick news update at the top of the hour. She noticed Lou had handwritten notes scattered across his desk, scribbled with time markers and reminders to mention sponsors, trending hashtags, and upcoming events.

"So, Lou," Penny said, lowering her voice so only he could hear, "why are you allowed bullet points while Rory and I have to follow fully scripted shows? I mean, it felt like we were reading off an autocue yesterday."

Lou chuckled knowingly, swivelling his chair to face Penny. "Ah, welcome to the Manic hierarchy, love. It all depends on your show's purpose, your audience, and, let's be honest, how much trust the bosses have in you. See, slots like mid-morning, early afternoon and the overnight ones, they're the 'quiet' slots, where nothing major happens."

"So, they're the ones where the freedom to experiment and show a bit of personality is allowed?" Penny asked, catching on quickly.

"Exactly," Lou replied, leaning back in his chair. "Shows like mine are about keeping the audience engaged but not too tightly scripted because people listening at this time want something a bit more laid-back. Drive shows, on the other hand, are prime time—biggest audience, biggest sponsors, and the bosses want control over every word. It's all about consistency and making sure nothing goes off the rails. You were a Bauer lass, right?"

Penny nodded, leaning in as Lou continued his explanation. "Yeah, Bauer Academy. We had Fleur East come in once for a guest session. She said the same thing—prime time is all about hitting the key points, no room for improvisation unless you're seasoned enough to pull it off without scaring the sponsors."

Lou nodded approvingly. "Fleur's spot on. You'll find it's a balancing act—bringing your personality while ticking all the corporate boxes. There's only 3 Drive shows where scripts aren't used, and that, like me, it's merely bullet points in the whole Manic network."

"Which three Drive shows get away with just bullet points?" Penny asked, her curiosity piqued.

Lou grinned, leaning in conspiratorially. "Well, there's Pete Smith on the Midlands Drive. He's a legend—thirty years in the business, and his audience would riot if they thought he was reading off a script. He's near enough unfireable as Birmingham is one of our key markets...

hang on, I need to do this quick link and I'll finish answering you in a sec." Lou swivelled back to the mic, smoothly transitioning into a pre-recorded split link for each region:

"Alright, hope you're enjoying your Tuesday afternoon! Coming up, we've got some big tunes to keep you going, plus I'll be giving you the lowdown on how you can win tickets to see Dua Lipa live—stay tuned to Manic Radio!"

As the split link rolled out across the different stations, Lou muted his mic again and turned back to Penny. "Right, where was I? Oh yeah, the Drive shows. Midlands Drive with Pete Smith, East Midlands Drive with Tim and Ellen—Ellen's got that no-nonsense vibe, and Tim's got the easy charm to match. Plus, both have been in their regions forever, so the bosses trust them to manage things their way. The third? Well, it's London Drive, obviously—Maya and Dante. They've got the audience numbers and the charisma, so they're given a bit more leeway. If you're in a key market like Brum or London, one where Bauer, Global and several independent stations are competing for every listener, the bosses let you play a bit looser—so long as you're delivering the numbers and not scaring off the advertisers. Maya and Dante are ex-Global, used to be on Heart London, so the bosses know they're safe hands, and Pete, Tim and Ellen are former Bones Network crew."

"Bones Network?" Penny asked, confused.

Lou chuckled, leaning back in his chair as "Welcome to the Black Parade" continued to play. "Ah, you wouldn't know unless you've been in the industry a while. Bones

Network was this small, independent radio group back in the day—proper grassroots stuff. They had a reputation for nurturing talent and giving presenters a lot of freedom. Woody Bones was the Ronan O'Rahilly of the ILR era, the guy who believed in radio being authentic, raw, and driven by the presenter rather than corporate scripts. Woody built a loyal following, but by the mid-2010s, the Bones Network got swallowed up by Breeze in 2010, and then in 2019 it all became part of Manic when Breeze Media was bought out. A lot of the old Bones Network crew ended up staying on because they had such strong local followings—Pete, Tim, and Ellen are part of that legacy. The bosses let them keep doing their thing because, well, it works."

"Ronan O'Rahilly? Who's he?"

Lou's eyes lit up with a mix of amusement and disbelief as Penny asked her question. He leaned forward, clasping his hands together as if he were about to tell her the secret to the universe.

"Ronan O'Rahilly? Penny, you've got to know this if you're going to survive in this business. He's practically the godfather of modern pop radio! The bloke who launched Radio Caroline back in the 1960s, one of the most famous pirate radio stations in the world."

Penny furrowed her brow, vaguely recognising the name but not entirely familiar with the story. "Pirate radio? Like the ships broadcasting from international waters?"

"Exactly!" Lou exclaimed, his enthusiasm infectious. "Back in the day, the BBC had a monopoly on radio, and they weren't exactly spinning the top 40 hits people actually wanted to hear. Ronan, being the maverick he was, got himself a ship, parked it in the North Sea, and started broadcasting what people loved—pop music, rock 'n' roll, you name it. He basically stuck two fingers up at the establishment and said, 'If you won't play it, I will.' Radio Caroline became a phenomenon. Changed the game forever."

Penny nodded slowly, her curiosity piqued. "So, what happened to him and Radio Caroline?"

"Well," Lou continued, leaning back in his chair, "the government didn't take too kindly to pirate stations undermining their rules. They passed the Marine Broadcasting Offences Act in '67 to shut them down. But by then, Ronan had already left his mark. The BBC was forced to change, creating Radio 1 to compete with the pirates. That's the legacy—he paved the way for commercial radio, even if it took a while for it to become what we know today."

"That's incredible," Penny said, genuinely impressed. "So, Woody Bones was like a modern-day version of him?"

"Sort of," Lou agreed with a grin. "Woody wasn't running pirate stations, his network of, towards the end, 12 stations in Central England, were all licenced stations in a market which was congested. He only got the licences because, as well as playing the hits of the '80s and '90s, the Radio Authority added conditions such as a requirement in Dudley to play Soul, or in Walsall to play Reggae, or in Derby to play local Folk music. Woody leaned into those niches, making each station feel authentic and deeply connected to its community. That kind of local focus gave him a die-hard audience. Even when Breeze Media bought the Bones Network, those stations kept their identity for a while. Manic inherited some of that legacy, but you'll notice it mostly survives in the personalities, not the playlists."

Penny nodded, absorbing the story. It was fascinating to see how radio's history still shaped the industry today. She glanced at the clock; there were just a few minutes left in the track, and she realised her impromptu appearance on Lou's show was coming to an end.

"Thanks for the history lesson, Lou," she said with a smile. "I'll have to look up more about Woody Bones and Ronan O'Rahilly. It's inspiring to hear about people who really shook things up in radio."

Lou chuckled, tapping a button to unmute the mic. "Anytime, Penny. And speaking of shaking things up, let's wrap this up with some classic Manic energy."

He leaned into the mic, effortlessly switching back into his on-air persona. "That was Lady Gaga and Poker Face, here on the Manic Radio network. Now, after the news, I'll be telling you how to enter the £500k Money Drop, and then we'll be going in the mix with this week's Top 15 hits."

Penny noticed that the next few minutes were scheduled to be advertisements, with split advertisements across the different Manic Radio stations depending on their regions, and Lou gestured for Penny to follow him out of the studio as the show continued on autopilot for the moment.

"Right, Penny," Lou said as they stepped into the corridor. "Word of advice—if you want to survive at Manic, you've got to learn how to balance the chaos with the structure. For Drive and Breakfast, they want Hattie Pearson and Mike Toolan clones, people who have the perfect mix of personality, polish, and professionalism. But for other slots, like mid-morning or evening, there's more room to breathe and find your voice. Keep that in mind, and you'll do just fine."

Penny nodded, her mind buzzing with all she'd learned so far. She was beginning to understand the intricate balancing act that came with being part of a quasi-national CHR station like Manic Radio. The station demanded high energy, tight control during peak hours, and a willingness to embrace its unpredictable culture off-air.

As she made her way back to her desk, Penny checked her watch. Her meeting with Alan Hamilton was fast approaching. Taking a deep breath, she reminded herself of Lou's advice: confidence and authenticity were key. No matter what curveballs Manic Radio threw at her, she was determined to find her place in this vibrant, chaotic world.

With that thought, she squared her shoulders and headed for the lift, ready to face whatever came next.

* _ * _ * _ *

If Penny had three words to describe her meeting with Alan Hamilton, then sex, cocaine and champagne would be the exact three words that summed it up perfectly. Alan Hamilton's office on the second floor was nothing short of impressive. It combined sleek modernity with a sense of laid-back cool—glass walls adorned with awards, photos of legendary presenters, and a minibar in the corner stocked with everything from water to top-shelf whisky. Penny stepped inside, immediately hit by the smell of fresh coffee brewing on Alan's personal machine.

Walking out of the office after the meeting, the taste of cocaine on her lips, cum leaking from her knickers, and the lingering taste of champagne in her mouth, Penny couldn't help but marvel at just how far removed this world was from the buttoned-up professionalism she'd experienced at Bauer.

The fact that the sex had been consensual, and that she had, surprisingly, initiated it and not Alan, added a new layer of complexity to her perception of Manic Radio. It was unorthodox, wild, and definitely not covered in any employee handbook. But the raw, unfiltered atmosphere was oddly liberating, even if it was wildly outside her comfort zone.

That it wasn't just Alan in the room but a fellow newbie, Weston O'Rourke, a Ballymena native who had joined the Western Ulster Vibes Breakfast team as a producer from Bauer Media Ireland, from Cool FM, one of the few Hits Radio stations that hadn't changed its name, and he had double teamed her with Alan, which she had enjoyed.

Weston, she learned, was 26, so four years older than her, a Catholic Unionist, an oxymoron in itself as most

Unionists in Ireland were Protestant and carried himself with a quiet confidence that contrasted sharply with the over-the-top chaos she had seen elsewhere in the building. His voice had that soothing Northern Irish lilt that could probably calm the most chaotic of days, and during their... unconventional introduction, he'd maintained an easy charm that was equal parts disarming and intriguing.

The irony that he was a redhead and looked like Ed Sheeran made Penny laugh, especially as he was rocking an Ed Sheeran t-shirt, ripped jeans and trainers that looked like they'd been pulled straight from a photoshoot for a trendy Belfast magazine. As Penny adjusted her skirt and tried to compose herself in the lift back to the ground floor, she couldn't help but reflect on just how surreal her first two days at Manic Radio Liverpool had been.

Turning round, she chuckled as she saw a grin on Weston's face as he was texting on his phone, that look of smug satisfaction plastered all over him. Penny shook her head, biting back a laugh as the lift pinged open on the ground floor.

"You alright there, Weston?" she teased, adjusting her

bag on her shoulder and giving him a knowing smirk.

Weston glanced up from his phone, his grin widening as if he had been caught out but didn't care. "Aye, never better," he replied, his Northern Irish lilt warm and casual. "Y'know, that was my second time shagging someone. First time was with my flatmate... a couple of evenings ago after she finished work."

Penny's laugh came out before she could stop it. "Wait, wait, you're telling me that after one day at Manic, you're already a serial seducer? What is it about this place? Is there something in the air—or is it just the champagne?"

Weston shrugged nonchalantly, slipping his phone into his pocket. "Could be the champagne. Could be the fact that this place seems allergic to the concept of 'boundaries.' Or maybe it's just the charm of us Manic newbies, eh?"

She rolled her eyes but couldn't suppress a grin. "Alright, Casanova. Just don't make a habit of it. You're going to get a reputation. Out of curiosity, who's your flatmate?"

"Toni Green," Weston replied nonchalantly, as if it were the most normal thing in the world. Penny's jaw nearly dropped as her mind immediately flashed back to her own whirlwind introduction to Toni the day before.

"Toni Green?" she repeated, incredulous. "You mean our Toni Green, network evenings Toni Green, coke and chaos Toni Green?"

Weston gave her a cheeky wink, clearly enjoying her reaction. "Aye, that Toni Green. She rents out the spare room in her flat. Don't look so shocked, Penny. She's actually grand once you get past the... larger-than-life exterior."

Penny shook her head in disbelief. "This place is unreal. I've been here less than 48 hours, and I've already kissed her, been thrown into a live studio, and now I find out she's your flatmate."

"Yeah. She's dating another Manic presenter funnily enough, but they're in an open relationship, so it's not a big deal," Weston finished with a shrug, as if this level of chaos was standard operating procedure. "She's got her... unique way of doing things, but she's a good laugh. Keeps things interesting."

Penny leaned against the lift wall, laughing softly as the doors closed. "Interesting is definitely one way to describe it. You know, I had my first Manic experience with her yesterday."

Penny shared her story of her whirlwind introduction to Toni Green as the lift hummed down to the ground floor, punctuated by Weston's occasional chuckles and wide-eyed expressions of disbelief. By the time they stepped into the bustling reception area of the Speke hub, Penny realised just how quickly she was adapting to the sheer unpredictability of her new workplace.

The chaotic energy of Manic Radio was palpable, from the hurried producers juggling schedules on their phones to the presenters laughing loudly over coffee in the corner. Penny adjusted her bag, glanced at Weston, and smirked. "Well, I suppose this is our normal now."

Weston laughed, his Northern Irish lilt making even the simplest comment sound charming. "Aye, Penny. Normal's a bit of a stretch, but I reckon we'll survive. Or we'll go mad trying. Y'know, we're alike in a way... both of us being former Bauer, you in their academy and me former Cool FM. We've seen the polished side of CHR radio, and now we're thrown into... well, this." Weston gestured broadly at the buzzing chaos of the Speke hub around them.

Penny chuckled, nodding in agreement. "Yeah, this definitely isn't what I expected when I signed up for a 'quasi-national CHR station.' But I guess that's the charm of Manic, isn't it? Total unpredictability. Anyway, I've got an hour until my meeting with Rory and Abby for my show, so fancy a quickie in Studio 2?"

As Penny's cheeky offer hung in the air, Weston laughed, his face lighting up with a mixture of surprise and mischief. "Studio 2, you say? I reckon you're getting the hang of the Manic way faster than I did. Let's go!"

****

# CHAPTER 3 – Unravelling Weston & The Scouse Divide
### Friday 6th September 2024

"Yo, Carmicheal, come here," Penny heard from Sue Parkinson, the early afternoon host who partnered Kyle Robinson on the Manic Radio network show that followed Big Lou. Looking up from her social media posts on her new profiles that Manic had encouraged her to create with the Penny Lane name, she saw the 35 year old Birmingham native beckoning her over with a grin that was equal parts friendly and mischievous. Sue had a reputation for being quick-witted and sharp-tongued, and Penny was equal parts curious and wary as she approached.

“What’s up?” Penny asked, trying to keep her tone casual as she joined Sue near the coffee machine.

Sue leaned against the counter, her freshly filled mug in hand. “First off, welcome to the madhouse,” she said, her Brummie accent softening the sarcasm. “Secondly, I hear you’ve already been inducted into the Manic way, courtesy of Toni and Lou. Fair warning, they’re just the tip of the iceberg.”

Penny chuckled nervously, unsure how much Sue knew— or how much she was joking. “Let’s just say it’s been a... memorable few days.”

Sue smirked. “That’s one way to put it. Anyway, I wanted to give you a heads-up. Kyle was digging into that Weston... and he seems to have made Kyle's antennas twitch a bit. You know, all the contradictions about him, such as being a Catholic who's a Unionist, producing the Breakfast show for Western Ulster Vibes. It's not sitting right with Kyle. He's been around long enough to smell when something doesn't add up."

Penny frowned, glancing over at Studio 2 where Weston was recording some content for the overnight show that airs across the two Northern Ireland stations, as there was some regional variation there, like Scotland and Wales, outside the standard regional Breakfast and Drive shows to the Network schedule. She knew that, in Scotland, the late night show, the early Breakfast and 2 other shows on weekends were locally produced from the Dundee hub, with Cardiff producing a pan-Wales Sunday evening show and Northern Ireland having its own early-breakfast show and 1am-4am slot. She knew that Bauer and Global had slight regional variations for their own Scottish, for Bauer, and North Wales, for Global, and it seemed that Manic followed a similar pattern. The quirks of these variations had fascinated Penny, but Sue's comment about Kyle's suspicions snapped her out of her thoughts.

"What do you mean, 'doesn't add up'?" Penny asked, lowering her voice.

Sue sipped her coffee, her expression thoughtful. "Kyle's got a good radar for bullshit, especially when it comes to people's backstories. His dad's West Midlands Police, so he's got a knack for spotting when someone's not entirely on the level. Weston's whole 'Catholic Unionist' thing has him raising an eyebrow. It's rare enough as it is, but to then find him jumping from Cool FM in Belfast to here, working on a station with a vibe that's worlds away from what he'd be used to? Kyle thinks there might be more to it. And then there's the quiet confidence yet he's shagging people as if it were about to be made illegal."

Penny tilted her head, intrigued but unsure how much to read into Sue's words.

"Maybe Weston's just one of those people who's good at adapting," Penny suggested, trying to keep the conversation light. "I mean, he's here, he's doing the work. Does it matter if he's a bit of an enigma?"

Sue chuckled, shaking her head. "You're sweet, Penny. But in this place, nothing stays an enigma for long. It's like a jungle—everything gets uncovered eventually, whether you like it or not. I did GCSE History when I was at school, and one of the things we learned about was The Troubles."

"The Troubles?" Penny interjected, her brows furrowing.

"What's that?"

Sue looked at her with mild surprise, setting her mug down on the counter. "You don't know about The Troubles? Alright, history lesson time. Sit tight, love."

Penny shifted her weight, leaning against the counter as Sue continued.

"The Troubles were a bloody conflict in Northern Ireland that started in the late '60s and dragged on until the Good Friday Agreement in '98. Basically, it was a violent political and sectarian conflict between two main groups: the unionists, mainly Protestants, who wanted Northern

Ireland to stay part of the UK; and the nationalists, mainly Catholics, who wanted it to join a united Ireland. It was a mess—bombings, shootings, protests. Lives torn apart on both sides."

Penny nodded slowly, starting to piece together the weight of what Sue was saying. "And Weston being a Catholic Unionist… that doesn't fit the usual narrative?"

Sue shook her head. "Not at all. Most Catholics would lean towards nationalism. Weston's position is like a unicorn in Irish politics—rare and usually controversial. Kyle's uncle is a British Army Colonel who's based in Northern Ireland, and Kyle said he's going to look into Weston's background because it feels too unusual to ignore. Not necessarily dodgy, but… peculiar. Kyle's seen enough to know there's usually a story behind someone like Weston."

Penny glanced back toward Studio 2, where Weston was now leaning back in his chair, headphones on, seemingly engrossed in his recording session. The idea that there might be more layers to her new colleague intrigued her.

"Well," Penny said after a moment, "if Kyle digs something up, I'm sure we'll all hear about it. But for now, Weston seems alright to me. A bit… unique, but who isn't in this place? I mean, you're a Brummie who moved to Liverpool when Manic networked your slot, and Toni's a Manc, so she's no stranger to shaking things up. Maybe being an outlier is just part of the Manic DNA."

Sue raised an eyebrow, her smirk returning. "Fair point. This place does seem to collect the misfits and the mavericks. Just keep an eye on Weston, yeah? Not in a suspicious way—more like… curious. People like him usually have a reason for being where they are."

Penny nodded, making a mental note to stay alert without jumping to conclusions. As unpredictable as Manic Radio was, it was also full of surprises—some welcome, some less so. She grabbed her own mug of coffee and headed back to her desk, her thoughts now a tangle of curiosity about Weston and the peculiar dynamics of her new workplace.

* _ * _ * _ *

It was 3:55, 5 minutes until Penny's fifth Drive show with Rory of her career at Manic, and she was worried, as there had been several comments on X complaining that a Hoylake girl like her shouldn't be hosting on the Liverpool station, with one saying that she should "stick to hosting on Chester & The Wirral Vibes where she belongs." The comment gnawed at Penny as she glanced at her laptop, refreshing the stream of messages coming through.

"Should stick to Chester & The Wirral Vibes?" she spat as she read the message aloud, her frustration bubbling over. "Honestly, like Liverpool hasn't had presenters from further afield before. Does nobody remember when Tony Snell did Breakfast on Radio Merseyside? He's from Birkenhead!"

Rory, lounging in his chair opposite her in Studio 2, raised an eyebrow at her outburst. "First online trolls getting to you, Penny?"

Penny sighed, running a hand through her hair. "It's not even the trolls, Rory. It's just... I'm here to do a job, to connect with the audience, and this divide—it's like a brick wall. The Wirral isn't the moon! It's right there!"

She jabbed a finger toward the window as if pointing out the Mersey.

Rory chuckled, spinning his chair lazily. "Welcome to Scouse radio, love. The Mersey divide's been around forever. Liverpool versus the Wirral, North versus South, Everton versus Liverpool. It's practically a sport here. You're just the latest player on the pitch."

Penny shot him a look. "That's not very reassuring."

He smirked, leaning forward conspiratorially. "Here's the thing, Penny. They're giving you grief because they don't know you yet. Scousers are fiercely loyal to their own, but once they let you in, they're yours for life. You've just got to prove you're not some posh bird from Hoylake looking down her nose at them."

"I'm not posh!" Penny protested, indignant. "Just because I'm from Hoylake doesn't mean I spent my weekends at polo matches! Hell, my great-granddad on my mum's side was from Vauxhall, worked on the Overhead Railway before it shut down in the 1950s and then he got a job at Anfield as a groundskeeper. My gran on my dad's side was from Southport, worked for Merseyside County Council in the '70s before it got dissolved, and my dad himself grew up in Bootle before moving to the Wirral after he met my mum at a gig at Eric's Club." Penny's voice rose with frustration, her Scouse pride bubbling to the surface.

Rory leaned back, clearly amused by her rant. "There you go, love. That's what they need to hear. You've got roots, connections. Drop those nuggets on air, and they'll warm to you. Scousers love a good story, especially one that ties into their history."

Penny stared at him, considering his advice. "You really think that'll work?"

"Absolutely," Rory said with a confident nod. "Make it part of your on-air persona. Be open about your background, but don't shy away from the Wirral thing either. Own it. Make a joke about it—show them you're not taking yourself too seriously."

Before Penny could respond, Abby's voice crackled through the studio intercom. "Alright, you two, we're live in two. Penny, you've got the opener today. Make it count."

Penny took a deep breath, adjusting her headphones as she glanced at the PlayoutONE screen displaying the countdown to the live broadcast. The intro music began, and the familiar energy of a live show buzzed through her veins.

As the music faded, Penny leaned into the mic, her voice bright and engaging. "Good afternoon, Liverpool! It's Penny Lane and Rory Carter here on your Drive show, keeping you company as you navigate the end of the workday. First up, it's the news with Anna Kincade, and then I'm going to drop some Scouse truths about me, because apparently some of you think I belong on Chester & The Wirral Vibes. Spoiler alert: I've got more Scouse roots than you might think, so stick around, and let's settle this once and for all!"

Penny grinned at Rory as the news jingle began, her heart pounding. She had thrown down the gauntlet live on air, deciding to tackle the criticism head-on. Rory gave her an approving nod, clearly enjoying her boldness.

As the news segment wrapped up, Penny prepared to dive into her planned response. Rory leaned over and whispered, "Remember—banter, not battle. Keep it light but own it."

The news ended, and Penny's voice filled the airwaves once more. "Alright, Liverpool, let's clear something up, shall we? There's been some verrrry interesting comments on my socials," she said, stretching the word for dramatic effect. "Apparently, being from Hoylake means I don't belong on Manic Radio Liverpool, that I'm a posh girl who should be broadcasting to Chester and the Wirral, that I should be sipping tea with my pinky out while discussing yacht prices on Chester & The Wirral Vibes and nipping down Cheshire Oaks to get Tommy Hilfiger handbags and that, right?"

Penny paused for a moment, letting the tension build as she leaned into the mic. She could see Rory grinning out of the corner of her eye, clearly enjoying her approach.

"Well," she continued, her voice bright with a touch of cheekiness, "let me tell you a little story..." she said, turning on a Scouse accent for dramatic effect, "Who knows who was born and brought up in the Scottie Road area of Vauxhall in the '40s, who's as Scouse as a Liver Bird and is buried in Allerton Cemetery? Clue, she had a hit with 'Something Tells Me (Something's Gonna Happen Tonight)'."

 Penny leaned into the mic, letting the silence linger for just a beat before delivering the punchline with a flourish.

"Cilla Black, of course! And guess what? My great-granddad on my mum's side lived... four doors down from her. Yep, he and her family were practically neighbours in the Scottie Road days. And guess what? He always said, 'That Priscilla White, she's got a voice that'll take her places.' So, there you have it—Scouse roots, right in the family tree! He was a Red all the way, and would sit in the Kop week in, week out, going to every home match at Anfield he could manage. He'd call out Shankly's bad decisions, Fagan's blunders and even Houlier's choices to bench Owen. He worked on the Overhead Railway for a bit in its final year, and then got a job down at Anfield as an assistant to the groundskeeper, keeping the pitch pristine for the likes of King Kenny and Rushie."

Penny watched as Rory then moved closer to the microphone. "Woah, so your great-granddad lived up the road from the legendary Cilla Black and worked on the Overhead Railway before tending the pitch at Anfield? Penny, you've just gone from 'posh Wirral girl' to bona fide Scouse royalty in one story!"

Penny laughed, feeling the tension ease as she continued, "And that's just one branch of the family tree! My gran on my dad's side was from Southport, worked for

Merseyside County Council until it got dissolved, and my dad grew up in Bootle before meeting my mum at a gig at Eric's Club. So, to all you lot on X giving me grief—how's that for Scouse roots?"

Rory chimed in, "There you go, Liverpool. Penny Lane, straight out of Hoylake but with more Scouse heritage than a Sunday roast in the pub after a win at Goodison—or Anfield, depending on your persuasion."

Penny grinned, riding the wave of momentum. "Exactly! Now, how about we put this whole Wirral-versus-Liverpool nonsense aside and get back to what really matters—keeping you lot entertained as you head home. Stick around, we've got the latest from Dua Lipa coming up, but first up, who'd like to win £500k?"

Penny leaned back in her chair as Rory read out the script for the £500k Money Drop competition, his polished delivery slipping seamlessly into the rhythm of the show. As he hit the final line, Penny took a moment to glance at the texts and tweets flooding in.

"Alright, Penny, you win this one—proper Scouse story there!"

"Never knew about Cilla Black's neighbours being Reds—class story, Penny Lane!"

"Fair play, love. Not a bad way to shut the trolls up!"

She couldn't help but smile. Rory caught her eye and gave her a thumbs-up, his grin widening.

"See?" he said once his mic was muted. "Told you they'd warm to you. You've just got to give them a reason to root for you. Scousers love a good underdog, and you've got a killer story to back you up."

Penny nodded, feeling a flicker of confidence take root. "Thanks, Rory. I'll admit, I wasn't sure if going straight for it was the right call, but... I think I'm getting the hang of this."

"Course you are," Rory said, leaning back in his chair. "Now let's see if you can handle the next hour—it's all you for the banter links. I'll just be here, looking pretty and letting you shine."

Penny laughed, rolling her eyes. "Oh, you're all heart, aren't you?"

The rest of the show went smoothly, the earlier tension melting away as Penny leaned into her natural charisma. By the time the final track faded out and the outro played, she felt a buzz of satisfaction—a sense that she'd taken a step closer to finding her footing in the whirlwind world of Manic Radio Liverpool.

****

# CHAPTER 4 – Toni's Secrets
## Monday 9th September 2024

Even though it had been 36 hours since her first Big Weekender, what the Manic presenters at the various hubs called their weekend social parties, where sex, orgies, drugs and copious amounts of alcohol flowed freely, Penny still felt like she was catching her breath. The Big Weekender had been a whirlwind of unfiltered chaos, equal parts exhilarating and exhausting. She'd spent most of Sunday trying to recover, curled up in her flat in Birkenhead, replaying the events in her mind.

But now it was Monday morning, and Penny was back at Manic Radio Liverpool, sitting in the break room, her hangover and lingering fatigue hidden behind a strong cup of black coffee and a pair of oversized sunglasses. Looking at her watch, it was half past 2, meaning she had an hour and half until her and Rory would be sat in Studio 2, ready for their drive show. She glanced around the break room, which was unusually quiet for this time of day. The usual buzz of the Manic office seemed subdued, but Penny suspected that everyone was still shaking off the effects of the weekend.

Toni Green sauntered in, her confidence as palpable as ever. Dressed in a cropped The Weeknd t-shirt and a short, leather, green skirt, with fishnet tights and a green hair scrunchie. Penny had to laugh at how effortlessly Toni embodied the chaotic energy of Manic Radio. She looked like someone who had stepped out of a music video, her every move oozing with the kind of confidence Penny could only dream of. Toni grabbed a can of Red Bull from the fridge, cracked it open, and perched on the edge of the table across from Penny.

"Survived the Big Weekender, did you?" Toni asked with a smirk, her voice teasing but warm. "You don't look half bad for someone who was dancing on tables at three in the morning and was deep throating cocks like it was about to go out of fashion. You know, babes, you looked hot with all that cum over you."

Penny nearly choked on her coffee, her cheeks flushing a deep crimson. Toni's audacious comments always left her scrambling for a response. She wasn't sure whether to laugh, blush, or hide under the table.

"Erm... thanks, I think?" Penny stammered, trying to muster a smile. "I guess that's... a compliment?"

Toni laughed, a full, throaty sound that filled the quiet room. "Oh, it's definitely a compliment, babes. You threw yourself into it like a pro. The Big Weekender's not for the faint-hearted, and you smashed it. Trust me, not everyone can handle their first one as well as you did. We've had newbies bolt halfway through or spend the night crying in the loos. But you? You were in the thick of it. That's proper Manic energy. I remember my first Big Weekender. I was 21, like you, a rookie in the world of radio, but unlike you, my ex was working at the same station at the time."

Penny tilted her head, curiosity piqued. Toni rarely let her guard down, and the mention of her past felt like a crack in the armour. "Your ex? That must've been... complicated."

Toni smirked, taking a sip of her Red Bull. "Oh, you've no idea. One thing that's not known about me is that Link, my son, isn't my first child."

Penny blinked, caught off guard by Toni's revelation. The room seemed to grow quieter, the hum of the vending machine the only background noise as Toni's words hung in the air.

"Wait… you've got another child?" Penny asked, her voice a mixture of curiosity and caution. She could sense that this wasn't a story Toni shared lightly.

Toni nodded, her usual bravado momentarily giving way to something softer, more vulnerable. "Yeah. I had a daughter when I was 15. Got preggers when I was in secondary school to my then boyfriend who was two years older than me. Cal, his name was. Callum Ellington. He's the Regional Head at Dudley now."

Penny leaned forward, her coffee forgotten. Toni's tone was different—quieter, more introspective. It was a stark contrast to her usual boldness, and it made Penny feel like she was witnessing a rare moment of unguarded truth.

"Wow," Penny said softly, not entirely sure how to respond. "That… must have been tough."

Toni shrugged, her lips curling into a half-smile that didn't quite reach her eyes. "Tough doesn't even begin to cover it, babes. I was a kid myself, barely old enough to understand what I was getting into. And Cal… well, let's just say he wasn't the epitome of maturity. You know the Skater boy in Avril Lavigne's song? That was him to a T. Full of dreams, no real plan, and not a clue about responsibility. When I found out I was pregnant, he said all the right things at first—'we'll get through it,' 'we'll be a family,' all that romantic crap. But reality hit hard and fast. He freaked out, left me to deal with the fallout, and vanished. Anyway, on my first day at Bee Manic, care to guess who I saw?"

Penny raised an eyebrow, leaning in slightly as her curiosity deepened. "Callum? You're kidding. He was there?"

Toni nodded, her expression a mix of exasperation and amusement. "Oh, he was there alright. Strutting around the Bee Manic office like he owned the place. Turns out he'd climbed the ranks while I was busy trying to piece my life back together. It was surreal, seeing him after all those years. And trust me, babes, he remembered me. You see, back then I was Cassie Longton, a name I've buried as deep as I could. I walked into Bee Manic on my first day, ready to reinvent myself as Toni Green, and there he was, like a ghost from my past, staring at me as if I was some sort of reminder of what he'd tried to forget."

Penny leaned back in her chair, absorbing the weight of Toni's story. The transformation from Cassie Longton to Toni Green suddenly made sense—more than just a rebranding, it was an escape, a reclamation of her identity.

"And he recognised you straight away?" Penny asked softly.

"Bastard didn't just recognise me, he was going to spill the beans on my past to all and sundry unless I slept with him," Toni said, her voice low but laced with a bitter edge.

She took another sip of her Red Bull, her gaze fixed on the table as if the memories were playing out in her mind like a film reel.

Penny's jaw dropped. "He what? That's… that's horrible, Toni. What did you do?"

Toni shrugged, her nonchalance clearly an act to mask the hurt. "What could I do, babes? I was 21, fresh into the world of radio, and terrified of being outed as this messy little girl from Alty with a kid in care. So, I... I gave him a blowjob. I... I remember thinking how much I missed his cock as I sucked it, how I used to enjoy the intimacy back when we were teenagers, but it also made me hate myself. I did it to shut him up, to protect my new life as Toni Green. I told myself it was just one moment, one thing to keep my past from ruining everything I'd worked for."

Toni's voice trembled slightly, the bravado slipping further. She glanced at Penny, as though assessing her reaction, before continuing. "But you know what? It worked. He kept quiet. And I swore to myself that no one would ever have that kind of power over me again. That's when I decided to own the chaos, to embrace it. It was where I met Kyler, my now ex-husband, and we built something... intense. A marriage, a family, and eventually, a spectacular disaster. Covid led us to marry, and Covid... well, it kind of killed the spark between us too. Everything was magnified during the lockdowns— our passion, our fights, and eventually, the cracks in our relationship. But that's another story for another day. You know, it's funny, as Kyler was... well, he looked like the gay porn actor Roxy Red, but an older version."

Penny chuckled at the description of Toni's ex-husband, Kyler Thompson, as a gay porn star lookalike. Toni's ability to find humour in the chaos of her life was one of the many things that Penny admired about her. It wasn't just her confidence or boldness—it was her resilience, her ability to take the messiest, most painful parts of her past and wear them like armour.

"Roxy Red, though?" Penny laughed, shaking her head. "Ain't he the emo looking one with the wild hair? I often wank to him and Kyler Moss in that one vid they did."

Toni let out a laugh, a throaty, genuine sound that filled the break room. "Aye, that's the one! Wild hair, eyeliner like he's about to headline a My Chemical Romance tribute band, and the kind of cheekbones that could cut glass. Kyler had that same vibe back in the day—though he swore blind he wasn't trying to look like anyone in particular. But, babes, you're full of surprises. Didn't peg you for a gay porn aficionado."

Penny blushed but grinned, leaning back in her chair. "I mean, who isn't these days? I like the twink on twink stuff—there's just something about the energy, you know?" Penny said, her tone light and teasing, trying to steer the conversation back to humour after the intensity of Toni's revelations.

Toni laughed again, shaking her head in mock disbelief. "You're a dark horse, Lane. One Big Weekender and you're already showing your true colours. I like it."

The mood lightened, the camaraderie between the two women palpable. Penny felt a surge of warmth for Toni, not just as a mentor but as someone who had lived through more than her fair share of challenges and emerged stronger for it.

"Thanks for sharing all that with me," Penny said after a moment, her voice quieter. "I can't imagine it was easy. But it means a lot, Toni."

Toni gave her a small, genuine smile, the kind that made her seem less like the larger-than-life persona she projected on air and more like a friend. "You're alright, Lane. I see a lot of myself in you, you know? That mix of nerves and fire, wanting to prove yourself but not entirely sure how. You're going to do just fine here—just don't let the chaos drown you. Ride it. Make it yours."

Penny nodded, the words resonating with her. She wasn't sure what the future held at Manic Radio Liverpool, but for the first time since she'd started, she felt like she might just be able to find her place in the madness.

"Hey guys..." Lavender Cole, one of the Wirral Breakfast hosts said, walking in. "You heard what they're bringing back?"

Toni raised an eyebrow, turning to Lavender as she sauntered in. The Wirral Breakfast host had an air of effortless cool, her bright pink hair tied up in a messy bun, offset by a vintage Adidas jacket and ripped jeans.

"What are they bringing back?" Toni asked, her tone a mix of curiosity and mild scepticism. "Please tell me it's not the Manic Secret Sound."

Lavender grinned, shaking her head. "Nope, it's not the Secret Sound. It's worse." She paused for dramatic effect, savouring the moment as both Toni and Penny leaned in slightly, their curiosity piqued. "They're bringing back the Manic Marauder."

Penny chuckled, as she was 12 when Manic Liverpool had brought out the Manic Marauder, a treasure hunt-style promotion that had captivated listeners back in the day. The premise was simple but brilliant: listeners followed clues revealed on air to find out where the Manic Marauder was, and then they had to go round asking people if they were the Manic Marauder. The first round had been on the Wirral in Birkenhead market, and Penny remembered how she had been close, but the time had ran out before the person had been identified.

She knew that Toni, being an Altrincham girl, wouldn't have the same nostalgic connection to the Manic Marauder that someone like her might. Penny's eyes lit up with excitement, memories of the event flooding back. "The Manic Marauder? No way! I used to love that as a kid. It usually ran during the school holidays and aired on both Manic Liverpool and Chester & Wirral Vibes, and would have people running round like headless chickens. The first round was £50k and it rolled over every day until someone found the Marauder. In its first run, only 2 people got the cash prize, and... get this... they ran a round in Manc."

Toni raised an eyebrow at Penny's sudden enthusiasm, sipping her Red Bull as she leaned back against the table. "The Manic Marauder? Sounds like the sort of chaos I could get behind, though I don't remember it being a thing in Manc. What happened there?"

Penny grinned, her cheeks flushed with excitement. "It was legendary! They ran it across the city centre one Friday afternoon, but—get this—the Marauder was hiding in... Shudehill bus station. He was a bus enthusiast, surprisingly, the Marauder, which is why it was the perfect disguise, as who'd ask a saddo who photographed buses if they were the Manic Marauder?" Penny laughed, the memory flooding back. "People were running around the Arndale, Deansgate, you name it, looking for this guy while he was just photographing buses leaving Shudehill. It ran in one hour slots, twice a day, one in the morning after the peak and one before rush hour, and each time it was a different location."

"Ah, talking about my little creation?" Alan Hamilton's voice interrupted, his unmistakable North West accent carrying an air of authority as he stepped into the break room. The Regional Head of Programming for the North West was dressed in his trademark ripped jeans, a Madonna tour t-shirt and a blazer that somehow made the casual look feel oddly polished. His appearance was as much a statement as his programming decisions—bold, unorthodox, and unapologetically Manic.

"Alan!" Toni greeted him with mock enthusiasm, raising her Red Bull in a mock toast. "Come to grace us with your genius, have you?"

Alan smirked, leaning against the doorframe. "Don't be cheeky, Green. Anyway, I... did kind of nick the original idea from Orion Media back in the day. Their old Free

Radio Phantom. I was a young programming assistant back then, fresh out of Oxford, full of ideas and ambition but not much originality. Two ideas I had were Orion knock-offs, and one, funnily enough, is still around nowadays. You know House of Manic Live, our yearly music event? Yeah, that's just a rip-off of Orion's old 'Free Radio Live.' Same bones, just with the Manic branding slapped on. But the Manic Marauder? That was my personal twist on the Free Radio Phantom—a proper scavenger hunt on steroids, with bigger prizes and absolute chaos. We made the locations pay to host Marauder rounds, and if they didn't pay, then they didn't get the publicity boost from hosting the event."

Alan's grin widened as he noticed Penny's obvious excitement. "Looks like you've got a fan of the Manic Marauder here," he said, gesturing toward her. "Penny, I take it you remember the good old days of hunting down our elusive Marauder?"

Penny nodded enthusiastically. "Absolutely! I was 12 when it first launched. My mum drove me and my best mate round Birkenhead market during the first Wirral round. We got so close, but we ran out of time before we found the Marauder. It was like a mix of adrenaline and chaos wrapped up in one event."

Alan laughed, clearly pleased. "That's exactly the vibe we're going for, Lane. And now, with the rise of social media and the Manic Prime app, the Marauder's going to be bigger, bolder, and madder than ever. Clues will drop in real-time on air and on the app, and we're throwing in some live-streamed hints from the Marauder themselves—well, in character, of course."

Toni raised an eyebrow. "Sounds like a lot of effort. Who's going to be the Marauder? Don't tell me you're pulling one of us off our shows to don the disguise?"

Alan's grin turned sly. "We've got the original Marauder back to play the role again. He's still got the energy and knows how to keep the chaos controlled. And it's not going to be just on the CHR stations that the clues air... it's going to be on all the stations under the Manic umbrella—Goldies, Rock, Metal and Soul. The idea is to make it a network-wide spectacle."

Penny's eyes widened in surprise. "The original Marauder? The bus enthusiast guy from Shudehill? You're kidding!"

Alan chuckled, shaking his head. "Not a chance, Lane. He's back, and this time he's more than just a bloke hiding with a camera. We've got him mic'd up, social-media-ready, and raring to cause a proper stir. You see, nostalgia sells, but we're giving it a 2024 twist. Think augmented reality, QR codes, and live-streamed shenanigans. The Marauder's going viral, baby."

Toni raised an eyebrow, scepticism flickering across her face. "Sounds like a logistical nightmare, Alan. You sure you're ready to wrangle all that chaos? And more importantly, what's the prize this time?"

Alan's grin widened. "£100k to start. And if no one finds the Marauder by the end of the day, it rolls over to the next. Think of it as Manic's way of setting social media on fire—and making sure every listener in the country's tuned in to our stations. It's going to be starting the end of the month, as we're resting the £500k Money Drop for a week while the Marauder runs."

Penny couldn't help but marvel at the scale of Alan's vision. The Manic Marauder was no longer just a nostalgic childhood memory—it was a full-blown, modernised media event that promised to dominate airwaves and social feeds alike.

"I've got to hand it to you," Penny said, sipping her now-lukewarm coffee. "It sounds ambitious. But £100k? That's going to have people running around like headless chickens."

"That's the point," Alan said, his grin almost devilish. "It's all about engagement. We don't just want people listening; we want them living Manic. Following the clues, talking about it online, roping their mates in—it's all part of the experience. And trust me, when that pot starts rolling over, the buzz will be unstoppable."

Toni rolled her eyes but couldn't entirely hide her smirk. "You're a madman, Alan. But I'll admit, it's a clever way to keep people hooked. Just don't expect me to be running around Liverpool with a mic looking for the Marauder—I've got enough on my plate keeping my show on track."

"Don't worry, Green," Alan said, giving her a playful nudge. "You just keep doing what you do best—making chaos sound good on air. We're also reintroducing the Manic Canaries too... a gimmick from 2008."

Penny knew that the Manic Canaries were Manic's version of the GCap Black Thunders that Buzz 97.1, a GWR station that ended up becoming Heart Wirral, had introduced, a promotional vehicle concept that GCap Media used for prize giveaways and local events. Manic's Manic Canaries had been a similar concept introduced in 2009 and had become iconic for their bright yellow Ford Rangers with all sorts of low to mid value giveaways, from £10 cash prizes to Echo Arena tickets and even VIP tickets to the Liverpool v Everton match. Penny's eyes lit up with recognition at the mention of the Manic Canaries. She had vivid memories of spotting the bright yellow vehicles cruising around Liverpool and the Wirral as a teenager, always drawing a crowd whenever they parked up for a giveaway.

"Manic Canaries?!" Penny exclaimed, her excitement evident. "Oh, I remember those! They used to cause a proper buzz. One time, my cousin queued for hours at the Albert Dock to win VIP tickets to see Rihanna. He didn't win, but the whole thing was an event. Are they coming back properly, or is it just for the Marauder?"

"Well, put it this way, 20 cars have been ordered, all decked out in bright yellow with the updated Manic branding," Alan continued, a glint of pride in his eye. "Each major hub will have a fleet of them, ready to roll out for giveaways, stunts, and local events. It's all on the internal site if you haven't read it yet, Penny. Think of it as Manic going back to its roots, but with a modern twist. We want the Canaries to be as iconic in 2024 as they were back in the day. And yes, they'll play a big role in the Marauder campaign—imagine being in the right place at the right time and having a Canary pull up with a clue that could change everything."

Toni groaned playfully, shaking her head. "Alan, you're turning this place into a circus. Not that it isn't already, mind. But fair play—it's ambitious, and I can't say I'm not curious to see how it all plays out."

Lavender, who had been quietly listening, finally spoke up, her tone dry but amused. "I give it a week before someone crashes one of those Canaries trying to outrun a mob of listeners. You know what people are like when there's free stuff on the line."

The room erupted in laughter, and even Alan couldn't help but chuckle. "Well, that's part of the fun, isn't it? Controlled chaos, as always. But seriously, this is our chance to remind people what Manic is all about—energy, excitement, and being unashamedly larger than life. If we pull this off, it's going to be unforgettable."

Penny couldn't help but feel a surge of excitement. The Manic Marauder and the Canaries felt like a perfect encapsulation of the station's ethos—chaotic, engaging, and unapologetically bold. For the first time since she'd joined, she felt like she was part of something truly unique, a station that wasn't afraid to take risks and make a splash.

As Alan headed out, tossing a casual "get ready for a wild ride" over his shoulder, Penny turned to Toni, who was already halfway through her second Red Bull.

"Well," Penny said, her voice tinged with awe and a touch of disbelief, "I guess this is just another day at Manic."

Toni grinned, raising her can in a mock toast. "Welcome to the madness, Lane. Just remember—around here, if it's not a bit mental, it's probably not worth doing."

Penny smiled, her earlier nerves fading into a sense of anticipation. Manic Radio Liverpool might be chaotic, unpredictable, and unlike anything she'd ever experienced, but it was also starting to feel like home.

****

# CHAPTER 5 – Controversial Break Bumpers
## Wednesday 11th September 2024

Penny Lane sat in the production office of Manic Radio Liverpool, scrolling through the PlayoutONE system on her laptop. It was a relatively quiet Wednesday morning—if anything at Manic Radio could truly be called "quiet." She was reviewing the scripts and notes for that afternoon's drive show with Rory Carter when Abby Blue, her producer, burst into the room, holding a clipboard and looking unusually flustered.

"Have you heard the new break bumpers we're going to be trailing?" Abby said, her face ashen as she continued to scan the clipboard. Penny looked up, raising an eyebrow at Abby's unusually frazzled state.

"Break bumpers? No, what's the big deal?" Penny asked, closing her laptop and leaning back in her chair.

Abby sighed, dropping the clipboard onto the desk with a thud. "They're… well, something Clubland TV love using."

Penny furrowed her brow, picking up the clipboard and scanning the notes Abby had dropped. "Clubland TV? What, like those risqué bumpers with the nightclub vibes and cheeky double entendre?"

"Its ones like 'We must save our nation from decay, and deliver our children from the horrors of perversion' and 'Through this salacious material, these abnormalities are corrupting the minds and the hearts of our children',"

Abby said, frowning. "From the '60s film Perversion for Profit. If you go onto the 'New' menu on PlayoutONE and then 'Liverpool Test', you'll see."

Penny tilted her head, curiosity piqued, and quickly navigated the PlayoutONE system on her laptop to the specified folder. She clicked into the 'Liverpool Test' playlist and saw a set of files labelled 'PFP_Break_1', 'PFP_Break_2', and so on. With a click, the first file began to play through her headphones.

The voice was stern, authoritative, and undeniably dated.

"We must save our nation from decay and deliver our children from the horrors of perversion."

The irony that it then went into the upbeat 'Rory and Penny's Drive Home' jingle was not lost on Penny, who pulled off her headphones and stared at Abby in disbelief.

"You're telling me this is what they want us to trial as break bumpers?" Penny asked, her tone a mixture of incredulity and amusement. "Who thought dragging a 60s moral panic film into a CHR station's sound design was a good idea?"

Abby shrugged, slumping into a chair opposite Penny. "Apparently, it's Alan Hamilton's brainchild. He says it's all about creating 'contrast'—you know, something provocative to grab attention before launching into the usual high-energy jingles and ads. He wants Manic Liverpool to be edgier, unpredictable. Says it's all part of the brand."

Penny pinched the bridge of her nose, trying to process the logic—or lack thereof. "So let me get this straight. We're going to juxtapose this puritanical doom-mongering with Dua Lipa and a £500k Money Drop competition?"

Abby nodded grimly. "Pretty much. And guess who gets to explain it live when the listeners inevitably blow up X with confusion or outrage?"

"Of course," Penny muttered, tossing the clipboard back onto the desk. "It's always us who have to front the chaos, isn't it?"

The door to the production office swung open, and Rory Carter strolled in, holding a takeaway coffee and looking unbothered as ever. He took one look at Abby's stressed expression and Penny's exasperated face, raising an eyebrow.

"Alright, what's got you two in a tizzy this time?" Rory asked, taking a long sip of his coffee before flopping into the nearest chair.

Penny gestured toward her laptop. "The new break bumpers. Have a listen."

Rory leaned over, snagging her headphones and slipping them on. His expression morphed from mild interest to a grin in an instant. "That's epic! Clubland use these as a piss take over how some of the music videos that are more wankable. I can see this getting the voice notes on WhatsApp coming in from listeners. George Putnam was the guy who narrated these back in 1965 in the film Perversion for Profit, yeah? This is so absurd it's genius!"

Rory said, laughing as he pulled the headphones off. "Trust Alan to come up with something that's going to wind people up and have them talking about us all week."

Penny crossed her arms, unimpressed. "You seriously think this is a good idea? It's not just going to wind people up—it's going to confuse them. Imagine someone tuning in for Dua Lipa and hearing 'the horrors of perversion' right before the chorus kicks in."

Rory shrugged, still grinning. "That's the point, isn't it? It's Manic Radio. We live for this kind of chaos. And honestly, it's a stroke of marketing genius. You know how the listeners are—half of them will hate it, half will love it, but all of them will be talking about it. That's how you win in CHR radio."

*_*_*_*

"Gooooood afternoon Liverpool," Penny watched as Rory said the words into the microphone with his signature swagger. The opening jingle played out, a familiar rush of energy filling the studio as the first segment of their drive show kicked off.

"And welcome to Rory and Penny's Drive Home!" Penny added, her voice bright and engaging. "We've got a packed show for you today—big tunes, your chance to win £500k on the Money Drop, and, oh, some brand-new sound design that we're sure you'll have opinions about."

She watched as, on cue, Rory played "Think then of the consequences to the inexperienced youth who, in purchasing and studying this material, becomes a pawn for these misfits", one of the 10 bumpers that Alan

Hamilton had insisted on trialling. The sharp, vintage tone of the voiceover was followed by their usual jingle: "Rory and Penny's Drive Home—keeping Liverpool moving!" The juxtaposition was jarring, to say the least.

"Right, so first thing's first, we've got some news... a week Saturday, in a mystery location, the Manic Marauder is back!" Rory continued, his voice oozing with enthusiasm. "That's right, Liverpool, the legendary treasure hunt with a £100k jackpot to kick things off. We'll be dropping clues on air and in the Manic Prime app, so make sure you're ready to go full detective mode this weekend."

"Yes, this week is the last week of the £500k Money Drop, but this week is-"

"But psychiatrists believe that prolonged exposure of even the normal male adult to this type of publication, though he not be aware of its true nature, will nevertheless pervert," another bumper came out, and Penny could see Rory was grinning as he moved his finger from the button that had triggered the break bumper back to his script.

Penny took a deep breath, leaning into her microphone to recover the flow. "Yes, that, Liverpool! This week is your final chance to win the £500k Money Drop before we bring the Manic Marauder back into your lives. If you've got a detective streak—or just fancy a laugh—get involved!"

Rory chimed in, his voice rich with playful mischief. "And hey, if you're wondering how the Manic Marauder works, we'll be explaining all over the next week and half. First though, it's Lewis Capaldi with Forget Me," Rory announced smoothly, and Penny could see the countdown timer had 10 seconds left, and that Rory was about to press another of the break bumpers to transition into the song. As the bumper played—"Smut peddlers do not have the right to contaminate our society."—Penny couldn't help but glance at Rory, her expression caught between disbelief and amusement. He gave her a cheeky wink as the intro to Forget Me started, its mellow chords providing a sharp contrast to the stern, vintage voiceover that preceded it.

The track filled the studio, and Penny leaned back in her chair, pulling off her headphones for a moment. "This is either going to make us radio legends or get us cancelled," she said, shaking her head with a mixture of disbelief and reluctant admiration.

Rory laughed, spinning in his chair. "Is there really a difference in this business? Either way, people will be talking about us. And you know the golden rule of CHR radio—if they're talking, they're listening."

Penny couldn't help but chuckle at Rory's optimism. "You've got a point there. But I can already feel the complaints rolling in. I just hope Alan has a strong inbox filter."

The song faded, and Penny could see Abby typing away, adding clips of voice notes and amendments to the script into the PlayoutONE system as the show continued. Penny knew they were already generating listener reactions. As Rory queued up the next link, Abby's voice came over the intercom.

"Alright, you two, heads up. Listener messages are already flooding in on WhatsApp. Want me to play a few during the next break?" Abby's tone was a mix of excitement and mild apprehension.

Penny glanced at Rory, who nodded with a grin. "Go for it, Abs. Let's see what the people are saying."

The next song wrapped up, and Rory hit the mic button. "Alright, Liverpool, we know you've got questions—and maybe a few strong opinions—about the new voice..."

Penny watched as Rory played another Perversion for Profit bumper, "This rot, this depraved material, is too obscene to show" and had to chuckle at, despite how weird they weird, how seamlessly Rory managed the absurdity of it all. He leaned into the mic, his voice smooth and teasing.

"Don't worry, folks, we hear you loud and clear. These vintage soundbites are, shall we say, a bold choice. But here at Manic Liverpool, we like to keep things interesting—and judging by the messages flooding our WhatsApp, you've got plenty to say about it. Scott in Bootle, what did you think?"

Penny noticed that there were half a dozen pre-selected voice notes ready to play, and that the first one was ready to go.

"Rory, Penny, what's goin' on with that voice? Prolonged exposure of even the normal male adult to this type of publication? Is some smut about to hit the airwaves? Proper mad, that is! But fair play—it got me laughing on my way home!" Scott's voice crackled through the speakers, his Scouse accent thick with amusement.

Rory laughed, leaning into the mic. "Glad to hear it, Scott! Don't worry, there's no smut here—just a bit of cheeky nostalgia to keep you on your toes."

Penny chimed in, her tone light and teasing. "And hey, if you think that was wild, wait until you hear the next one. We've got plenty more where that came from—Manic Liverpool keeping it unpredictable, as always."

Rory grinned as he hit the button for the next voice note, a woman's voice cutting through the airwaves. "Hi Rory and Penny, this is Claire from West Derby. I nearly swerved my car when I heard that break bumper—what even was that? I had to check I wasn't accidentally tuned into Radio 4 or something. But you know what? I'm hooked. Keep it coming!"

Rory clapped his hands together, clearly enjoying the listener reactions. "Claire, you're a legend! That's exactly the energy we're going for—keeping you on your toes while you navigate the end of the workday."

Penny nodded, picking up the rhythm. "And don't forget, Liverpool, we want to hear from you! Drop us a message on WhatsApp and let us know what you think of our bold new experiment. Love it? Hate it? Confused by it? We want it all."

Abby's voice came over the intercom again, her tone urgent but amused. "You've got another twenty messages waiting. This is blowing up faster than we thought."

Rory hit the mic button again, his voice brimming with enthusiasm. "You heard Abby—keep those messages coming! Up next, we've got more reactions, plus your chance to win that £500k Money Drop jackpot. But first, here's Becky Hill with 'Side Effects,' right here on Manic Liverpool."

* _ * _ * _ *

Penny was on her way back to her Birkenhead flat, a paradox in itself, when she noticed on her phone a post on Weston's private Instagram account. It was a selfie of him in a Confessional at a local Catholic church, his trademark cheeky grin and ginger curls visible under the dim lighting of the booth. The caption read: "Forgive me, Father, for I have sinned... again."

Penny couldn't help but laugh, shaking her head at Weston's knack for mixing irreverence with his unique charm. The comment section was already filling with replies from colleagues and friends:

**Toni Green**: *And yet you still look saintly, O'Rourke. Teach me your ways.*

**Rory Carter**: *Confession doesn't work if you keep sinning, mate. #Amateur*

**Abby Blue**: *Wait, you're actually in a church? Bet the priest is loving the tea.*

Penny quickly added her own comment.

**Penny Lane**: *At least you're honest about surviving the madness. #TeamManic*

It was then that she noticed that another person with the same surname had commented under the post: "Weston, you eejit, yer a disgrace to the family and the Republic."

The comment caught Penny's eye, making her pause mid-step on her way to the front door of her flat. She clicked on the profile of the commenter, whose name was "Michael O'Rourke." His profile picture was a grainy old family photo, and his bio read, "Proud son of Ballymena, defender of truth, faith, and freedom."

Looking further at the photos, she noticed that one was of Michael dressed in an IRA uniform standing next to a flag, a caption of how the IRA shouldn't be demonised and how he was proud to serve. The date on the watermark of the photo was 11 August 1971, and that the caption also said "50 Years of British Terror in Ballymurphy. #RIPBallymurphy11".

Penny stared at her phone, the realisation hitting her like a cold gust of wind. The comment, paired with the photo on Michael O'Rourke's profile, painted a picture that was deeply unsettling. Weston's connection to a figure associated with the IRA was a detail she hadn't expected—not after hearing about his proudly Unionist stance and his unapologetically Catholic identity.

Her thumb hovered over the "like" button on his comment before she thought better of it. The last thing she needed was to wade into an online rabbit hole of political controversy. Instead, she made a mental note to ask Weston about it the next time she saw him. If he was going to be a fixture in the whirlwind of her life at Manic, she needed to understand the full story behind his enigmatic persona.

Her thoughts were interrupted by a notification from the Manic Liverpool group chat. Abby had posted an update.

**Abby Blue:** *FYI, Rory and Penny's break bumpers are trending on X. We've officially gone viral. Half the posts are calling us unhinged; the other half think we're geniuses. Welcome to Manic, Penny Lane.* 😄

Penny smirked, letting out a small laugh. Despite her earlier reservations, it seemed Alan's gamble was paying off. The absurdity of the break bumpers had captured attention, just as Rory had predicted. She scrolled through some of the reactions on X:

**@ScouseJoe95**: What in the George Putnam hell is going on at @ManicLiverpool? Those bumpers are WILD. Can't stop listening though. #ManicMadness

**@MissRachaelL**: *I was just trying to vibe to Becky Hill and got hit with 'prolonged exposure to smut corrupts youth'. Is Manic Radio OK?* 😄

**@RedTillImDead**: *Manic Liverpool is the best thing on the airwaves right now. Those bumpers are like a fever dream and I'm living for it.* @RoryMiserysideDrive @PennyLaneManic

Rory had already replied to a few tweets, playing up the chaos with his usual charm.

**@RoryMiserysideDrive**: *We're fine, thanks for asking. Just saving the nation from the horrors of perversion, one Dua Lipa track at a time.* 😏 *#ManicLiverpool*

Penny felt a pang of pride seeing her name tagged in some of the posts. The chaos was working, and she was slowly finding her place in it.

****

# CHAPTER 6 – Weston's Confessions
## Thursday 12th September 2024

Penny was sat in Studio 3, the Cumbria studio, recording some split links as she had been asked to cover the 1am-4am show, one that was pre-recorded and voice-tracked, for the Manic network. She knew that, for the overnight slots, automated and pre-recorded content was the norm, given the limited listenership at those hours. However, it felt like an odd milestone in her budding career—her voice would be carried to listeners far beyond Liverpool, reaching across the Manic network to places she'd only visited on family holidays or heard about in passing.

As the clock on the PlayoutONE screen ticked closer to 11am, an odd hour to record the overnight show, Penny found herself distracted by a text from Weston O'Rourke. It popped up on her phone, which was propped up against the studio console.

**Weston O'Rourke**: *Fancy a coffee after your stint in the Cumbria booth? Need to pick your brain about something. Bring your Scouse sass, Lane.* 😏

Penny smirked, rolling her eyes at Weston's cheeky tone. He'd been a constant presence in her whirlwind introduction to Manic Radio Liverpool—sometimes a confidant, sometimes a chaos catalyst. Typing a quick reply, she agreed to meet him in the break room once she wrapped up her voice-tracking.

She leaned back into the mic as the next split link counted down, her voice smooth and cheerful as she recorded another intro.

"Coming up on Western Ulster Vibes, we've got Calvin Harris and Ellie Goulding, plus your chance to win tickets to The Belfast Ma: A Crackin' Christmas at The Old Courthouse in Antrim this December, but first, here's Clean Bandit and the brilliant Jess Glynne, with "Rather Be," right here on Western Ulster Vibes—keeping your late nights lively and your mornings mellow."

Penny leaned back, watching the waveform render on the screen as she hit save. She took a sip from her water bottle and sighed, the vodka infused orange juice that she'd poured in that morning kicking in slightly. The thrill of being part of a quasi-national network like Manic Radio had its perks, but the grind of pre-recording overnight content was undeniably tedious. Penny glanced at the text Weston had sent again, curious about what he wanted to discuss.

Hearing a knock on the door, she turned to see Alex Le Mantre, one of the Manic Dance hosts, a 23 year old blonde male who she had slept with on her first Big Weekender, the term used for the sex parties that were hosted by the various Manic Radio hubs every week, in the doorframe, a grin on his face and a condom in his hand, as though it were a cheeky invitation rather than a practical accessory. Penny rolled her eyes, a smirk tugging at her lips as she turned back to the console.

"Alex, don't you have some deep bass tracks to curate or a mic to spit over?" she teased, her tone playful but dismissive.

Alex chuckled, stepping into the room and leaning casually against the doorframe. "Deep bass can wait. I'm not due on until 1, so I've got some time to kill. Thought I'd cum in ya."

Penny grinned, as she knew that he was the king of double entendres, but decided to play along. "Alex, you're as subtle as a sledgehammer. And no, I've got an overnight show to wrap up, so unless you fancy voice-tracking some split links with me, I suggest you keep it zipped... unless you want me to gag you with my stockings?"

Alex chuckled and smiled, and Penny groaned, as she knew he was into the gagging kink, having seen Toni Green and Weston teasing him about it during the last Big Weekender.

"Are they fresh on, or are they day old ones?" Alex asked, and Penny knew that they were the same ones that she had worn the previous day, but she wasn't about to give him the satisfaction of an answer. Instead, she shot him a look of mock exasperation.

"Alex, you're impossible. Go find someone else to torment—I've got a show to finish," she said, shooing him toward the door with a wave of her hand.

Alex laughed, holding up his hands in mock surrender. "Alright, alright. But don't say I didn't offer to make your morning more... memorable."

As he sauntered off, Penny shook her head, smiling despite herself. Alex was nothing if not consistent in his cheeky antics. She refocused on the console, finishing the final few links for the overnight show. When the last track was queued and ready, she packed up her things and headed toward the break room, where she knew Weston would be waiting.

* _ * _ * _ *

The break room buzzed with quiet activity as Penny entered, spotting Weston sprawled in one of the chairs by the coffee machine. His signature Ed Sheeran-esque ginger curls were slightly tousled, and he wore a navy jumper with the sleeves pushed up, exposing forearms that he undoubtedly knew were a feature. He grinned as she approached, holding up a takeaway coffee cup.

"Hey, Lane, fancy a latte? It's a caramel latte—I figured you'd need a little sugar to keep up with me," Weston said, his Northern Irish lilt as disarming as ever.

Penny rolled her eyes but took the coffee, a small smile tugging at her lips. "You know, you're dangerously close to being my favourite Manic colleague. What's the catch?"

Weston leaned back, smirking. "No catch, just... well, me mam's come over from Ballymena, and I'm trying to avoid her."

Penny raised an eyebrow, intrigued. "Your mam? What's she doing in Liverpool, then? And why are you avoiding her? Surely, she didn't come all this way just to chase you around the studio?"

Weston sighed dramatically, taking a sip of his own coffee. "Ah, you've never met me mam, have you? She's lovely—don't get me wrong—but she's also got a knack for asking questions that no one in their right mind wants to answer. Like, 'Weston, when are you going to stop gallivanting around on the radio and get a proper job?' Or, 'Weston, why haven't you settled down with a nice Catholic girl yet?' She's relentless."

Penny chuckled, imagining a fierce Northern Irish matriarch grilling Weston over tea and biscuits. "So, what you're saying is, you'd rather hide out here with me than face the inquisition?"

"Exactly," Weston said, his grin widening. "Besides, you're much better company. Mam's only in Liverpool to see some family friend who's just had a baby. She's using it as an excuse to 'check in' on me. That and me granddad, me dad's dad, is pressuring her to 'put me in line'."

Penny smirked, taking a sip of the caramel latte. "Ah, the classic 'family intervention disguised as a social visit.' Gotta love it. And let me guess—she's got a laundry list of things you should be doing with your life?"

Weston nodded, chuckling. "Oh, absolutely. Top of the list is quitting radio and coming back to Ballymena to work in the family's business. Never mind that I'd rather shove pins in me eyes than spend my days arguing about stock deliveries and balance sheets. Mam thinks this radio gig is a phase, like I'm going to wake up one day and decide to swap microphones for spreadsheets. It's just me dad's dad who's worse. You saw me Insta, right?"

Penny nodded, recalling the Instagram post from the previous night and the comment from Michael O'Rourke, the older relative with the staunch Republican stance. "Yeah, I saw it. The whole 'forgive me, Father' thing was classic Weston. But that comment from your granddad caught my eye. 'Disgrace to the family and the Republic'—that's pretty intense."

Weston snorted, running a hand through his curls. "Aye, that's Granddad Michael for you. Always been the family's old-school Republican firebrand. Former IRA Commander, believes London should burn to the ground for what they've done to Ireland and that Sien Fein is the true leadership for a United Ireland, all that craic. He thinks I've sold out by even considering working in England, let alone embracing a Unionist stance. There again, he's one of those who's proud of both the Provisional and the 'Real' IRA, having been involved with both at different points. You know the Manchester Bombings?"

Penny knew that she had never heard of that bombing in 1996, so her head shook slightly as she leaned in closer. "What, the one in the Arndale? The Provisional IRA planted that one, right? The massive evacuation, no fatalities but a ton of damage?"

Weston nodded, his expression a mix of pride and discomfort. "Aye, that's the one. Me granddad was involved—one of the coordinators on the ground. He's always spoken about it as a victory, a show of power, though he's not the kind to admit his involvement outright unless he's had a pint too many. Growing up, those stories were like bedtime tales in our house, passed off as part of the fight for freedom. He's even admitted that he held his head high when he got thrown in prison for several years after being linked to another bombing in Belfast. It's not something I like to advertise, obviously. He was 21 back in '71, when the Ballymurphy massacre happened, a junior IRA member, and it made him more radical than ever before. Then Bloody Sunday happened."

Weston leaned back in his chair, his expression darkening as he continued. "Bloody Sunday was a turning point for Granddad. He always said it was the day he truly committed to the cause. He was in his early 20s then, and he saw it as a betrayal—a massacre of innocent people. It radicalised him, pushed him deeper into the Provisional IRA. He became someone who believed violence was the only language the British government understood."

Penny sipped her latte, her brow furrowing as she absorbed the weight of Weston's words. "That's heavy, Weston. To grow up with those kinds of stories... it must have shaped how you see things, even if you've gone a different way."

Weston nodded, his expression thoughtful. "It did. For a long time, I believed everything Granddad said. I thought the British government was the enemy, that unionism was a betrayal. But then I started to see the cracks—how his version of the world didn't fit with what I experienced. I worked with Protestants, Unionists, people who didn't fit the narrative he'd hammered into me. And then, well, there's the Church. I'm Catholic, I go to Mass three times a week, go to Confession, Holy Communion and all the other rites, but that doesn't mean I agree with everything the Church, or what my granddad stands for. Me brother's a priest in the Church, has a flock just outside Derry, and he's like Granddad, staunch anti-Brit, wants a united Ireland and believes in the old ways. Funny thing is, my brother was a choir boy back in the day, and the father...

he... well, let's just say there's some things about the Church that..." Weston trailed off, glancing around the break room before lowering his voice. "Let's just say the Church isn't perfect, and leave it at that, yeah? Dad killed the bastard though."

Penny froze mid-sip, her mind trying to process what Weston had just said. She set her cup down carefully, glancing at him with wide eyes. "Wait... your dad killed someone? Like, actually?"

Weston nodded slowly, his expression unreadable. "Aye. It's not exactly family dinner conversation, but it's true. He was a devout Catholic, believed in God and all that, but when he found out the priest had... well, hurt my brother and other kids in the parish, he lost it. Him and a few of his Constabulary mates."

Weston paused, his normally cheeky demeanour replaced with something much heavier, a mix of anger and sorrow. He took a deep breath, the kind of inhale that carried the weight of years.

"Him and a few mates from the Constabulary found the priest. They didn't take it to court, didn't trust the system to handle it properly. They took justice into their own hands. It wasn't clean, it wasn't legal, but... it was done. The priest disappeared, and for years it was just whispers in the parish. No one spoke openly about it, but everyone knew."

Penny stared at Weston, unsure of what to say. The light-hearted banter they'd usually shared felt miles away now, replaced by a raw, unfiltered glimpse into the complexities of his life.

"And your dad?" she asked softly. "What happened to him?"

Weston gave a small, bitter smile. "He carried on. Stayed in the Constabulary for a while, but you could see it changed him. The guilt, the weight of what he'd done, it ate away at him bit by bit. He was already in the shadows with the family for being in the PSNI, the police force. Dad told me once it was so he could protect the Catholics from the few PSNI coppers who hold on to the sectarian prejudice, but that didn't stop Granddad from seeing him as a traitor to the Republican cause. Dad said that, while he did agree with Sinn Féin and some of their beliefs about a united Ireland, he believed the violence had to stop for the sake of the next generation. He stayed in the PSNI for another ten years, then retired early. You see, Damien, my eldest brother, as I'm one of 5, is 20 years older than me. Dad had him when he was 16 and Mam was 18, so I'm not as close to Damien as I am to the others. Cathy, me one sister, she's 4 years older than me, so 29 now, and we're closest in age and in thinking. I'm the youngest."

Weston leaned back in his chair, swirling the dregs of his coffee in the cup, his gaze distant. Penny watched him carefully, her mind reeling from the sheer complexity of his family history. It was a lot to process—the radical grandfather, the priestly brother, the vengeful father. Each layer added another dimension to Weston's already enigmatic persona.

"What's worse is that Damien... he's... he's like the priest who did... that... to him," Weston then stopped mid-sentence, his voice faltering as his eyes met Penny's. A heavy silence fell between them, and Penny realised that whatever Weston was about to say wasn't just difficult—it was devastating. "His wife is only 20 as well."

Penny's breath caught as she stared at Weston, the weight of his words sinking in like stones in water. "His wife's... twenty?" she asked softly, trying to tread carefully. "But he's… what, forty-six, right?"

Weston nodded, his jaw tightening as he ran a hand through his curls. "Aye, forty-six. Met her when she was seventeen. Mam and Dad were furious, Granddad thought it was a joke—said it was the 'old ways' coming back to life. But me? I couldn't stand it. Cathy's the only one who really sees it like I do. She called him out, said it was wrong, but no one else in the family dared to back her up. There again Cathy, like me, doesn't subscribe to certain aspects that the Church want, like the mortal sin of sex before marriage or using contraception. She... does pornos."

Penny blinked, struggling to keep up with the whirlwind of revelations Weston was throwing at her. Each new piece of his family story felt like another twist in a gripping but deeply uncomfortable drama.

"Wait... Cathy does what now?" Penny asked, leaning forward slightly, her tone a mix of disbelief and intrigue.

Weston let out a dry chuckle, rubbing the back of his neck. "Aye, you heard me right. Cathy's in the adult film industry. She's been at it since she was 21. Lives in Dublin, keeps it all under a pseudonym—'Ciara Flame.' She's actually pretty successful. Bit of a feminist in her own way, saying it's about owning her body and her choices. Mam pretends it's not happening, Dad doesn't care as long as she's happy, and Granddad thinks it's the ultimate betrayal of everything Irish Catholic women are supposed to stand for. Me Gran, however, is like me Dad, that as long as we're happy with our careers, be it producing films or working on radio, she doesn't care about the rest."

Penny leaned back in her chair, sipping her now-cold latte as she absorbed yet another curveball in Weston's family saga. "Your family sounds like a soap opera, Weston. A very dark, complex, slightly unhinged soap opera."

Weston laughed, the sound lighter this time, as if the weight of their conversation was finally starting to lift. "Aye, it's a bit of a circus. But it's mine, for better or worse. And honestly, Lane, having you hear all this without running for the hills is a relief. You're alright, you know that?"

Penny smirked, setting her cup down on the table. "I'll take that as a compliment. But seriously, Weston, thanks for sharing all that. It's... a lot, but it explains so much about you. Like why you've got this... duality. Confident and cheeky on the surface, but clearly carrying the weight of a million family secrets underneath."

Weston shrugged, his usual grin returning. "What can I say? We all have our baggage. Mine just happens to be shaped like a dysfunctional Irish Catholic family with more skeletons in the closet than a Halloween store."

Penny chuckled, the tension in the room finally easing. "Well, for what it's worth, I think you've turned out alright. A bit of a rogue, sure, but not a bad one."

"High praise coming from you, Lane," Weston said, raising his empty coffee cup in a mock toast. "Alright, enough about me and my family's questionable life choices. What about you? How's the Wirral gal holding up in the lion's den of Manic Liverpool?"

Penny grinned, shaking her head. "Let's just say it's been a learning curve. But I think I'm starting to find my rhythm. The chaos doesn't feel quite so overwhelming anymore."

"That's the spirit," Weston said, his tone genuinely encouraging. "Manic's all about embracing the madness, finding your place in the chaos. And you're doing just fine, Lane. Better than fine, actually."

Penny felt a flicker of warmth at his words, the sense of camaraderie between them growing stronger. She raised her cup in return, the caramel latte long forgotten but the gesture still meaningful.

"Here's to surviving the madness," she said with a grin. "And maybe even thriving in it."

Weston clinked his cup against hers, his smile genuine. "Here's to that, Lane. And don't worry—if the chaos ever gets too much, you've got me in your corner. Even if I am a rogue."

Penny laughed, feeling a little lighter as the conversation shifted to more light-hearted banter. The heaviness of their earlier discussion lingered in the back of her mind, but for now, she was grateful for the distraction and for the unlikely friendship she'd found in Weston O'Rourke.

As they left the break room and returned to the bustle of the station, Penny couldn't help but feel like she'd gained a deeper understanding of her enigmatic colleague. Weston was far more complex than his cheeky exterior let on, and while his stories left her with more questions than answers, one thing was clear—life at Manic Radio Liverpool was never going to be boring.

****

# CHAPTER 7 – New Software Blues
## Monday 16th September 2024

The Speke hub at Manic was buzzing with a palpable mix of anticipation and dread. Over the weekend, the network had officially completed the rollout of new software: the station was switching from PlayoutONE, a trusted favourite among presenters, to the seemingly all-encompassing RCS suite. This included Zetta for playout, GSelector for music scheduling, and RCS News for newsroom integration. While the leadership team praised the new system as a "game-changer for efficiency and engagement," the rank and file were less enthused.

Penny knew that Zetta and GSelector had been used by Bauer, and so she, along with Weston, was familiar with it, her having been part of Bauer's training program at the Bauer Academy and Weston having been at Cool FM, it meant that they both had a slight advantage over their Manic Liverpool colleagues when it came to adapting to the change. Penny had fond memories of her training sessions with Zetta and GSelector—albeit in a much less chaotic environment than Manic—but she knew how finicky it could be, especially under pressure.

The fact that the announcement had come as apparently some hubs, such as Huddersfield, a former Lite Group hub and was running on Genesys, and Dudley and Stratford, former Breeze Media bases, which had never had the PlayoutONE system and had been a RCS stronghold for years, only added to the complexity.

"How the fuck did we manage to network everything bar drive and breakfast while using 3 different systems," she heard Anna Long, the North Wales Sound breakfast host, say as she walked past the break room where Anna was animatedly chatting with another presenter. Penny couldn't help but smile at the chaos Manic seemed to thrive on—three playout systems somehow operating under one roof for years, and now the inevitable upheaval of consolidating everything under the RCS umbrella.

"Morning Penny," she heard Weston say. Turning around, she saw he had a grin on his face and a coffee cup in his hand. "Good day for us former Bauer lot, isn't it?"

Penny couldn't help but laugh at Weston's comment as she adjusted her bag on her shoulder. "Good day for us, maybe," she replied, her Scouse accent lilting with amusement. "But judging by the faces around here, it's like someone's asked them to host live while juggling flaming batons."

Weston chuckled, falling into step beside her as they walked toward the production office. "Can't blame them, though. Switching systems is a pain in the arse at the best of times, and this place? Chaos on a normal day. Throw in new software, and it's bound to be a circus."

Penny nodded, glancing around at the sea of colleagues, some huddled around screens, others furiously scribbling notes as IT staff flitted between desks. It was as though the entire station had been thrown into a survival course with no clear instructions.

"What's your money on, then?" Penny asked as they reached the office. "First major crash, or someone accidentally airing dead air because they can't figure out Zetta?"

"That's already happened. Lou crashed the system an hour ago on his show, ended up blasting out a repeat of the same Teddy Swims track for half an hour. I walked in, tapped a few buttons, and sorted it. Poor bloke looked like he'd aged ten years," Weston said, grinning. "You know the one advantage is that the bosses in the offices next door can tighten the network playlists even more."

Penny knew that the office building next to the studio building was where the Head Offices of Manic's network team were based, including the Head of Music, Head of Programming, and other senior figures who had a direct say in what went on air. She knew, however, that, to compete against Bauer and Global, Manic needed a tight playlist to ensure listeners stayed hooked.

"Let me guess, because we're the fresh meat, having only been here two weeks, and because we're ex-Bauer, we've been 'volunteered' to help out," Penny finished, rolling her eyes as they stepped into the production office. "Of course we have. Nothing screams welcome like being thrown into the deep end of a software rollout. What does the internal chat board say from the other hubs?"

Weston laughed. "Dudley and Stratford are laughing, as they've had RCS stuff since the Woody Bones days. Huddersfield's staff are losing their minds because they've gone from Genesys to this overnight and don't even know what a segue is in Zetta yet, and Cardiff, Exeter and Dundee are in panic mode as they're former PlayoutONE sites like us but they've got no one with RCS experience on their teams. I mean, PlayoutONE is alright for indie stations and small regional setups, but let's face it—this lot aren't ready for Zetta's 'bells and whistles' vibe. You know, they had me, instead of producing my own show, helping set Zetta Splits up so our regional variations here have the ads set up for the early afternoon show with Kyle and Sue. Ah well, it's only half hour until 1, so I'm knocking off in a bit."

Penny chuckled. "Have we had Zetta2GO logins issued yet or are we still on the desk setups for accessing Zetta remotely?" she asked, settling into her chair and powering up her workstation.

Weston pulled out his phone and tapped through a few screens. "Zetta2GO logins are live, the techies at Dudley issued them, as they've had RCS kit for 15 years, so they're essentially the RCS gurus of the Manic network. Check your inbox, you should have your login details. Handy for when you're stuck at home and need to tweak your pre-records or fix a rogue segue."

Penny opened her email and found the login instructions Weston mentioned. "Well, at least something's going smoothly," she said, typing in her details and setting up her access. "Though knowing this place, it'll only be a matter of time before someone accidentally wipes the ad log or schedules an hour of dead air."

Weston smirked. "Thank goodness I'm not your producer then. Oh, and by the way, Abby said those bumpers you had last week are no longer going to be played... apparently it was all a prank... on you."

Penny froze mid-setup, her fingers hovering over the keyboard as Weston's words sunk in. She turned to face him, narrowing her eyes. "What do you mean a prank? Those bumpers went viral! People thought we were some edgy, avant-garde station pushing boundaries!"

Weston grinned, clearly revelling in her reaction. "Apparently, it was Rory and Abby's idea to mess with you, the newbie. It seems, according to Kyle and Sue, there's a tradition to, within the first fortnight, prank the newbies. Niamh and Lorcán got me this morning with their prank. Bloody eejits got me with a recording of a fake listener complaint about me mispronouncing Ballymena. Said I'd called it Ballymonkey. I nearly fell for it before Niamh burst out laughing. Classic prank. But hey, it's all in good fun, right?"

Penny groaned, leaning back in her chair as she processed the revelation. "Unbelievable. I was stressing about those bumpers, thinking Alan had lost his mind, and it was all just a big joke. I mean, I knew Manic was chaotic, but I didn't realise it doubled as a comedy club."

Suddenly Penny felt a cramp, and, wincing, she knew what was happening—it was her time of the month. Penny grimaced, muttering under her breath as she shifted uncomfortably in her chair. She glanced at Weston, who was busy scrolling on his phone, oblivious to her discomfort.

"Great," she mumbled, reaching into her bag for a paracetamol packet and a small chocolate bar she always kept for emergencies. She popped two pills into her hand

and washed them down with the last dregs of her now-cold coffee.

Weston looked up, noticing her wince. "You alright there, Penny? Let me guess, period?"

Penny shot Weston a glare that could have stopped a train. "Brilliant deduction, Sherlock. What gave it away? The paracetamol or the death stare?"

Weston smirked, leaning back in his chair. "Hey, don't shoot the messenger. I've got three sisters and a mum who think I'm their personal errand boy for chocolate and tampons. I know the signs. Put your feet on the desk."

Penny sighed but complied, sliding her chair back and propping her feet on the desk. "This better not be another prank, O'Rourke," she muttered, though her tone was more playful than serious.

Weston stood by her feet, and Penny noticed him taking her heels off with an exaggerated flourish, carefully placing them on the floor. "Mind if I take your stockings off?"

Penny raised an eyebrow, her expression a mixture of bemusement and disbelief. "Weston, if you're trying to be chivalrous, this isn't the way to do it."

"Hey, I was going to give you a foot massage, but if you're not keen, I can just leave you to your misery," Weston replied, grinning cheekily as he leaned against the desk.

Penny chuckled despite herself, shaking her head. "You're lucky I'm too tired to argue. Fine, go ahead. But if you start making weird noises or anything, I swear you'll regret it."

Weston crouched down and carefully slid her stockings off, his expression surprisingly sincere as he began to gently massage her feet. Penny let out a surprised sigh, the tension in her muscles easing slightly under his touch.

"Alright, I'll admit," she said, her voice tinged with reluctant gratitude, "you're not completely useless."

"High praise from you, Lane," Weston quipped, his grin returning. "My sisters used to get me to do it when I lived in Ballymena, as, when I was 16, I may have done an 8 week course on how to massage properly. Long story short, they figured I was better at it than Dad. Ever since, I've been the family masseuse. Look, I know you're on your period, but if you need satisfying in any other way?"

Penny grinned, as she had to admit, out of all the blokes at the Speke hub, Weston was the most hung among them, and she was starting to get used to the sex parties at Manic.

"Well, if you don't mind me giving you a blowjob after you've massaged the tension out of my feet, we might just have a deal," Penny quipped, a mischievous glint in her eye as she leaned back into the chair, clearly playing along with Weston's cheeky vibe. "That or fuck my arse. I need a good release today," she continued with a smirk, testing Weston's reaction.

Weston burst out laughing, leaning back on his heels. "Lane, you're a one-woman comedy show. If you weren't already brilliant on air, I'd suggest you moonlight as a stand-up."

Penny rolled her eyes, chuckling despite herself. "You wish. Now finish the massage before I change my mind."

As Weston resumed massaging her feet, Penny noticed Rory sauntering in, with Mags O'Leary in his arms, his erection filling the wife of the regional programming director with the gusto of a man who clearly had no concept of discretion. Penny had realised, over the past two weeks, that Manic was a hotbed of sex, drugs and booze, and that she, like Weston, had got hooked on all three. It was part of the wild, unfiltered culture that defined Manic Radio—an environment where boundaries were blurred, and indulgence was almost a prerequisite for survival. Penny couldn't decide whether to laugh, cringe, or cheer at Rory and Mags' blatant disregard for any semblance of professionalism.

Or is it fitting in with the peers?

*No*, the irrational side of Penny's mind whispered, *it's thriving in the chaos.*

Manic wasn't just a workplace—it was a living, breathing soap opera, complete with scandal, drama, and the occasional moment of unhinged brilliance.

The fact that HR didn't care, as long as consent was clearly established, was both shocking and oddly liberating. Manic Radio's culture was like a rollercoaster without safety rails—thrilling, unpredictable, and occasionally leaving you questioning your life choices.

Penny shifted in her chair as Weston finished the massage, a little too aware of Rory and Mags in the corner, obliviously wrapped up in each other. Weston caught her glance and smirked, leaning in conspiratorially.

"Another day at Manic," he whispered, nodding toward the amorous pair. "You know, Bauer would have a field day at Manic's HR policies. Especially the coke and sex policies. Talking of which, Harry has had a new batch of coke come in."

"Yeah, they taught us at the Bauer Academy not to even joke about stuff like this," Penny finished with a smirk, shaking her head. "But here at Manic, it's like HR actively encourages it as part of the onboarding process."

Weston laughed, settling back into his chair as he watched Rory and Mags disappear into the next room, their laughter echoing down the corridor. "You've got to hand it to them, though—Manic really leans into the 'work hard, play harder' philosophy. And hey, it makes for great stories. In a way, I miss working at Bauer, but... well, I had to leave."

Penny glanced at Weston, sensing there was more to his comment. "Had to leave? Why? Did you piss someone off?"

Weston hesitated for a moment, running a hand through his ginger curls as if weighing whether or not to elaborate. Finally, he leaned forward, his voice dropping slightly. "Let's just say, you know the other day I told you about my family, right?"

Penny nodded, leaning in slightly. She could sense this was about to be one of those moments where Weston's cheeky exterior cracked, revealing something deeper. "Yeah, your family's like a live episode of Line of Duty—what about them?"

Weston chuckled softly, though his usual humour was muted. "Well, it's not just my family that's... complicated. Let's just say that I got accused, wrongly, of sexual harassment at Bauer. It wasn't true, but the rumour spread like wildfire. One of the girls on the team—she was new, and I thought we were mates—misinterpreted my offer of a massage as something it wasn't. I'd done it for loads of people on the team before—nothing dodgy, just trying to help when someone was stressed. I tried to explain that I was a trained masseur, and it was purely platonic, but once HR got involved, it spiralled out of control. Even after I was cleared, the damage was done. My reputation there was ruined, and I knew I'd never be comfortable working in that environment again. So, when the opportunity at Manic came up, I grabbed it. Now, how's that?"

Penny noticed that in the 10 minutes Weston had been massaging her feet, she hadn't noticed the cramps she normally had from her period had all but disappeared. She stretched her legs out and gave Weston a sincere look. "Honestly, Weston, you've got magic hands. If this radio thing doesn't work out, you should open a spa."

Weston laughed, but his expression softened. "Glad to be of service, Lane. And thanks for not laughing me out of the room with all my drama earlier. You're a good egg."

"Yeah. Now, O'Rourke, get those jeans and boxers down as I'm going to give you a blowjob you'll never forget," Penny said with a mischievous grin, clearly teasing but enjoying the light-hearted banter. She watched as Weston dropped his Levi jeans without hesitation, revealing his boxers underneath, and grinned.

* _ * _ * _ *

"This bloody thing is like ancient Greek," Penny heard Rory complain. It was half past 3, half hour until their drive show started, and Penny was back in Studio 2 with Rory. He was gesturing dramatically at the Zetta interface on the computer screen, his frustration palpable. "Looks all shiny and clever, but it's all just smoke and mirrors. Where's the 'make my life easy' button?"

Penny smirked as she adjusted her headphones. "You should look at the internal chat board. Al over at Dudley is saying how it's about time the rest of Manic caught up with Dudley and Stratford. What do you need doing?"

"Well, as everything has been centrally programmed, I'm trying to just understand why it's not allowing me to get a word in edgeways on the show intro for when we start." Rory said, and Penny chuckled.

"Have you looked at the script, Rory?" Penny said, clicking on the SharePoint link for the drive show's rundown and opening script. She scanned it briefly and grinned. "It's because I'm to take lead on the show. Didn't you listen to Abby's brief this morning?"

Rory blinked, leaning back in his chair as if trying to piece together the conversation he'd evidently tuned out.

"Wait—you're leading? Why didn't anyone tell me? And more importantly, why didn't Abby stop me from making a complete fool of myself just now?"

Penny grinned, enjoying the rare moment of having the upper hand. "Because, Carter, the world doesn't revolve around you. Plus, Abby did tell us during the morning briefing—you were too busy giving Danny a blowjob to attend. You know, it's funny how most of us are bi but before we joined Manic, we didn't realise that we're attracted to both genders. Didn't you say that before you joined Manic 4 years ago, you were as straight as a ruler?" Penny teased, her grin widening as Rory groaned and slumped back in his chair.

"Alright, alright," Rory said, raising his hands in mock surrender. "I'll admit, Manic has... broadened my horizons. When I left Uni 4 years ago, I thought I had it all figured out—straight as an arrow, focused on climbing the radio ladder. Then Manic happened, and suddenly, everything I thought I knew about myself went out the window. But hey, it's been... an education."

Penny chuckled, leaning back in her chair. "An education? That's one way to put it. I'd call it a crash course in chaos with a side of self-discovery. Honestly, I think Manic should offer therapy vouchers as part of the onboarding process."

Rory grinned, adjusting his headphones. "Therapy vouchers? Nah, they'd just hand out more cocaine and tell us to crack on. Welcome to Manic—where the chaos never ends, and HR is just a suggestion."

As the minutes ticked down, Penny saw Abby sitting in her chair at the desk, instead of the production booth, and knew that the producer, who was today sporting a dyed yellow hairstyle instead of her regular look, was preparing for just in case things went wrong.

"You know," Abby said with a chuckle. "I still don't know what the fuck I'm doing here half the time. I swear, Zetta's interface has more buttons than the cockpit of a Boeing, and every one of them is just waiting to blow something up."

Penny laughed, shaking her head. "Abby, you're the glue holding this circus together. If you weren't here, Rory would probably be trying to run the show from Spotify on his phone."

"Hey, I resent that!" Rory chimed in, grinning as he leaned into his mic for a soundcheck. "It'd be Apple Music, thank you very much. I'm classy like that."

Abby rolled her eyes, adjusting her monitor as she checked the running order. "Alright, clowns, focus up. We've got the intro locked, Penny's taking the lead, and Rory, you're on colour commentary duty. Don't forget to mention the Manic Marauder instead of the Money Drop, and that we're giving away WWE Live tickets for their upcoming show at the M&S Bank Arena," Abby finished, her tone brisk but not without a hint of amusement. "Now let's make this sound like we actually know what we're doing."

Penny glanced at the countdown timer on the Zetta screen, her fingers hovering over the keyboard as the clock ticked closer to 4pm. She could feel the familiar mix of nerves and excitement bubbling up, the pre-show adrenaline sharpening her focus.

"Right, Liverpool," Penny said into the mic as the intro jingle began to fade, her voice bright and full of energy. "It's Monday, the start of a new week, and-"

Before she could say anything else, the sting for the news unexpectedly cut in, its dramatic chime filling the studio.

Penny glanced at Rory, her eyebrows raised, and mouthed, "What the hell?" Abby, seated at her console, frantically clicked through screens, her fingers flying over the keyboard.

"Sorry!" Abby's voice crackled through the studio intercom. "Zetta's auto settings are overzealous—it triggered the news sting early. Give me a sec to fix it."

Rory leaned back in his chair, stifling a laugh as Penny muttered, "New software blues, indeed." She adjusted her headphones and straightened her posture, waiting for Abby to regain control. Then the pre-recorded Wirral and Merseyside news that was the norm came on, as with part of the changes, the Chester & Wirral Vibes and Manic Radio Liverpool news broadcasts had merged, with one pan-Merseyside bulletin for the region instead of the two hyper-local ones that had previously existed. As the smooth, professional voice of Anna Kincade, the newsreader, filled the studio, Penny exchanged a glance with Rory, both of them trying not to laugh at the irony of their slick, high-energy intro being cut short by an overzealous news automation.

"Right, let's try that again," Penny said with a grin as the news ended and Abby signalled that they were back on track. "It's Monday, Liverpool, the start of a brand-new week, and we've got a show packed full of chaos, prizes, and more questionable decisions than your average visit to the Cavern Club. Now, we've had some new tech here at Manic, and it seems-"

Suddenly the playout system went into Espresso by Sabrina Carpenter, and Penny knew that it would not just be the Liverpool station, but the whole network, as music playout was controlled by the programming team as a whole and not the local presenters.

Looking at the screen, Penny noticed that there was a triple header of back-to-back tracks scheduled, with no room for their next link. Rory leaned into the mic, muting his laughter as the first notes of Espresso blasted through the speakers.

"Well, looks like Zetta's decided it's time for a coffee break," Rory quipped, his grin widening as Penny tried to keep a straight face.

Abby's voice came through the intercom, a mix of frustration and amusement. "Triple-header override. The whole network's got it—someone in programming must've hit the wrong button. You've got a good eight minutes to regroup."

Looking on the Manic Prime app, the app which Manic promoted and was their Global Player and Bauer Rayo equivalent, Penny saw that some of the CHR stations in Manic's roster, like Midlands Manic, Northern Vibes,

Oxford Manic, London Vibes and East Midlands Hits, ones which were Stratford and Dudley based ones, was showing a completely different song, Texas Hold 'Em by Beyoncé, while other Dudley and Stratford stations, ones which had the network drive with Danny O'Neil, along with the other hubs, were playing Sabrina Carpenter's Espresso. Penny realised that the split in song playout was likely a remnant of the system integration teething problems, with Dudley and Stratford being RCS strongholds prior to the Manic-Lite merger, and carrying the correct playlist, while the stations previously using PlayoutONE or Genesys were stuck with a default fallback list. It was the kind of chaos that only Manic could manage—half the network operating on one playlist while the other half played a completely different set of tracks.

Reading the script that she and Rory were meant to be using, Penny saw that the correct order of tracks was Texas Hold 'Em, a three minute link, then Sabrina Carpenter's Espresso, Calvin Harris's I'm Not Alone and Madonna's 4 Minutes, before the traffic and weather break, followed by the local ads and promos for Manic Liverpool.

Having been trained properly on Zetta and the rest of the RCS suite during her Bauer Academy days, Penny leaned forward and typed quickly into the Zetta interface, trying to correct the playout sequence before the next song began. "Rory, we're pulling this back. Give me a sec," she muttered, her fingers flying over the keyboard.

"Should I just sit here and look pretty, or do you want me to do something useful?" Rory quipped, leaning back in his chair.

"Try being useful for once," Penny shot back with a smirk, not taking her eyes off the screen. "Check with Abby if we've got the network-wide override permissions or if we're stuck local. I can only fix our station unless the Dudley lot give us a pass."

Rory spun his chair toward the intercom. "Oi, Abby! Are we in full control here or just babysitting Liverpool?"

Abby's voice crackled back over the speakers. "Liverpool only. Dudley's programming team is sorting the network issue. Just keep the energy up and roll with it. We're all flying blind for the next ten minutes."

Penny groaned but quickly added the correct sequence into Liverpool's local playlist. "Alright, I've got it. When Espresso ends, we'll do a 6 minute link, then go into Calvin Harris's I'm Not Alone and Madonna's 4 Minutes."

Suddenly an error message flashed on Penny's screen: "Unable to queue tracks due to conflicting automation commands. Contact Network Admin."

"Of course," Penny muttered, throwing her hands up in exasperation. "The one time I actually manage to fix something, and the system decides to block me."

Looking on the WhatsApp group for the various Manic hubs, she saw that presenters from both Huddersfield and Cardiff were chiming in about similar issues, their messages a mix of frustration and gallows humour

"Apparently, we're playing Espresso, but we've had tweets saying that we're playing Texas Hold 'Em on the app, but on the FM stream its Sabrina!" Hannah Potter, one of the Huddersfield crew who presented White Rose Vibes's drivetime, had written, and Penny had to chuckle at how disjointed everything was. Looking at the WhatsApp feed that the studio used, Penny noticed that the consensus from listeners was that Espresso was playing no matter how people in Liverpool were listening. Clearly, the chaos of the system transition wasn't confined to just one hub; it was a network-wide reality.

Eventually Espresso went straight into I'm Not Alone, and Penny could see that the system had decided to insert a 3 minute gap after the Calvin Harris track, obviously someone in the building having overridden the local playlist to allow time for local links. Penny knew that that meant there was nearly 4 minutes until the first link, and then hopefully enough time to regain control and make the show sound seamless to the listeners. Penny adjusted her headset and motioned to Rory, who was checking his reflection in the studio glass as though preparing for a photoshoot.

"Rory, focus!" Penny called, pointing at the countdown timer on Zetta. "We've got a gap coming up after this track—time to salvage this circus and remind Liverpool why they tune into us."

Rory spun back around, grinning. "Relax, Lane. Chaos is our brand, remember? Let's roll with it."

As the last beats of I'm Not Alone faded out, Penny leaned into the microphone, her voice confident and upbeat despite the technical chaos. "Alright, Liverpool, we're back! Apologies if your Monday is feeling as chaotic as ours right now—right, we want you to WhatsApp in with all your experiences of technical chaos at work. Ever had a system update go so wrong it makes Monday feel like a holiday? Let us know, and we'll share the best ones on air."

Rory chimed in, his voice dripping with playful sarcasm. "And if you're wondering what's going on here, welcome to Manic Liverpool, where the new software is giving us more surprises than a Christmas cracker. But don't worry, we've got tunes, laughs, and a big prize to keep your afternoon rolling."

Penny leaned back, glancing at the monitor to make sure the next track was queued correctly. The timer ticked down steadily, and she felt a flicker of hope that the worst of the chaos was behind them.

"So, Rory," Penny began, her tone teasing, "how would you rate our new software on a scale of 'mild headache' to 'complete meltdown'?"

Rory laughed, playing along. "Oh, it's definitely a 'why did I come into work today?' kind of vibe. But hey, at least the music's good. Speaking of which, we've got Madonna coming up with 4 Minutes, followed by your chance to win those WWE Live tickets at the M&S Bank Arena."

Penny smiled, the flow of the show slowly returning to normal. "That's right, Liverpool. WWE are coming to Liverpool as part of their European tour, and you could win VIP tickets to see WWE Superstars in action, including Undisputed WWE Champion "The American Nightmare" Cody Rhodes, WWE Women's Champion Bayley, WWE Women's Tag Team Champions Bianca Belair & Jade Cargill, Randy Orton, LA Knight, AJ Styles, Queen of the Ring Nia Jax, Kevin Owens, The Bloodline, Bobby Lashley, The Street Profits, and many more. We'll be giving out 5 pairs of tickets over the next week, so make sure you stay tuned for your chance to snag those tickets! And remember, if you're not in it, you can't win it."

Rory leaned in, his cheeky grin returning. "And don't forget to practise your wrestling moves at home—safely, of course. No blaming us if your living room turns into WrestleMania and your mum gets body-slammed onto the sofa!"

Penny chuckled, shaking her head. "Rory, I'm not sure encouraging family wrestling matches is the kind of chaos we need right now. Let's leave the heavy lifting to the pros, shall we?"

The countdown timer ticked down to the next song, and the familiar opening beats of 4 Minutes began to play. Penny glanced at Rory, who was already preparing a one-liner for the next link.

"Alright, Liverpool," Penny said as the song played, leaning back in her chair with a satisfied smile. "It looks like we're back on track... for now."

Rory smirked, sipping his coffee. "Back on track? Lane, this is Manic. The only track we're on is the runaway kind, and we wouldn't have it any other way."

As 4 Minutes filled the studio, Penny felt a small sense of accomplishment. Despite the chaos, the mishaps, and the occasional inappropriate quip, they had managed to hold it together. It wasn't perfect, but it was Manic—unpredictable, messy, and unapologetically alive. And for the first time since joining, Penny felt like she was exactly where she belonged.

****

# CHAPTER 8 – Breaking News
## Wednesday 18th September 2024

Penny didn't know why, but as she sat on the bus from Birkenhead to Liverpool city centre, there was a feeling that something was about to go wrong. The usual chatter of the morning commuters and the gentle hum of the engine felt subdued today. She glanced out of the window, watching the familiar streets roll past, her coffee cup clutched tightly in her hands.

The unease wasn't helped by the constant buzz of her phone. The Manic Liverpool WhatsApp group was alive with activity—far more than usual for this hour. Penny unlocked her phone and skimmed through the messages. Abby, Rory, and a few others were discussing some sort of major incident happening at Liverpool One, the main shopping district in the heart of the city.

**Abby Blue**: *Can anyone confirm what's going on? I've just seen a tweet about a stabbing at Liverpool One. Anyone in the city centre?*

Penny looked out the window and saw that her bus was about to enter the Herbert James Rowse built Queensway Tunnel. The familiar art-deco surroundings passed by, but the usually buzzing anticipation of reaching Liverpool's city centre was overshadowed by a sense of dread. Penny quickly typed a message into the group chat.

**Penny Lane**: *I'm on the bus to the city centre now. Should be in town in 10 mins. Do you want me to head down?*

Abby's response was almost immediate.

**Abby Blue**: *Which way are you coming from?*

Quickly typing, Penny knew that Abby needed to know her location for clarity. She replied swiftly:

**Penny Lane**: *Coming in through Queensway Tunnel. Bus stops near Lord Street. The bus to Speke stops at Liverpool One so I can head straight there if needed.*

**Abby Blue**: *Brilliant, Penny. Can you check it out and see if it's as bad as the tweets are making it sound? Rory's commute is from Runcorn, so he won't be here for at least another 20 minutes, and I'm tied up with the newsroom team prepping bulletins. Keep us updated.*

Penny felt a knot tighten in her stomach. She wasn't a journalist, but working in radio, she understood the importance of being first on the scene. She tucked her phone into her pocket and leaned back in her seat, mentally preparing herself for what she might find.

As the bus emerged from the tunnel and navigated through the bustling streets, Penny headed downstairs, her preferred seat on the number 1, the Stagecoach service that ran from Chester to Liverpool, being the upstairs left front, over the doors, meaning that she had access to the staircase when she needed to move quickly. By the time the bus pulled into its stop on Lord Street, Penny was already on edge. She stepped off into the crisp morning air, the sounds of the city rushing around her. Ahead, the towering shops of Liverpool One came into view, but something was off—there was an unusual cluster of police vehicles near the main entrance, their lights flashing silently.

Donning her Manic Radio ID card, one that showed she was a presenter for the station, she walked along the Paradise Street side of the centre, and noticed where, at the Wall Street junction where the Nando's was, police tape blocking access to the main square near John Lewis. Penny slowed her pace, her heart pounding as she took in the scene. Several uniformed officers were directing people away from the area, and a small crowd had gathered, their faces a mix of curiosity and concern.

Pulling out her phone, Penny snapped a quick photo of the scene—not close enough to be intrusive, but enough to capture the gravity of the situation. She sent it to the group chat with a brief update.

**Penny Lane**: *Police tape up at Liverpool One. Looks serious. Lots of officers. Heading closer but staying out of the way.*

The response came almost immediately.

**Abby Blue**: *Thanks, Penny. Be careful, and don't do anything that'll get you in trouble. Give the news desk a ring, as the 12 noon news might want a live eyewitness update from you if you're comfortable with it.*

Penny's nerves jangled at the thought. She'd never done a live update before—not like this. But she didn't have much time to dwell on it. As she edged closer to the police cordon, a uniformed officer stopped her.

"Sorry, miss. This area's restricted. Please move back," the officer said firmly, gesturing for her to join the rest of the onlookers who had gathered across the road. She then noticed he saw her ID card and raised an eyebrow. "Manic

Radio, eh? Hang on, aren't you that Penny Lane from the drive show? Me missus listens to you and Rory every day," the officer said, his tone softening slightly. "You've got a cracking show, love. But this here is serious—can't let anyone through."

Penny gave him a polite smile, her heart still racing. "Thanks, officer. Do you know what's happened? I'm not here to interfere, just trying to keep the public informed."

The officer hesitated for a moment, glancing around before leaning in slightly. "There's been a stabbing, two dead, one is the assailant, and one is the victim. Off the record, they both look related. Possibly Irish related as the victim has a phone in a tricolour phone case... and is associated with your lot, as he had a Manic ID card hanging off his jeans belt. Red headed fellow, looks like Ed Sheeran."

Penny felt a wave of nausea wash over her. Red-headed, Irish, looked like Ed Sheeran... the officer's description struck her like a bolt. Weston. Her mind raced, trying to piece it all together. No, it couldn't be Weston—she'd just seen him yesterday. He'd been fine, his usual cheeky self, teasing her about her show prep...

...and how he had feelings for her.

Real feelings. The kind that one could, in two weeks of chaos and camaraderie, never quite process amidst the whirlwind of Manic Radio Liverpool.

Penny's heart raced, her hand trembling as she clutched her phone. Her mind replayed Weston's grin, his voice, the way he could make even the most stressful situations seem light-hearted. But now, standing here, staring at the scene unfolding before her, the possibility of him being gone felt crushing.

"Are you alright, Miss?" Another PC asked, noticing Penny's pale face and unsteady stance. She quickly nodded, masking her emotions as best she could, though her voice betrayed her when she spoke.

"Y-yes, I'm fine. Just... just a lot to take in," she said, forcing a weak smile.

The officer gave her a concerned look but didn't press further. Penny stepped back from the cordon, her legs feeling like jelly as she moved away from the crowd. Her phone buzzed again—this time, it was a call from Abby.

"Penny! What's happening?" Abby's voice was sharp, filled with both urgency and concern. "We're hearing bits on Twitter, but no solid details. Do we have a connection to this?"

Penny hesitated, her throat dry. She wanted to tell Abby everything but wasn't sure if she could trust herself to speak without breaking down.

"There's been... a stabbing," she said finally, her voice trembling. "Two people dead—one's the assailant. And... and the victim..." She swallowed hard, her hands shaking as she gripped the phone. "They said he's red-headed, Irish, looks like Ed Sheeran. Abby, what if it's Weston?"

The silence on the other end of the line was deafening. Finally, Abby spoke, her tone softer but still steady. "We don't know that yet, Penny. Don't jump to conclusions.

Weston could be anywhere. Anyway, his shift ended an hour ago... shit, I bumped into him in the production office, and he said he was getting the bus into town as he needed to get something for Toni's birthday. Maybe it's just a coincidence, Penny. Don't panic yet."

Penny took a shaky breath, trying to steady herself. Abby was right—jumping to conclusions wouldn't help. But the officer's description had been so specific, so eerily close to Weston's appearance, that she couldn't shake the sinking feeling in her gut. Looking round, she saw Alfie Harrison, one of the reporters from Manic who covered local news for the Speke hub, coming down Paradise Street with his press badge prominently displayed. He was already holding his phone to his ear, speaking rapidly, likely coordinating with the newsroom team back at the hub.

"Penny!" Alfie called out as he spotted her. He jogged over, his face a mixture of curiosity and concern. "What's the situation? Abby said you were here. Any updates?"

Penny hesitated for a moment, trying to collect her thoughts. "The police are saying two dead—one's the assailant, the other the victim. They've mentioned the victim's Irish and... they described him in a way that sounds a lot like Weston."

Alfie's expression darkened, his usual journalistic composure wavering for a brief second. "Shit. You think it's him?"

"I don't know," Penny admitted, her voice barely above a whisper. "But I've got a horrible feeling. Abby said that he was coming into town as his shift on the Western Vibes Breakfast was over as it's Toni's birthday this Big Weekender."

Alfie nodded grimly, his phone still pressed to his ear. "Right, let me see what I can find out. I've got some contacts with Merseyside Police—they might be able to give us a name. But Penny, don't lose your head just yet. Could be someone else entirely. Do you know how long ago the stabbing happened?"

Penny shook her head, her thoughts still swirling. "I don't know. The officer didn't give me a timeline, but the scene looks recent—there are still paramedics around." Her voice wavered as she glanced back toward the police cordon, where a group of officers was gathered, speaking in hushed tones.

Alfie nodded, his journalist instincts kicking into high gear. "Stay here, Penny. I'll see what I can get from the scene. You focus on keeping it together, alright? Have you tried phoning Weston to see if it is him?"

Penny's breath caught as Alfie's words cut through the fog of her thoughts. Weston. She hadn't even thought to call him—her mind had been so consumed with the worst-case scenario that the most obvious solution had escaped her.

Quickly, she pulled out her phone and navigated to Weston's contact. Her thumb hovered over the call button, hesitating for just a moment. What if he didn't answer? What if his phone rang from somewhere within that taped-off scene?

*No. Stop. Don't think like that*, she told herself, pressing the button and holding the phone to her ear. The ringing tone felt agonisingly loud in her ear, each ring stretching out like an eternity. *Come on, Weston. Pick up.*

"What's the craic, its Weston here, can't come to the phone right now, but leave a message and I'll get back to ya. Cheers!"

Penny's heart sank as Weston's voicemail clicked in. The cheery, familiar tone of his recorded message felt like a cruel mockery of the panic churning inside her. She ended the call without leaving a message, her hands trembling as she stared at her phone. It didn't mean anything, she told herself. Maybe he was just busy. Maybe his phone was on silent, or the battery had died.

But maybe wasn't enough to stop the storm of dread building in her chest.

Alfie was still talking to someone on the phone, his expression serious as he jotted down notes in a small pad. Penny took a deep breath, willing herself to stay calm. If it wasn't Weston, she'd laugh about this later. If it was... she couldn't let her thoughts go there just yet.

It was then she noticed Alfie writing 'New IRA?' on his notepad and 'email from anonymous source sent to Western Ulster Vibes' as part of his notes. Penny's stomach twisted further. The New IRA? What the hell was going on? She felt like the ground beneath her feet was shifting, each new piece of information dragging her closer to the edge of a dark and overwhelming pit.

And then she remembered.

Weston's grandfather was a former IRA commander, someone whose shadow loomed large over his family's history and his own narrative. The knot in Penny's stomach tightened further. *Could this really be connected to Weston's family?* The anonymous email Alfie had jotted down, the possible involvement of the New IRA— it was all too much to process.

Penny's phone buzzed in her hand, pulling her out of her spiralling thoughts. It was Abby again.

"Penny, any update?" Abby's voice was calm, but there was an edge of urgency.

"No," Penny said, her voice strained. "I tried calling Weston, but it went to voicemail. Alfie's here—he's digging into the scene, but..." She hesitated, her eyes darting toward the police cordon. "Abby, this is starting to feel bigger than just a random incident. There's talk of the New IRA, and... you know about Weston's family, don't you?"

Abby was silent for a moment before letting out a low sigh. "I've heard bits and pieces, yeah. But Penny, don't jump to conclusions. Let Alfie do his job. We'll know more soon."

Penny nodded, even though Abby couldn't see her. "I know. It's just... I've got this horrible feeling, Abby. I can't shake it."

"Take a deep breath," Abby said firmly. "If it is Weston, we'll deal with it. But right now, we don't know anything for sure. Just keep an eye on the situation and keep us updated, alright?"

Penny mumbled a quiet agreement before ending the call. She felt a pang of gratitude for Abby's level-headedness, but it did little to quell the storm of emotions raging inside her.

Alfie approached her, his face grim. "Penny, the email that came through to Western Ulster Vibes—it's looking like a possible New IRA claim. The email said they were targeting someone who had 'betrayed their heritage.' They haven't released any names yet, but..." He trailed off, his expression heavy with unspoken words.

"But it fits," Penny finished for him, her voice barely above a whisper. "If the victim was Irish, and if they had a Manic ID card... hang on, doesn't Weston also have a cousin who's an IT guy in the main building next to the studio building?"

Alfie nodded slowly, his brow furrowing in thought. "Yeah, I remember Weston mentioning him—Cillian, wasn't it? Works with the corporate IT team, deals with the website side, looks like Weston if he had an identical twin."

Alfie's words landed like a slap, jolting Penny out of her spiralling thoughts. Weston's cousin. Cillian. The similarities between them, from the striking red hair to the shared O'Rourke features, had always been a point of humour within the team. Could it have been Cillian, not Weston, caught in this nightmare?

The fact that Cillian was a Protestant Unionist, and Weston was a Catholic Unionist, while the two both shared a grandfather who was a former IRA commander, added a complicated layer to the story. Penny's mind raced, trying to connect the dots. The New IRA email, the victim's description, the family's tangled history—it was like a web of threads pulling tighter with every moment.

"Alfie," Penny said, her voice trembling, "if it's Cillian, it could make sense. He's so similar to Weston. And if someone was targeting their family, maybe they mistook him for Weston. Do you think that's possible?"

Alfie sighed, his expression conflicted. "It's possible. But without more information, it's all speculation. Look, Penny, we need to wait for confirmation from the police or the email's claims. Anything we say on air needs to be precise—we can't risk getting it wrong."

Penny nodded, her grip tightening on her phone. The logical part of her brain agreed, but her emotions were spiralling. She needed to know. She needed to see Weston or hear his voice, anything to confirm he was safe.

"What's the craic, its Weston here, can't come to the phone right now, but leave a message and I'll get back to ya. Cheers!"

Penny ended the call once again, the familiar voicemail message leaving her both relieved and frustrated. It wasn't confirmation, but at least it meant Weston's phone hadn't been confiscated as evidence—or so she hoped. Her thoughts were interrupted by Alfie, who tapped her shoulder gently.

"Look, Penny," he said, his voice softer now, "you're not going to get any answers standing here torturing yourself.

Go to the station. Rory's probably there by now, and Abby will want you close in case we need you live."

"I would, but I don't know where the buses will be going from, as the 82 stops the other side of the cordon and doesn't seem to be running from here," Penny muttered, glancing at the disruption caused by the cordoned-off streets. "Unless... hang on, I'm an idiot, I could just head to Liverpool Central, get the Northern line down to Aigburth or Cressington and get an 82A or 500 to the office, get off at Speke Hall Avenue like normal. My pass is a Trio, so I'm covered on the train. I've lost the plot, ain't I?"

Alfie chuckled, though his face still carried the weight of the situation. "You haven't lost the plot, Penny. You're just stressed, and no wonder. Look, head to Central, get yourself on that train. The fresh air and a bit of quiet might do you good."

Penny nodded, grateful for Alfie's practicality. The logical solution gave her something tangible to focus on amidst the chaos. She pulled her bag onto her shoulder and turned toward the direction of Central Station.

"Let me know if you hear anything more," she said over her shoulder. "And Alfie... if it is Weston's cousin, or worse, Weston himself, make sure the newsroom knows before it breaks anywhere else."

Alfie gave her a firm nod. "You've got it, Penny. And don't overthink this—you'll get through it."

With that, Penny walked briskly through the city centre, her steps quick but her mind racing. The bustle of

Liverpool One was replaced by the quieter hum of Bold Street as she approached Central Station. The city felt strangely heavy, like everyone around her could sense the weight of the day but were too distracted by their own lives to acknowledge it.

"We are sorry to announce that the 11:59 Merseyrail service to... Hunts Cross... has been cancelled. This is due to a staff shortage," the automated voice echoed through Liverpool Central Station as Penny arrived on the platform. She groaned inwardly, gripping the strap of her bag as she scanned the departure board. The next train to Hunts Cross was scheduled for 12:14, giving her a frustrating fifteen-minute wait.

She pulled out her phone again, refreshing the group chat to see if there were any updates. Abby had posted a short message.

**Abby Blue**: *Newsroom is saying police will give a statement in 30 mins. Alfie is staying on the scene. Penny, head back to the hub—we might need you for the lunchtime bulletin.*

**Penny Lane**: *On my way—train delays. Should be there by 12:45 if all goes well.*

She shoved her phone back into her pocket, the knot in her stomach tightening. She hated the uncertainty, the not knowing. And while Alfie's theory about Cillian being the victim provided some hope, the idea that Weston's family was at the centre of a potentially politically motivated attack was horrifying.

"We are sorry to announce that the 12:14 Merseyrail service to... Hunts Cross... has been cancelled. This is due to a staff shortage," the automated voice droned again, cutting through Penny's thoughts. She clenched her fists in frustration, her mind racing for alternatives. The disruption was more than an inconvenience—it was another barrier between her and the answers she desperately needed.

"If you see anything that doesn't belong to you, then report it to the British Transport Police or a member of staff," the automated announcement continued, adding to Penny's rising frustration. She glanced at her phone again, quickly typing into the group chat.

**Penny Lane**: *Seems Miseryfail has lived up to its nickname. Two cancellations in a row. Something to do with staff shortages.*

**Alana Kettlehurst**: *Yeah, I'm waiting for the 11:59 from Conway Park to get to Moorfields, and that's decided to do a runner. Thank goodness its every few minutes from here to get to Moorfields and I can jump a Northern Line from there to Aigburth.*

Penny knew that Alana, one of the Lancashire drive hosts who, like the other North West stations apart from the Manchester ones, were based at the Speke hub, would probably end up on the same train as her, as Moorfields was before Central on the Merseyrail Northern Line towards Hunts Cross. Penny sighed, knowing the delays were another layer of chaos to an already tense day. She turned her attention to the station announcements, hoping the next train would run on time.

Finally, the board updated: 12:29 service to Hunts Cross – On Time.

Penny exhaled in relief. It was a small victory amidst a day of frustration. She glanced around the platform, spotting a few other commuters with the same weary expressions, their patience wearing thin.

The train arrived, and Penny quickly boarded, finding a seat near the door. As the train rattled out of the station, she pulled out her phone to check for updates.

Her thoughts drifted back to the earlier conversation with Alfie. *New IRA, family betrayal, Weston's cousin... or Weston himself?* The possibilities swirled in her mind, each one heavier than the last.

"Hey, Penny," she heard, and saw that Alana was walking through the train, latte in hand, balancing it precariously as the train jolted slightly. She plopped into the seat across from Penny with an exasperated sigh.

"Miseryfail strikes again, eh?" Alana quipped, her Lancashire accent cutting through the low hum of the train.

Penny managed a faint smile. "Yeah, today's been one for the books already, and it's barely lunchtime."

Alana tilted her head, studying Penny's expression. "You alright? You look like you've seen a ghost."

Penny hesitated, debating whether to unload the swirling thoughts in her mind. But Alana was a colleague, and more importantly, she was someone Penny trusted to keep things in perspective.

"There's been a stabbing at Liverpool One," Penny began, her voice low. "Two dead. One's the attacker, the other's..." She swallowed hard, her hands gripping her bag tightly. "The other might be connected to someone I know. It's all so unclear right now, but the description... it matches Weston."

Alana's eyes widened, her latte forgotten as she leaned in closer. "Weston? As in ginger-haired Weston from Western Ulster Vibes? As in 'Irish Hottie Who We Both Fancy' Weston?"

"Yeah, that Weston," Penny confirmed, her voice barely above a whisper. She glanced around the train carriage, the muted conversations of other passengers a stark contrast to the storm swirling in her chest. "It could be him... or it could be his cousin, Cillian. The victim fits the description, but we don't have confirmation yet."

Alana leaned back, her expression shifting from shock to determination. "Right. First thing's first—we're not jumping to conclusions. Until we know for sure, you've got to keep it together. Weston's a smart guy. He wouldn't get caught up in something like this unless... unless it's as mad as it sounds."

"Mad doesn't even begin to cover it," Penny said, her voice trembling despite her efforts to stay composed. "There's talk of the New IRA being involved. Alfie mentioned an anonymous email sent to Western Ulster Vibes claiming they targeted someone who betrayed their heritage. If that's true, and if it's Weston or his cousin, this isn't random, Alana. It's personal."

****

# CHAPTER 9 – Confessions in Chaos
## Wednesday 18th September 2024

Penny stormed through the doors of the Manic Radio Liverpool building, her heart pounding with a mix of anxiety, confusion, and relief. The news had broken only minutes earlier when she was on the bus from Aigburth station—Weston had been found, and it was the most embarrassing find ever.

He had been stuck in the third-floor lavatory, and the lock on the toilet door had got jammed that bad, it had to be removed by maintenance.

As for his phone going to voicemail? It was because Weston had accidentally dropped it and the screen had shattered, rendering it unusable...

And the worst bit? When trying to retrieve it from the floor, his jeans had ripped at the rear of them, meaning that he had been sitting there, stranded and humiliated, with numb legs from having to sit on the toilet for hours. Penny could hardly believe it as she ascended the stairs to the third floor, her emotions a chaotic mix of exasperation, amusement, and sheer relief.

As she approached the break room where Weston was reportedly recovering, she heard familiar voices—Rory and Abby were clearly relishing the situation.

"You're telling me," Rory was saying between fits of laughter, "that Weston O'Rourke, the so-called king of smooth talk, was stuck on the bog for hours with a shattered phone and split jeans? Mate, you couldn't write this!"

Abby snorted. "Honestly, I think this tops the time Kyle got locked in Studio 2 because he forgot how the new keypad worked."

Penny pushed open the door, her presence immediately silencing the pair. Weston sat slouched on the sofa, his ginger curls tousled and a distinct flush of embarrassment colouring his face. His jeans were now patched together with hastily applied gaffer tape, and he held a mug of tea as though it were his only source of comfort.

"Penny," he began, his voice sheepish but laced with that familiar Northern Irish charm. "Before you say anything, just know... I've had better mornings."

She folded her arms, raising an eyebrow as she stepped into the room. "Better mornings? Weston, I thought you were dead! I was at Liverpool One, staring at police tape and hearing about a red-headed victim with a Manic ID. I was ready to—" She stopped herself, realising her voice had risen far beyond her usual tone. She took a deep breath, willing herself to calm down. "I thought it was you."

The she saw Weston's face drop, and she knew that something was wrong. His usual cheeky grin was gone, replaced with a look of genuine guilt and sadness.

"Penny," Weston said softly, setting down his mug. "I didn't mean for this to happen. I had no idea what was going on outside. I've been stuck in here since early this morning. And Cillian..." He hesitated, his voice breaking slightly. "I phoned his phone when a cleaner rescued me off the landline here, and the Police answered. I... he's gone. My favourite cousin's gone. What's funnier is... well, the person who killed him is one of me granddad's New IRA men. Can you believe it? Someone from our own bloodline, someone meant to be family, took him out. All because Cillian didn't toe the line of the 'old ways.' I can't wrap my head around it, Penny."

Weston's words hung heavy in the air, his usual carefree demeanour shattered. Penny took a hesitant step forward, unsure how to bridge the gap between the Weston she knew—the cheeky joker with an answer for everything—and the Weston sitting before her, raw and vulnerable.

"I don't know what to say," Penny admitted softly, lowering herself into the chair opposite him. "This... it's horrific, Weston. But it's not your fault. None of this is."

He gave her a faint, humourless smile. "I wish I could believe that. But you know my family's history, Penny. It's all tangled up in politics, religion, and feuds older than both of us combined. I thought I'd escaped it, left it behind when I chose this life—radio, Manic, all the madness here. Cillian... he was a Protestant Unionist, who'd moved here to the mainland back in '15 with my aunt and uncle, as they felt they couldn't stay in Ballymena any longer. Too much pressure, too many threats. Me? I stayed because I thought I could prove I was different, that I could be the Catholic O'Rourke who didn't live by our grandfather's rules. But now..." Weston trailed off, his hands gripping the mug so tightly Penny thought it might crack. "Now I wonder if any of us can really get away from it."

Looking at Weston's phone, which was sat next to him, charging up, Penny could see it pinging that much that it was lighting up like a Christmas tree. Weston noticed her glance and let out a bitter chuckle.

"Probably the family WhatsApp group blowing up," he muttered, reaching for the shattered device. "Or worse—Granddad Michael trying to spin this into some kind of 'martyrdom' for the cause. He always was one for dramatics."

Penny leaned forward, her voice firm. "Weston, you don't have to read those. Not now. You've been through enough today. You're allowed to take a breath before diving into whatever chaos your family is stirring."

Weston shook his head, unlocking the cracked screen with some difficulty. "You don't understand, Penny. If I don't, it'll just haunt me. Better to face it head-on, you know?"

She stayed silent, watching as Weston scrolled through his messages. His face shifted between anger, sadness, and something else—an expression she couldn't quite place. Finally, he let out a frustrated sigh, setting the phone down.

"Half of them are calling Cillian a traitor," Weston said, his voice tinged with disgust. "The half led by my granddad that is. The other half are saying that Cillian will meet the Lord with his head held high, and that he'd meet the Lord knowing that he had lived his life by his own principles."

Penny reached across the coffee table and placed a hand on Weston's, her touch firm but gentle. "You know what's true, Weston. You know Cillian wasn't a traitor, and he didn't deserve this. What your granddad thinks or says— it doesn't define who Cillian was or the choices he made."

Weston looked at her, his eyes glistening with unshed tears. "You didn't know him, Penny. He was the best of us—sharp, kind, always saw the bigger picture. He wasn't perfect, but he had this way of making you believe in better things, better people. And now... he's gone because of the same twisted ideology that tore our family apart in the first place. You know, Carmichael, I... I came to a realisation. I... I'm in love with someone."

Penny froze, the weight of Weston's sudden confession rendering her momentarily speechless. She could feel the air between them shift, the gravity of the situation pulling them into an unspoken moment of clarity. The vulnerability in Weston's voice was unlike anything she'd heard from him before.

"You're… in love?" she managed to say, her voice softer than she expected. She searched his face for a hint of his usual cheeky grin, some sign that he was about to crack a joke or spin this into one of his trademark quips. But his expression was earnest, raw, and completely serious.

Weston nodded, setting his mug down on the table with a shaky hand. "Aye. It's not something I've been good at saying out loud, Penny. I mean, you know me—I'd rather laugh my way out of awkwardness than face it head-on. But after today, after losing Cillian... it hit me how short life is. And how much time I've wasted dancing around my own feelings."

Penny's heart was pounding, her mind racing to keep up with the flood of emotions swirling in the room. She opened her mouth to respond, but Weston held up a hand, stopping her.

"Before you say anything, let me finish," he said, his voice steady but laced with a nervous edge. "I know this probably isn't the best time or place, and I'm not expecting anything from you. But you've been there for me these past couple of weeks—through the madness, the chaos, even when I've been a complete eejit. And every time I look at you, Penny, I feel... I don't know, like I've finally found someone who gets it. Who gets me."

Penny swallowed hard, her throat dry as she processed his words. She felt a mix of emotions—flattered, overwhelmed, and deeply conflicted. Weston was her colleague, her friend, and now, apparently, the man harbouring feelings for her.

"Weston…" she began, her voice barely above a whisper. She wasn't even sure what she was about to say, but the intensity in his gaze held her words in place. Then, deciding to grab the bull by the horns, she kissed him, her lips melting into his as the chaos of the day dissolved into the background. For a brief moment, there was no grief, no shattered phones, no broken families—just the two of them and the quiet relief of something real amidst the madness.

Weston responded gently, his hands trembling slightly as they came to rest on her arms. It was a tentative kiss, filled with the unspoken weight of their shared history and the whirlwind that had brought them to this point. When they finally broke apart, Penny could see the surprise and a flicker of hope in Weston's eyes.

"Penny…" he said softly, his voice trailing off as though he couldn't quite believe what had just happened.

She leaned back, her cheeks flushed, and let out a small, nervous laugh. "Well, that's one way to stop you rambling, O'Rourke."

Weston grinned, the warmth returning to his features for the first time that day. "I didn't see that coming. And Penny... the Big Weekenders... I... I don't mind you getting fucked by other blokes or women, but I want you to know… you're the one I care about. The one I'll always come back to." Weston's voice was sincere, his usual cheeky tone replaced with quiet intensity.

Penny laughed softly, shaking her head. "Leave it to you to bring up the Big Weekenders in the middle of an emotional confession. But Weston… I don't know what this is or where it's going. I don't even know if we can figure it out with all the madness going on around us."

Weston leaned forward, his gaze steady. "We don't have to figure it all out now, Penny. But today made me realise I can't keep running from what I feel. If this—us—is something, then I want to see where it goes. And if it's not, well… I'll still be here. Your chaos companion. Your late-night foot masseur. Whatever you need."

Penny smiled, feeling a warmth, one that she hadn't expected. "You're impossible, you know that?"

"Comes with the territory," Weston replied, his grin returning. "Comes with the territory."

* _ * _ * _ *

Penny was sat in Studio 2 with Rory next to her, and Abby sat on the opposite side of the desk instead of her usual production booth as the clock ticked down, her dyed yellow hair catching the studio lights. The tension in the room was palpable as they prepared for the 4pm drive show. It wasn't just the chaos of the day hanging in the air but the unspoken undercurrent of everything that had transpired earlier. Penny had barely had time to process Weston's confession—or her own impulsive response—before diving back into the relentless rhythm of live radio.

"Alright, Liverpool," Rory said, leaning into his mic as the opening jingle played out. "It's your favourite duo, Rory and Penny, here to brighten up your Wednesday. And let's just say—it's been one of those days. If you've had a bit of chaos in your life, you're not alone."

Penny forced a smile, her professional persona slipping into place as she leaned into her mic. "Absolutely, Rory. First, it's the news with Mary O'Shea, and then we've-"

Looking at her screen, Penny noticed that Zetta had queued the wrong news clip—a bulletin from an hour ago and not the most recent one, and that Abby, who was sitting opposite on the station which a third presenter would normally occupy, was frantically trying to correct it.

Quickly typing a quick message to Abby, Penny knew that the odds nobody would notice that it was the previous hour's news unless something significant had changed since then. Abby gave her a subtle nod, signalling that she'd patched it through, and the pre-recorded bulletin began to play.

As Mary O'Shea's voice filled the studio, calm and authoritative, Penny exhaled, trying to shake the lingering tension. She glanced at Rory, who was scrolling through the script on his screen, and trying hard not to laugh at how the system, in its third day of operation, was still causing chaos. Rory leaned over to Penny, muttering just loud enough for her to hear.

"Zetta's got a mind of its own, doesn't it? If it keeps this up, we might as well let it host the show."

Penny chuckled softly, grateful for the humour to lighten the mood. "Yeah, maybe we can take an early night and let Zetta handle the drive slot. I'm sure it'd make as much sense as we do."

The bulletin ended, and Abby gave them a thumbs-up from her position. Penny adjusted her headphones and leaned into the mic.

"Right, Liverpool, thanks for bearing with us," Penny said smoothly. "Now, today was a bit of a rollercoaster, wasn't it? Firstly, we're sending our thoughts to the family of our colleague here at Manic Radio, Cillian O'Rourke, who was tragically taken from us earlier today in an incident at Liverpool One. Cillian was part of the team that kept this station running behind the scenes, working his magic in our IT team, keeping our website up to date and making sure the Manic Prime app never missed a beat. He'll be deeply missed, and our thoughts are with his family and friends at this incredibly difficult time.”

Penny’s voice remained steady, but the weight of the words hung heavy in the air. Rory gave her a reassuring glance before jumping in.

“And, you know, it’s in moments like these that we’re reminded of how important it is to cherish the people around us,” Rory added, his tone unusually solemn. “So, Liverpool, if there’s someone you haven’t spoken to in a while, someone you’ve been meaning to reach out to—why not send them a message today? Let them know you’re thinking of them.”

Penny nodded, grateful for Rory’s thoughtful addition. “Well said, Rory. And as always, we’re here to keep you company through it all—whatever kind of day you’re having. Coming up next, we’ve got Calvin Harris and Ellie Goulding with Miracle—because sometimes, we all need one.”

As the familiar opening beats of Miracle filled the studio, Penny leaned back in her chair, finally allowing herself a moment to breathe. The weight of the day still pressed heavily on her, but the routine of live radio offered a strange comfort, a semblance of normalcy amidst the chaos. Rory, ever the expert in lightening the mood, leaned over and gave her a cheeky nudge.

"Lane," he whispered, his tone conspiratorial, "you’re the rock of this station today. If Abby and I had to deal with what you’ve been through, we’d have cracked by now. I’d probably be halfway through a bottle of gin in Studio 3."

Penny smirked despite herself, shaking her head. "Don't tempt me, Carter. Anyway, Weston and I... we've kind of admitted that we're more than just colleagues."

Rory's eyebrows shot up, and a grin spread across his face. "Oh, well, well, well! The Wirral gal and the Ballymena boy, huh? You've got to spill, Lane—did this revelation happen before or after his legendary toilet debacle?"

Penny rolled her eyes, fighting the blush creeping into her cheeks. "After, obviously. I mean, who wouldn't fall for someone in that situation? Stuck on a toilet, shattered phone, ripped jeans… the height of romance."

Rory stifled a laugh, leaning back in his chair. "I knew there was chemistry there, but I didn't expect it to come out like this. Manic Radio really does bring people together, doesn't it? Or, in your case, forces them to confront their feelings after a family tragedy and a plumbing disaster."

Abby, who had been monitoring the show's flow from her spot, smirked. "I'd say 'only at Manic,' but trust me, there's been bets on when you two would bite the bullet since you pair started here two weeks ago."

Penny groaned, dropping her head into her hands. "Bets? Seriously? You lot are unbelievable."

Abby shrugged, her smirk widening. "What can I say? It's part of the Manic way. We thrive on chaos, whether it's technical glitches, workplace romances, or Weston's ability to turn even a toilet disaster into a headline."

Rory chuckled, adjusting his mic. "Well, speaking of headlines, I think we've just found our next listener topic— 'Embarrassing Moments That Turned Into Love Stories.'"

Penny shot him a warning glare, though a small smile tugged at her lips. "Don't even think about it, Carter."

"Oh, come on, Lane," Rory teased. "The listeners would love it. Weston's toilet tale could become the stuff of Manic legend. And think of the content—it's a win-win!"

Before Penny could respond, Abby tapped her pen against her notepad to refocus them. "Alright, lovebirds, let's keep it professional for now. We've got a show to run. Save the romantic revelations for after the last track of the day."

Penny sighed, sitting up straighter in her chair. "Fine. But if anyone brings this up on air, I'm blaming you, Carter."

Rory held up his hands in mock surrender. "Wouldn't dream of it. Well, not yet, anyway."

The light banter was a welcome distraction as the show rolled on. Despite the lingering tension from earlier events, Penny found herself easing back into the rhythm of the drive slot. The familiar flow of links, music, and audience interaction reminded her why she loved radio— it was a chance to connect, to bring a little levity even in the darkest moments.

"So, Liverpool," Penny said as the half past 6 news finished, and she had two minutes until the next track was scheduled to playout, "We've got... a clue."

The jingle for the Manic Marauder and the pre-recorded voice of the Manic Marauder host, a deep and mysterious tone, echoed through the studio:

"Your next clue, Liverpool... The Marauder's treasure lies where history and tides collide. Seek the merchant who never sailed. Find me there Saturday... if you dare."

Penny grinned as the studio lights dimmed slightly for effect. The Marauder campaign had been a stroke of genius by the marketing team, blending nostalgia with a fresh twist, and the audience engagement was off the charts. She leaned into the mic, her voice warm and inviting.

"Alright, Liverpool, you've got the clue—where history and tides collide. Wherever the clue may lead you to will be the location, this Saturday between 12 and 1, somewhere in the Merseyside area. It's a network campaign, so all Manic stations across the UK will be playing this game here in Liverpool this weekend. Remember, the jackpot stands at £50,000, so get your thinking caps on and start piecing it together. Only 1 person can win it, and it'll roll over to the next round later that day. Entry is free as all you have to do is ask one question to everyone you see, and what is that question, Rory?"

Rory leaned into his mic, his trademark cheeky grin audible in his voice.

"And that question is... 'Are you the Marauder?' Simple, Liverpool. Ask everyone you see on Saturday at the mystery location. Remember, the Marauder will only respond to the correct question. If you're the lucky one who figures it out first, you could be walking away with a cool £50k. No pressure, eh?"

Penny chuckled, playing along. "No pressure at all. And remember, Liverpool, the Marauder isn't just hiding—it's blending in. So, keep your eyes peeled and your wits about you. And hey, if you see someone dressed like they're ready for a pirate convention, maybe give them an extra nudge."

"And we'll be at that location, reporting live on Manic Radio Liverpool and across the Manic Radio network," Rory added, his tone brimming with excitement. "Penny and I will be there, soaking up the madness and cheering you on as you hunt down the elusive Marauder. So, if you're in the area, come say hi—just don't forget to ask us the question too. You never know, we might have a few surprises up our sleeves."

Penny laughed, leaning back in her chair as the next track began to play. "You, surprises? Rory, the day you stop being predictable is the day I'll eat my Manic mug live on air."

Rory feigned offence, clutching his chest dramatically. "Predictable? Penny Lane, I'm hurt. I'll have you know I'm full of mystery and intrigue. You just haven't cracked the code yet."

As the beats of Let's Go by Calvin Harris and Ne-Yo pulsed through the studio, Penny allowed herself a moment to reflect. The events of the day—Weston's confession, the tragedy of his cousin, the surreal mix of humour and heartbreak—had left her emotionally drained but also strangely grounded. Life at Manic Radio Liverpool was unpredictable, messy, and often overwhelming, but it was also vibrant and alive in a way she'd never experienced before.

****

# CHAPTER 10 – Visit to Ballymena
## Thursday 19th September 2024

The early morning ferry from Holyhead to Dublin rocked gently on the Irish Sea, the low hum of the engines blending with the soft chatter of passengers and the occasional clink of coffee cups. Penny sat at a small table near the window, gazing out at the expanse of grey water that stretched endlessly towards the horizon. The journey was calm, but her thoughts were anything but.

Next to her, Weston O'Rourke nursed a steaming cup of tea, his ginger curls slightly tousled from the early start. His usual cheeky grin was absent, replaced by an expression of quiet contemplation. Penny glanced at him, wondering what was going through his mind. It wasn't every day you travelled to confront the ghosts of your family's past—and present.

"You alright?" Penny asked softly, breaking the silence. She'd asked the question several times since they'd boarded, but it felt necessary each time.

Weston nodded, though his gaze remained fixed on the horizon. "Aye, I'm grand. Just... thinking, you know? It's been a while since I've been back to Ballymena. Feels like a lifetime, but it's only been a couple of years."

Penny nodded, wrapping her hands around her own cup for warmth. She'd agreed to come with Weston without hesitation when he'd suggested the trip the previous night. After everything that had happened with his cousin Cillian, he felt compelled to return to Northern Ireland, to face his family and pay his respects. Penny didn't know what she could offer beyond her presence, but she hoped it would be enough.

The ferry docked in Dublin as the sun began to rise, casting a golden glow over the bustling port. Weston had rented a car for the next leg of the journey—a drive north to Ballymena, a small town steeped in history and marked by its proximity to the complex politics of the region.

Penny had never been to Ireland, neither the Republic or Northern Ireland, and knew that the stereotype of Irish people were that they were alcohols, had red hair, fought a lot, like to talk and talk and talk and were obsessed with religion, with the stereotype that those who lived in the Republic were Catholic and those who lived in Northern Ireland were Protestant. She also knew that such stereotypes were overly simplistic and outdated, but as they walked into the car hire station, the first of those were totally and utterly shattered.

The man at the desk greeted them with a warm, welcoming smile, his accent a lilting blend of Dublin charm. "Mornin'," he said cheerily, "Have ya reserved a car, or do you need to sort one out here?"

Weston frowned. "It was a bit of a last minute thing, so I didn't manage to book ahead," he admitted, his Northern Irish lilt softening slightly, likely out of habit when speaking with someone from the Republic.

The attendant nodded knowingly, tapping away at his keyboard. "Not to worry, lad. We've a good few options left. You're headin' up north, yeah?"

"Aye," Weston replied, glancing at Penny. "Up to Ballymena."

The man raised an eyebrow. "There's going to be an extra charge leaving the Republic, and the insurance is gonna cost ya."

"What? Your website says-"

"That's the British one, not the Irish one," the man said with an air of amusement, clearly accustomed to dealing with cross-border travellers. "What driving licence do you have?"

"A British-"

"Ah, that's going to cost even more," the man interrupted with a wry smile. "British licences come with a higher insurance premium when you're hiring in the Republic. Something about 'cross-border liabilities.' Bureaucracy, eh? And if you want to add the missus to-"

"Let me guess, you'll add another surcharge for adding a driver with a British licence?" Weston interjected, his tone caught between irritation and amusement.

The attendant laughed, clearly unfazed. "You've got it, lad. And if she's under 25, there's a youth driver fee as well."

"Damn, I'm 22, so that surcharge would be mine to cover," Penny said, raising an eyebrow. "Guess I'm not driving this time, then."

Weston let out a chuckle, shaking his head as he handed

over his documents. "We'll manage with just me behind the wheel, thanks. You've got a grand little racket going here, though."

The man laughed again, handing over the keys to a compact black hatchback. "Enjoy your trip and watch out for the Gardaí down here—they don't take kindly to speeding tourists. Once you cross the border, though, I hear the PSNI have bigger fish to fry."

Weston smirked, taking the keys. "Cheers. We'll keep it steady."

* _ * _ * _ *

As they left Dublin city centre, Penny noticed Weston wasn't driving from a satnav or a map book, but from memory, relying on an instinctive knowledge of the roads and landmarks that had been ingrained in him from years of navigating the area during his childhood.

Looking at the radio, Penny noticed that Weston had turned it to Cool FM, a Bauer station known for its high-energy CHR format similar to Manic Radio. The upbeat tracks filled the car, but the tension between them was palpable. Penny stole a glance at Weston, who seemed lost in thought as he drummed his fingers on the steering wheel in time with the music.

"You've not forgotten how to get there, have you?" Penny teased lightly, hoping to ease some of the tension.

Weston smiled faintly, his eyes still fixed on the road. "Not a chance. These roads are burned into my memory. I know how to get from Dublin to Belfast as, when Bauer brought the Communicorp Ireland stations, they moved their IT servers to the UK offices. Spent many a long weekend travelling this route when I was freelancing for Cool FM back in the day."

Penny chuckled, as she knew that Weston was a former Bauer employee who was a producer for Cool FM before joining Manic Radio, and that he had left because of an allegation of sexual misconduct that had been proven false but left him deeply disillusioned with his previous role. He had mentioned it to her once and compared it to Manic's more libertarian attitudes towards interpersonal relationships and station culture.

Crossing the border into Northern Ireland, the landscape subtly changed. Road signs switched from kilometres to miles, and the prevalence of Northern Ireland cars appeared.

"We've got a choice," Weston said, as they passed Newtowncloghoge. "We can go via Belfast, and I can show you the Titanic Quarter, or we can take the back roads through the countryside. The latter's longer as we have to go through Cookstown, but our flight is from Belfast International tomorrow morning, so we could save the sightseeing for then. What do you fancy?"

Penny pondered the options. The allure of Belfast's Titanic Quarter was tempting, but the idea of experiencing the countryside, especially in such a deeply personal and reflective journey, felt more fitting.

"Let's take the back roads," she decided. "I'd like to see more of the place that shaped you—and maybe get a better feel for Ballymena before we dive into the deep end."

Weston nodded, a faint smile tugging at the corners of his lips. "Good choice. It's not all beauty and charm, mind—there's a reason they call Ballymena 'the buckle on the Bible Belt.' But the countryside's something else entirely. You'll see."

They turned off the main motorway, the car now winding through narrow roads bordered by sprawling green fields and occasional clusters of houses. The world outside the window felt slower, quieter, a stark contrast to the high-energy chaos of Liverpool and Manic Radio.

Penny gazed out at the passing scenery, the rolling hills and grazing sheep lending an almost dreamlike quality to the journey. "It's beautiful," she murmured, more to herself than Weston.

"It is," he agreed, his voice carrying a tinge of nostalgia. "But beauty can be deceiving. Ballymena's a place of contradictions. It's where I learned to love, to fight, to stand my ground. And it's where I realised I didn't fit in."

Penny turned to him, her expression soft. "Do you miss it?"

Weston hesitated, his hands tightening briefly on the wheel. "Parts of it, maybe. The simplicity, the sense of community—even if it came with strings attached. But I don't miss the politics, the judgment, or the constant pressure to pick a side. That's why I left. I wanted more than what Ballymena could offer."

Penny nodded, understanding the complexity of his emotions. "And now, going back… does it feel like you're stepping into the past?"

Weston glanced at her, his expression thoughtful. "Aye, it does. But it's not just my past—it's my family's past too. And no matter how much I've tried to distance myself, I can't escape it. Especially not now."

His words hung heavy in the air, a reminder of the gravity of their journey. Penny reached over, placing a hand on his arm briefly. "You're not facing it alone, Weston. I'm here."

He gave her a small, grateful smile before returning his focus to the road. "Thanks, Penny. That means more than you know."

* _ * _ * _ *

They arrived in Ballymena in the early afternoon, the town unfolding before them with its mix of historic charm and modern touches. Weston navigated the streets with an ease born of familiarity, his years of living in the town just outside Belfast showing.

"And this is the Wrightbus factory," Weston said, gesturing toward a large industrial building as they drove past. "They're one of the biggest employers around here—make buses for cities all over the world. The buses in Liverpool that Arriva use were built here. When I was younger, there was a friend of mine who was a bus spotter, used to hang around the factory gates and take pictures of the new models before they were shipped off. Thomas his name was, Thomas McAllister. Proper bus nut, he was. I still chat to him on the phone. He drives for Ulsterbus nowadays, based out of their depot in Antrim. Always said he wanted to work for them, and he made it happen. Still sends me pictures of buses sometimes—bit of nostalgia, I guess."

Penny smiled at the fondness in Weston's tone. "Sounds like a good mate. Did you ever think about staying here, you know, keeping things simple?"

Weston chuckled, shaking his head. "Not really. Ballymena's fine if you want a quiet life, but I was never built for that. I wanted more than what these streets had to offer. And once I got a taste of radio, there was no going back. My first job was as a 13 year old, a tea boy for Q107 FM Ballymena—me uncle Len was a local presenter there. He let me tag along one summer, and I fell in love with it all—the music, the energy, the connection with people. Even the smell of the studio had something magical about it. Ballymena couldn't hold me after that. When I was 16, I got a job with the BBC, as a trainee studio technician at BBC Radio Ulster. That was my ticket out, you know? I used to commute into Belfast every day after school, and when I left sixth form, I went full-time. They wanted me to go to uni, do the proper training, but I'd already fallen in love with the practical side of it all. I was learning more by being there than I ever could in a classroom. When I was 20, I got a job at Bauer as a junior producer on their Downtown Radio and Cool FM brands. Technically, Downtown and Cool are part of the Hits network, but they've always had their own identity here in Northern Ireland. It felt like a step up from the BBC, more fast-paced, more commercial. But then…

well, you know the rest. False allegations, the fallout, and my move to Manic."

Penny nodded, her eyes following the passing houses and shops as Weston drove. His story was one she had heard in bits and pieces, but this journey seemed to peel back more layers, revealing the raw emotions and memories tied to his home.

"Do you think your family's changed since you left?" Penny asked hesitantly, unsure if the question would hit a nerve.

Weston shrugged, his expression unreadable. "Some have, I suppose. My sister Cathy, for one. She's always been her own person, not afraid to challenge the family's expectations. But others… like my granddad Michael, they're set in their ways. He's stuck in the past, in the ideals of the 'old guard.' And that's what worries me most—how much his influence still lingers."

As they approached Weston's family home, Penny could feel the tension in the air. The house was modest but well-kept, unlike those of her native Wirral where decay seemed to be a common feature in certain parts, with neatly trimmed hedges and a whitewashed facade. The driveway was flanked by a small garden, where roses bloomed defiantly against the chill of the autumn air. Weston pulled the car to a stop, switching off the engine and exhaling deeply.

"This is it," he said, his voice quieter than usual. "Home sweet home… or something like that."

Penny glanced at him, sensing his unease. "Ready?"

He nodded, though his expression betrayed his doubts.

"As ready as I'll ever be."

They stepped out of the car, the gravel crunching beneath their feet as they approached the front door. Before Weston could knock, the door swung open, revealing a man in his 80's who Penny recognised as Weston's grandfather, Michael O'Rourke, his presence imposing despite his advancing years. His sharp eyes darted between Weston and Penny, a flicker of recognition and perhaps disapproval crossing his face as he took in the scene before him. Michael stood tall for his age, his silver hair neatly combed and his stance reminiscent of the authority he had once wielded in his younger days.

"Well, I thought you were dead. The lads must have got the wrong traitor," the elder O'Rourke said gruffly, his voice carrying the weight of years and judgement. "Yer a disgrace to the cause, Weston, and yer'll burn in hell for yer betrayal. Get out, yer not welcome."

Weston froze for a moment, the sting of his grandfather's words visible in his taut shoulders and clenched jaw. Penny, standing beside him, felt her own pulse quicken. She had braced herself for tension, but the outright hostility in Michael O'Rourke's voice caught her off guard.

"Granddad," Weston began, his voice calm but strained, "I'm not here to argue. Cillian and I worked together, and he's family. He's been dead less than 36 hours and yer accusing him and me of treachery? Have some bloody respect, Granddad!" Weston's voice cracked slightly as he spoke, the weight of his emotions pressing down on him.

Michael's eyes narrowed, his lips curling into a sneer. "Respect? For a boy who turned his back on his own blood? Who sided with the Brits and took a Unionist's path? Yer no grandson of mine, Weston O'Rourke. And don't even get me started on that Protestant sympathiser Cillian. He got what was coming to him—an O'Rourke who forgets his heritage doesn't deserve the name."

Penny's heart clenched as she watched Weston's fists tighten at his sides. The man standing before them was a relic of a past that Weston had spent his life trying to escape—a man who saw loyalty as black and white, with no room for nuance or individuality.

"Cillian was your grandson too!" Weston snapped, his voice rising. "He wasn't a traitor—he was a good man, better than any of us. He didn't deserve to die, and he sure as hell didn't deserve to be killed by someone who should've been protecting him!"

Michael's gaze flicked to Penny, his expression hardening. "And who's this, then? Another English lass come to corrupt ya? What's the matter, Weston? Couldn't find a nice Catholic girl to settle down with? Let me guess, yer've deflowered her before you even brought her to Mass. Typical of ya to drag someone else into yer disgrace."

Penny bristled at the man's audacity, her temper rising alongside Weston's. But before she could speak, Weston stepped forward, his voice low and steady, the anger barely concealed.

"Don't you dare," he said, his Northern Irish accent thick with emotion. "Don't you dare talk about Penny like that. She's here because she cares, not that you'd understand what that means. She's got more respect in her little finger than you've shown your own family in years. Anyway, it's not as if I'm the only sinner in the family. Damien enjoys using his choir boys like he had been used as a kid, and you condone him abusing them the same way the priest who hurt him did. You can't stand the truth, can you, Granddad? You've built your whole life on loyalty and honour, but all you've done is destroy the people who needed you the most. Cillian's dead because of people like you—your 'cause,' your so-called 'heritage.' You didn't protect him. You left him to be a target."

Michael's face darkened, his posture stiffening as if every fibre of his being resisted Weston's accusations. His voice, cold and unyielding, cut through the tension like a knife. "Mind your tongue, boy. Yer've no right to speak to me like that in my own home."

Weston's laugh was bitter, his eyes blazing with a mixture of anger and pain. "Your home? Actually, it's Dad's name on the deeds, not yours, so he decides who can enter and leave. You've been living off everyone else's goodwill for years, Granddad. Playing the hero of a war that's long over, spinning your tales to anyone who'll listen while tearing your own family apart. And what was that about the 'lads' not getting me? Was I meant to be the target of their attack instead of Cillian? Was that it, Granddad? You've sunk so low that you'd rather see one of your own blood killed than let them live a life you don't approve of?"

Michael O'Rourke's face flushed with anger, his fists clenching at his sides. The old man was clearly not used to being challenged so openly, especially not by his own grandson. "Watch yer tongue, Weston. You don't know what you're talking about. The cause—our cause—was about freedom, about dignity for our people. Cillian forgot that, and yer've been forgetting it too."

"No, Granddad," Weston shot back, his voice breaking slightly. "The 'cause' was about survival and unity—at least that's what you told us when we were kids. But you've twisted it into something else, something toxic. Cillian didn't forget anything. He made his own choices, just like I have. And if that makes me a traitor in your eyes, then so be it. I'd rather be a 'traitor' than live with the hatred and bitterness that's consumed you."

Penny stood rooted to the spot, the sheer weight of the confrontation leaving her momentarily speechless. She felt a surge of admiration for Weston—his courage in standing up to his grandfather, his refusal to let Michael's words go unchallenged. But she could also see the toll it was taking on him, the raw pain etched into his features.

Michael's gaze shifted to Penny again, his expression hard and unrelenting. "And what about you, lass? Yer standing there, watching all this—thinking you know us, know our lives. What do yer think of yer boyfriend now, eh? Still think he's some kind of saint, or have yer seen the blood on his hands?"

Penny took a step forward, her voice calm but firm. "Weston doesn't have blood on his hands, Mr O'Rourke. And neither did Cillian. The only blood here is on the people who think violence is the answer to everything—people who would rather destroy their own families than let them live their lives in peace. If you can't see that, then I feel sorry for you."

Weston shot her a grateful look, the faintest flicker of a smile crossing his lips. Michael, however, looked as though he'd been slapped. His eyes narrowed, and for a moment, it seemed as though he might lash out again. But instead, he turned away, his voice gruff and dismissive.

"Yer've made yer choice, Weston. Don't come crying to me when it all falls apart. And don't expect me to shed any tears for yer when it does."

****

# CHAPTER 11 – The Return of the Marauder

## Saturday 21st September 2024

"The Marauder's treasure lies where history and tides collide. Seek the merchant who never sailed. Find me there Saturday... if you dare."

That was one of four clues that had aired as part of the nationwide Manic Marauder promotion, a flagship campaign that had listeners across the network on edge with excitement. The mysterious treasure hunt, blending cryptic riddles and local history, had proven a stroke of genius. Each Manic hub across the country had aired the same clues, with stations outside of Merseyside and the Wirral having hinted that the clue was a Liverpool region as a fifth clue. The anticipation had been building all week, and now the day had arrived.

Sitting in one of the cars was branded for the Manic Canaries, the newly rebranded promotional crew that was now a feature of all the Manic stations, a fleet of BYD Dolphins painted in neon green, yellow and white, all electric cars that were making their debut as part of Manic's sustainability push, Penny was sat in the driver's seat next to the person who was playing the Marauder, a Manic Radio Cumbria runner who was, funnily enough, a bus enthusiast, the last person that people would assume was the mysterious Marauder.

Penny glanced at the time on the dashboard. It was just past 11:30 am, and the streets of Liverpool were already buzzing with activity. Listeners had been speculating online all week about the location of the Marauder's treasure. Social media was awash with theories, ranging from the Albert Dock to the Liver Building, but the consensus was starting to settle on Birkenhead Market— a location rich in history and perfectly aligned with the cryptic clue.

Unfortunately, the guesses for Birkenhead were wrong, as it was Canning Place, where the Liverpool One bus station and Canning Dock intersected. The "merchant who never sailed" referenced the historic connections of Canning Dock, once a hub for goods and trade but also a sobering reminder of Liverpool's involvement in the transatlantic slave trade. "History and tides collide" was a nod to Liverpool's maritime legacy, and the location's proximity to the River Mersey made it the perfect choice.

Penny adjusted her headphones, as she was acting as an on-the-scene reporter for the Network show that was on on a Saturday, Papa Wolf's Wake Up, the Saturday morning show that ran from 9 in the morning to 1 in the afternoon, presented by the charismatic "Papa Wolf," real name Harry Wolfe. The show had a reputation for its wild antics, high-energy banter, and ability to draw listeners into the thick of Manic Radio's chaos. Broadcast from Studio 2 at Speke, where Penny and Rory normally did their local drive show, Papa Wolf's show was a network favourite, pulling in listeners from across the UK. Today, his lively voice boomed into Penny's earpiece as she prepared for her live report.

"It's quarter to 12, and we're gearing up for the first appearance of the Manic Marauder, and today he's somewhere in Merseyside. We've got Manic Radio

Liverpool's Penny Lane somewhere in the Merseyside area to give us a run down of the clues that have aired across the Manic network all week. Penny, where are you, and what's the vibe like this morning?"

Penny took a deep breath and leaned into her mic, her voice smooth and confident despite the mild chaos around her. "Good morning, Papa Wolf, I'm here somewhere in Merseyside, ready to give you the clues again. The first clue, which appeared on Monday during Kyle and Sue's early afternoon show was 'In the shadow of the stone sisters, a legacy of trade endures.' Tuesday, during Big Lou's mid-morning show, the clue was 'Where the past meets the present, and the waters hold their secrets.'. On Wednesday during Drive, the clue was... 'The Marauder's treasure lies where history and tides collide. Seek the merchant who never sailed.' and during Toni Green's evening show on Thursday, the final clue was 'Where two worlds meet, and stories are told, the secrets of the dock unfold.' Finally, on Friday, the clue was 'Two giants, a park apart, the Marauder's treasure lies within their gaze.'"

Papa Wolf chuckled, his tone brimming with excitement. "Cracking clues, Penny. Those sound like they've been driving the listeners wild all week. So, what's your guess at where the Marauder could be hiding? Give us your expert deduction, Penny Lane!"

Penny grinned, leaning into the mic as she glanced at the buzzing scene around her. "Well, Papa Wolf, if I were the Marauder—and sadly, I'm not—I'd say the clues point to a place steeped in Liverpool's rich history. Where history and tides collide? That screams our waterfront. And as for the 'merchant who never sailed,' my money's on somewhere like Canning Dock, near Liverpool One. It's got the maritime connection and the perfect mix of old and new."

"Brilliant deduction, Penny," Papa Wolf replied. "And for those listeners just joining us, the first person to find the Marauder and ask them the all-important question, 'Are you the Marauder?' wins today's jackpot of £50,000. It's a life-changing amount, and we're counting down to when the hunt officially begins at noon. Penny, keep us posted, and don't let the excitement sweep you away!"

"I'll try not to, Wolf," Penny said with a laugh. "But let me tell you, the energy here is electric. I've already seen a few groups gathering, all eager to crack the clues and find the Marauder. It's shaping up to be a fantastic day."

Looking out of the window of the car, however, she knew that there wasn't as many people at the expected location as Manic might have hoped. A few clusters of eager listeners loitered nearby, chatting animatedly and glancing at their phones, likely cross-referencing the clues with maps and online theories. Penny's radio crackled in her earpiece, and Papa Wolf's voice came through once more.

"Alright, Lane, I hear it's a bit quiet where you are. Do you think the listeners have overthought the clues, or are we looking at a sneaky late arrival for the big prize hunters?"

Penny smirked, leaning into her mic. "Could be either, Wolf. Liverpool's a big place, and these clues are as cryptic as ever. Some might be scouting the wrong spots first, but I reckon we'll see a surge as we get closer to noon. The £50,000 prize is definitely enough to bring people running."

At 11:55, her phone buzzed with a message from Alan Hamilton, the Regional Head of Programming.

Alan Hamilton: "Crowd light at Canning Dock. Stay upbeat but improvise if it's a no-show situation. Don't worry, Penny—you've got this."

Penny sighed inwardly, glancing at the Cumbria runner sitting beside her, who was dressed like an average person on the street, and could see on the chat that various Manic Canary crews were dotted around Merseyside, as they were required to document the hunt's progress in real-time. Her heart raced slightly as she considered the possibility of a lukewarm turnout for the big event. Still, she knew how to roll with the punches—that was the Manic Radio way.

As the clock struck noon, Penny spoke again, her voice steady and enthusiastic. "Alright, Wolf and listeners, the time has come! The hunt for the Marauder is officially on. We're here at the docks, where history and tides collide, and the excitement is building. Remember, all you need to do is find the Marauder and ask, 'Are you the Marauder?' But time is ticking, so get moving, Liverpool!"

The Cumbria runner stepped out of the car, blending seamlessly into the scattered crowd. He meandered around the bus station area, his demeanour calm and casual, as if he were just another passerby. Penny had to chuckle as he started taking photographs of the buses exiting the bus station from the Canning Dock exit of Liverpool One, blending into the public without drawing suspicion. The thrill of the treasure hunt was palpable now, even if the turnout wasn't as massive as anticipated.

Getting out the car, Penny knew that she had to start making posts on social media, hyping the event to draw in more participants. She pulled out her phone and snapped a few pictures of the bustling waterfront, making sure to include the dock and a few cryptic angles of the area without giving too much away.

**@PennyLaneManic:** *The hunt is on! The Marauder is somewhere in Merseyside right now. £50,000 is at stake. Where history and tides collide… could it be here?* 👀 *Get searching, Liverpool!* *#ManicMarauder #TreasureHunt*

As the post went live, she saw notifications instantly start pinging—listeners tagging their friends, debating locations, and speculating on the clues. Chuckling, she noticed that, out of all the people that were being asked, Louis, the person who had been selected to be the Marauder, was the only person not being asked by people if he was the Marauder. His clever disguise as an unassuming bus enthusiast had paid off, and it seemed even the most eager participants had overlooked him entirely.

By 12:15, the crowd had started to swell as more participants arrived, phones in hand and eyes scanning the area for any sign of the elusive Marauder. Penny kept her commentary lively, juggling updates to social media with her live reports for Papa Wolf's show.

"Wolf, it's starting to pick up here," Penny reported, weaving through the growing crowd with her mic in hand. "People are finally zeroing in on this spot, and I can see a few determined faces. I've even overheard some theories being shared—everything from 'It's someone dressed as a pirate' to 'It's definitely a dockworker.' The speculation is wild!"

Papa Wolf's laugh boomed in her earpiece. "I love it, Penny. The Marauder could be anyone—and that's what makes it so brilliant. Keep those updates coming; the whole nation is hooked."

Penny caught sight of a group of teenagers approaching Louis, their excitement evident as they gestured animatedly. She paused, watching closely as they asked him something—but it wasn't the magic question. Louis simply nodded politely and continued taking photos of the buses.

"Looks like someone just missed their chance," Penny said into her mic, a smile tugging at her lips. "The Marauder's blending in perfectly. If you're listening, Liverpool, remember the question: 'Are you the Marauder?' That's all it takes!"

The tension built as the minutes ticked by. Penny noticed a young woman, perhaps in her late twenties, hesitating near Louis. She appeared deep in thought, clutching her phone as she glanced between the clues on her screen and the man before her. Penny could almost see the wheels turning in her mind. But then the clock ticked 1pm, and the hour was over, the game rolled on to its next phase. Penny's heart sank slightly as she realised that Louis, the bus enthusiast Marauder, had gone undiscovered for this round. Yet, the thrill of the event and the energy of the crowd around her still buzzed with excitement.

Papa Wolf's voice came through her earpiece once more, his tone upbeat and playful. "Alright, Penny, the first round is officially over, and it seems the Marauder's treasure remains unclaimed! But that just means the jackpot rolls over. Now, he's going to be in Merseyside later this afternoon, and you have the next clue. What is it?"

Penny knew, looking at her cue card, that the next location, at 5pm, would be at John Lennon Airport, and that the clue would lead listeners there. She leaned into her mic, her voice calm but enticing, as she read off the scripted lines.

"Alright, Wolf, here's the next clue for our Merseyside treasure hunters. Listen closely: 'Where journeys begin and memories take flight, seek the shadows of the famous face in the spotlight.' The Marauder's next location is set for 5pm, and this time, the jackpot stands at an incredible

£52,000. Yes, its rolled over and increased from £50,000 to a whopping £52,000. So, Britain, get your thinking caps on and start piecing this one together. My colleagues from Manic Radio Liverpool, Abby Blue and Rory Carter will be live from that location at 5pm on the Manic Rock Takeover on Manic Radio England, the Big Scotland Footie Phone-in on Manic Radio Scotland and Sŵn y Sul on Manic Radio Wales. Wherever you are, you can tune in and follow the action as it unfolds. Who knows—this time, the Marauder might just be caught!"

Papa Wolf chimed in with his signature enthusiasm, "That's what we love to hear, Penny. The tension builds, the jackpot grows, and the hunt continues! A huge shoutout to everyone who came out for the first round—don't give up yet. You've got another chance this afternoon, and £52,000 is nothing to sniff at. Penny, thanks for keeping us on the edge of our seats. We'll catch up with Abby and Rory at the next spot. Meanwhile, I'm here to keep the tunes going and the vibes high. Stay sharp, Britain—the Marauder's out there, and they're waiting for you! Anyway, I'm off, its 'Saturday Power' up next with Mike Peters here on Manic Radio!"

Penny smiled as Papa Wolf signed off, her adrenaline still pumping from the event. Despite the lack of a winner in the first round, she knew the campaign was far from over. The rolling jackpot and the growing buzz on social media guaranteed that the excitement would only increase as the day went on.

She walked back toward the branded Manic Canaries car, Louis already inside, looking somewhat relieved to have made it through the round unnoticed. "Well, that went smoothly," he said with a grin. "Not a single person guessed it was me. I was half-expecting to get mobbed!"

Penny laughed, shaking her head as she buckled into the driver's seat. "You're good at blending in. The photos of buses were a nice touch. You could probably do this full-time if the running gig doesn't work out."

"Hey, I'm a genuine bus enthusiast, so it wasn't even an act," Louis quipped, a cheeky grin spreading across his face. "Are we off to the hub now for a lunch break or a quick prep before heading to John Lennon Airport?"

Penny started the car, glancing at the time. "We've got a bit of time before the next round kicks off, so let's head back to the Speke hub. I could use a bite to eat, and we'll go over the plan for this afternoon. Abby and Rory are already gearing up for the airport round, so we'll join the briefing there."

Louis nodded, leaning back in his seat with a content sigh. "Sounds good. I've got to say, it's been 10 years since I last did the Marauder gig - last time it was ran, I'd been with Manic only a year and was the youngest runner in the team and had been asked to do the various rounds for an extra day's pay. Funny how, 10 years ago, I was working in Carlisle and had to uproot myself for a fortnight to work down here in Liverpool for the Manic Marauder campaign. Nowadays with the hubs it's a case of basing myself at a hub for a few days while I work through the list. You know I'm doing Chester tomorrow for the Marauder?"

Penny chuckled as she navigated the car through the busy streets of Liverpool, heading back toward the Speke hub. "Chester, eh? That's a good one—plenty of historic spots to work with there. You'll blend right in again, especially if you pull out that bus enthusiast act. I can see it now: 'The Marauder, a master of disguises, hiding in plain sight with a camera photo'ing buses."

"Yeah, the downside, however, is I can't tell my family where I'm going or why, just that its work related and that from Tuesday I'll be away from here until the campaign wraps up at the end of the month. We're doing rounds all over the country, so I'll be on the road quite a bit. After Chester, I'm heading to Manchester on Monday, Edinburgh for the Tuesday to Thursday rounds, and then Brum for the Friday to Monday rounds, with London and then South Wales bringing up the final legs of the campaign." Louis stretched his legs out, settling into the passenger seat as they drove. "It's a bit of a whirlwind, but it's all part of the job. And honestly, I love the buzz of it all. Keeps things exciting, you know?"

Penny nodded, her thoughts already shifting to the upcoming round at John Lennon Airport. The Marauder campaign was proving to be an exhilarating mix of tension, creativity, and community engagement. Even with the lighter turnout at the docks, the energy surrounding the event had been contagious, and she had no doubt that the afternoon round would draw an even bigger crowd.

"You know," Penny said, glancing at Louis as they pulled into the Speke hub's car park, "this campaign might just be the best thing Manic's done in a long time. It's not just about the prize—it's the way it's bringing people together, getting them out and exploring their cities."

"Like Pokémon Go used to be at the height of its popularity," Louis finished, laughing. "Except instead of catching Pokémon, they're chasing me around trying to figure out if I'm the Marauder. And I've got to say, it's much less tiring than running from gyms to Pokéstops."

Penny grinned as she parked the Manic Canaries car. "Ah, that's going back a few years. I miss the days of randomly bumping into strangers and bonding over a Pikachu or a rare spawn. But hey, who needs Pikachu when you've got £52,000 on the line and a nationwide audience waiting to see who cracks the clues first?"

The two stepped out of the car and headed inside the Speke hub, greeted by the familiar hum of activity. Abby Blue was already in the break room, sipping a coffee and scrolling through her tablet, likely reviewing details for the 5pm broadcast. Rory Carter leaned against the counter, his easy-going smile lighting up the room as he saw Penny and Louis enter.

"Well, well," Rory said, raising his mug in a mock toast. "If it isn't Liverpool's own Sherlock Holmes and the elusive Marauder. How'd it go at the docks? Any close calls?"

Louis shook his head with a grin. "Not even a little. I was hiding in plain sight, mate. Apparently, looking like a bus nerd is the ultimate disguise. No one batted an eyelid. Plus, I kind of managed to photo a few brand new buses on their first weekend in service, so I'm happy that I've got those photo'd. Can't beat a brand new Enviro200EV in the new Merseytravel Metro livery that's going to be more frequent when franchising kicks in next year."

Rory let out a laugh, clearly enjoying the banter. "Mate, you've got it all figured out. Blend in, get your kicks, and keep the jackpot safe. Honestly, you should write a book on the art of being invisible—'The Disguised Marauder: A Masterclass.'"

Penny rolled her eyes but couldn't help smiling as she grabbed a sandwich from the break room fridge. "You're all ridiculous. But honestly, it's genius. No one suspects the quiet bus enthusiast snapping photos. It's the perfect way to keep people guessing. Anyway, I'm knocking off after I've had a brew, as my day is over."

"Meanwhile, Abby and I will be the ones braving the airport chaos," Rory said, chuckling. "You know how much I love transport hubs. Nothing like fighting through a sea of stressed-out travellers while trying to broadcast live."

Abby snorted, setting down her coffee. "Oh, come on, Rory. John Lennon Airport's not that bad. And you're forgetting—the clue's brilliant. 'Shadows of the famous face in the spotlight'? It's got Lennon written all over it. The listeners will be swarming the place in no time."

Penny raised her mug in mock solidarity. "Well, good luck with that. I'll be cheering you on from the comfort of my sofa as I get dolled up... we've got the Manc lot coming for another Big Weekender, ain't we?" Penny said, leaning against the counter with a smirk.

Abby nodded, a grin spreading across her face. "You bet. Spence has got us the VIP Lady Chapel at Alma de Cuba on Seel Street reserved from 9, and we're meeting up at Alan and Mags's place over in Childwall before we head out. You're coming, right? Can't have a Big Weekender without Penny Lane."

Penny laughed, setting her mug down. "Wouldn't miss it for the world. I've got to show those Mancs how

Liverpool does a proper night out. Plus, after the chaos of today, I could use a drink or three."

Louis leaned back in his chair, grinning. "Sounds like a cracking plan. Shame I'll be missing it—Chester calls tomorrow, and I've got an early start. But you lot have a pint for me, yeah?"

Rory raised his mug in a mock toast. "Consider it done, mate. And don't forget to throw some curveballs at the Chester crowd. Keep them on their toes."

Abby glanced at her tablet again, her fingers tapping on the screen. "Alright, Rory, we've got a briefing in ten minutes for the airport round. Penny, enjoy your evening off—you've earned it. And Louis, thanks for being the most convincing Marauder we've ever had. Seriously, bus photos? Inspired."

Louis chuckled, standing up and stretching. "What can I say? I'm a man of many talents. Alright, I'll leave you pros to it. Penny, I'll catch you at the next round of chaos, whenever that may be."

As the team dispersed, Penny took a moment to savour the camaraderie that had become such a defining feature of her time at Manic Radio. Despite the chaos, the uncertainty, and the occasional misstep, she felt more at home here than she ever had anywhere else. The team wasn't just a group of colleagues—they were friends, partners in crime, and, in a way, family.

And tonight, as the Big Weekender loomed, Penny knew one thing for certain.

Whatever chaos the night brought, it was going to be unforgettable.

****

# CHAPTER 12 – Blame It On The Night

## Sunday 22nd September 2024

Stumbling out of Alma de Cuba at closing time, 3am, Penny knew that the night had been both a blur and an unforgettable riot of laughter, dancing, and more than a few rounds of cocktails. Her heels clicked against the cobblestones as she leaned against Abby, the two of them giggling uncontrollably at a joke Rory had made earlier about Alan Hamilton's questionable dance moves.

The fact that, under her miniskirt, she was trying to hide a 14 inch strap-on, a dare by Toni Green to see if she could keep it hidden all night, only added to the ridiculousness of the evening. Penny couldn't help but laugh at the absurdity of the situation. The strap-on, and its accompanying dildo that was keeping the seed of Weston, Rory, half of the Manchester crew and some of the Speke crew inside her was a bit of an oxymoron in itself, as it was making her feel like she was constantly being filled.

Penny knew that she couldn't tell anyone about the strap-on unless they were going home with her, and that her chosen partner for the evening was Weston, meant that the couple was going to face a rather hilarious situation once they made it back to her flat. Penny could already imagine Weston's face when she explained the dare and the entire chaos behind it.

But ever since Thursday, when the two had visited his native Ballymena, and Weston had started to grow more withdrawn, more aware of the gravity of his family's history, Penny felt like she had been walking a tightrope. Tonight's chaos, though utterly ridiculous, had been a welcome reprieve from the weight of the past few days. Weston had let loose, joining in with the Big Weekender antics and laughing more freely than she had seen in weeks.

As the pair stumbled toward a waiting cab, Weston slung an arm around her shoulders, his balance slightly off from the cocktails and shots consumed over the course of the night.

"You know, Lane, he slurred, his Northern Irish accent thicker than usual before walking into a lamppost and falling as though he were in a Carry On film. "I reckon I need to return to Ballymena. Not for a visit, but to end it once and for all. To end me granddad."

Penny froze, her giggles dissolving into the crisp early morning air as Weston's words hung heavily between them. The laughter and lightness of the night suddenly felt a million miles away. She crouched beside him, the cobblestones cold against her knees as she helped him sit up. His face, usually lit with mischief or quiet confidence, now bore an expression of raw emotion that sent a chill through her.

"Weston," she said carefully, her voice low so as not to draw the attention of Abby or Rory, who were busy calling the cab a few feet away. "What are you talking about? You can't be serious."

He rubbed the back of his head where he'd hit it lightly on the lamppost, wincing before meeting her gaze. His eyes were bloodshot, and the alcohol had clearly loosened his tongue, but there was a dark sincerity in his expression that made Penny's stomach twist.

"Carmichael," he muttered, using the surname he often deployed when he wanted to sound more serious. "The man's poisoned everything he's touched. Cillian's gone because of him. My childhood—ruined by his legacy. And now he's still there, spouting his bile, controlling what's left of the family like some kind of warlord. Someone's got to stop him. I know a bloke who, fer the right price'll put him six feet under and make it look like an accident."

Penny's breath caught, her heart thudding as she tried to process what Weston had just said. The alcohol might have clouded his judgement, but the pain and anger behind his words were very real. She placed a hand on his shoulder, steadying both him and her.

"Weston," she whispered, her tone firm but gentle. "You're not that person. You're not a killer, and you're not going to solve this by sinking to his level. He's not worth it, and you know it."

Weston let out a bitter laugh, running a hand through his dishevelled curls. "What am I supposed to do, then? Let him keep ruining lives? Let him sit there in Ballymena, untouched, while the rest of us pick up the pieces? Ye know, when you nipped to the loo at me mam's place, he straight out told me that he actually had planned to have me killed and not Cillian, as Dad'd disinherited Damien and half the family, with only me, Cathy and Aldor being the ones left in his will. You see, even though my Dad's

PSNI, he won the lottery a few months ago, the Euromillions, £134 million, as part of a syndicate with some of his colleagues. Granddad's seething because Dad said the money was for our future, not his 'cause.' So yeah, Cillian got caught in the crossfire—literally."

Penny inhaled sharply, feeling a pang of sympathy for Weston's turmoil. She crouched lower to meet his gaze, her voice soft but resolute. "Weston, listen to me. I know this hurts—I can't even imagine how much. But you've survived this far because you're better than him. You've got your family, your life, and a chance to break free from all of it. Killing him—whether you mean it or not—only drags you deeper into his world. And I can't stand the thought of losing you."

Weston's expression softened slightly, his drunken bravado giving way to a more vulnerable sadness. "I just feel so... trapped, Penny. Like no matter what I do, he'll always have this hold over me. You know, Penny, sometimes I wished that I'd been adopted, that I'd been born into a family without this legacy, without all this pain and hate. But here I am, carrying all of it, and no matter where I go, it finds me."

Penny sat down beside him, her voice steady despite the swirling emotions in her chest. "Weston, you can't change where you come from, but you can choose where you're going. Look at what you've built for yourself—Manic, your life here, us. You've already broken free in so many ways. Don't let him pull you back into his world."

Weston leaned against her shoulder, his weight heavy but comforting. "You're too good for me, Carmichael. I don't deserve someone like you."

Penny gave a small laugh, wrapping an arm around him to steady them both. "Don't flatter yourself, O'Rourke. You're a pain in the arse most days. But I see you—the real you. And that's why I'm not letting you give up on yourself, even when it feels impossible."

Rory's voice called out from behind them, breaking the heavy moment. "Oi, lovebirds, cab's here! We've got 4. One for the Manic crew heading east towards Knowsley, one for the crew heading south to Speke and other points that way, one towards Bootle and northwards, and the final one for the Wirral."

Penny saw 20 of the 40 strong Manic crew that had joined them at the Big Weekender were already piling into the first three cabs, laughter and banter still flowing despite the early hour. She gave Weston a gentle nudge, helping him to his feet.

"Come on," she said softly, steadying him as they walked toward the last cab. "Let's get you home. We'll talk more when you're sober—and when you're not trying to win the award for most melodramatic declaration of the year."

Weston chuckled weakly, leaning on her as they climbed into the cab. "Fair play, Carmichael. But you can't deny it—you love me for it."

Penny rolled her eyes, her smile softening as she gave him a playful shove. "You're lucky you're cute, O'Rourke."

"Room for a little 'un?" Alana Kettlehurst asked, and Penny chuckled as the Lancashire Drive host and her partner for the night, one of the Manic network runners named Simon Pentmorgan, clambered into the cab alongside them. Alana was all smiles, her cheeks flushed from a mix of dancing and one too many shots. Simon, equally as rosy, was carrying what appeared to be a plastic flamingo that someone had swiped from the bar's decor as a memento of the night.

Joining them was Alistair Loken, one of the Ulster Vibes producers, who lived in Arrowe Park, and Lisa Doherty, a presenter from Manic Radio Cumbria who lived in West Kirby.

"So, driver," Lisa said with a grin, "we're going to 22 Elm Street, 24 Circular Road, both in Birkenhead, then 12 Fleet Croft Road in Arrowe Park, then finally 4 Grange Mount in West Kirby. Oh, and before you head to Arrowe Park, can you nip through a Maccies drive-thru as I'm starving, and I'm sure Alistair is."

"Yeah, I'm bloody starving too!" Alistair chimed in, his broad grin reflecting his slightly tipsy state. "Make it a double quarter pounder meal with a large Coke for me. Lisa, what about you?"

Lisa nodded enthusiastically, pulling a crumpled £10 note from her handbag. "Chicken nuggets, large fries, and a milkshake, please. Vanilla. And if they don't have that, Coke Zero."

The cab driver, a seasoned professional with Liverpool's nightlife, chuckled at the lively group. "Maccies detour it is. You lot are keeping me entertained tonight. We'll have to go through the Wallasey Tunnel as the Birkenhead Tunnel's closed for maintenance this morning. Hope you're not in a rush."

Penny leaned her head back against the cab's window, closing her eyes for a moment as the warmth of the laughter around her wrapped her in a comforting cocoon. Weston rested his head on her shoulder, his breathing evening out as the motion of the cab seemed to lull him toward sleep. Despite the heaviness of their earlier conversation, she felt a flicker of hope. They would get through this—somehow.

Suddenly she heard Lisa laugh and woke up to see Alistair stroking the tip of the strap-on that she was trying to keep hidden under her skirt. Her cheeks burned as she realised Lisa and Alistair had noticed her predicament. Penny shot a warning look at Alistair, who held his hands up in mock surrender, his grin mischievous.

"Don't look at me, Penny," he said, stifling a laugh. "I was just curious why you were smuggling a baguette under your skirt."

Penny groaned, her hand flying to her face. "Oh, for heaven's sake. It was a dare from Toni, alright? I've had to keep it hidden all night. Now, can we just... not?"

Alana burst out laughing, clutching her stomach as Simon leaned forward, clearly intrigued. "Toni's dares are legendary. You know she's got me wearing a butt plug, and Simon's got a chastity cage on because Toni dared us to not remove them until Monday morning!" Alana finished with a cackle, her cheeks flushed with laughter.

Penny then saw Weston reaching for the strap-on and sighed, as she knew that, despite being in a b barely 5 day relationship with him, but allowed to sleep with other men and women, she'd never live this down. Weston's fingers brushed against the strap-on as he mumbled groggily, his accent thicker in his inebriated state. "Carmichael, what's this, eh? Some kind of... tactical advantage for when we get to yours and fuck?"

Penny rolled her eyes, biting back a laugh at Weston's drunken curiosity. "Tactical advantage, O'Rourke? Not quite. It's a dare from Toni. I've been hiding this thing all night, and somehow you lot are just noticing now." She glanced at Lisa and Alistair, whose stifled laughter only added to the absurdity of the moment. "And yes, I was going to fuck your arse with it. After all, you let Rory stretch you out earlier at Alan and Mags's place, didn't you? Thought I might see how far your adventurous streak goes."

The cab erupted into laughter, with Lisa nearly choking on her drink and Alistair wiping tears from his eyes. Weston, despite his obvious embarrassment, managed a sheepish grin. "Aye, fair enough. But you'd better be gentle with me, Carmichael—I'm delicate, you know."

Penny shook her head, smirking as the group's banter filled the cab. The ridiculousness of the situation somehow felt fitting after such a wild and chaotic night. Alana leaned forward, raising an eyebrow at Penny. "So,

Lane, what's the plan when we get to yours? Aside from, you know, your tactical manoeuvres with O'Rourke."

Penny shrugged, adjusting her position as Weston slumped further against her. "Honestly? Get this lot fed, make sure Weston doesn't do anything daft, and maybe sleep for about twelve hours. What about you, Alana? Heading straight home, or is there more mischief planned?"

Alana grinned, glancing at Simon, who was fiddling with the flamingo in his lap. "I'm going to torture Simon by putting Fake Taxi on the widescreen and then tie him to the sofa so he can't get up while he watches 12 hours of pure torment. All in good fun, of course. You know me—I never let a dare go unfinished. And Simon's been such a good sport tonight, haven't you, love?"

Simon gave a half-smile, shaking his head in mock despair. "I'm beginning to question all my life choices, but sure, Alana. You do your worst. Say, I didn't see Louis or Kara this evening... morning... whatever time it is. Weren't they supposed to join us?"

Alana shrugged, her grin mischievous. "Louis is doing his Marauder routine around Cheshire tomorrow, and Kara is doing the OB for the first round, remember."

Kara Hamilton, one of the Cheshire and the Wirral Vibes Breakfast hosts, Penny knew, was scheduled to do the reporting, like she had done the previous lunchtime at Liverpool One, for the second day of the Manic Marauder campaign, focused on Cheshire. Penny couldn't help but admire Kara's energy—balancing breakfast radio with the chaos of these events was no small feat.

As the cab trundled into the McDonald's drive-thru, the surreal energy of the night lingered. The group placed their orders amidst more laughter and jabs at Penny's "tactical advantage," with Lisa teasingly asking the cashier if they had any extra-large straws to go with Penny's "equipment." The cashier looked utterly baffled, which only added to the hilarity inside the cab.

By the time they reached their first stop in Birkenhead, 22 Elm Street, near Conway Park station, Penny felt like the group's collective exhaustion was finally catching up with them. Alana and Simon were the first to hop out, Simon clutching his flamingo trophy and muttering something about needing a week to recover from the night. Alana gave Penny a cheeky wink before disappearing into the house with Simon in tow.

"Don't forget to take that thing off before you hit the sheets, Lane," Alana called back, her laughter echoing down the quiet street. Penny waved her off with a smirk, knowing full well the chaos Alana and Simon would be up to once the door closed behind them.

The cab set off again, winding through the quiet streets of Birkenhead. As they approached Circular Road, Penny knew that this was her and Weston's stop for the night. She gently nudged Weston, who had dozed off against her shoulder, his curls tickling her cheek.

"Weston," she whispered, "we're here. Time to get you inside before the neighbours wonder why I'm dragging a half-conscious Irishman into the house."

Weston stirred, blinking groggily as he sat up. "Carmichael, you're a saint," he muttered, fumbling with the door handle. "But if I'm to pass out somewhere, I'd prefer it's not in the cab."

Lisa, now nursing her milkshake with a bemused expression, smirked. "Don't forget your little... accessory, Penny. Wouldn't want to deprive Weston of his 'tactical advantage.'"

Penny rolled her eyes, her cheeks burning as she grabbed her bag and gently guided Weston out of the cab. "Thanks for the reminder, Lisa. I'm sure it'll come in handy."

Lisa winked, raising her milkshake in mock salute. "Enjoy your night, lovebirds. And Penny? Make sure to keep him on his toes. He needs it."

With a final laugh, the cab pulled away, leaving Penny and Weston standing in the dim light of the streetlamp. Penny fished her keys out of her bag, steadying Weston as he swayed slightly on his feet.

"Alright, O'Rourke," she said, unlocking the door and pushing it open. "Let's get you some water and into bed before you start waxing poetic about revenge plots again."

* _ * _ * _ *

The afternoon sunlight greeted Penny, and she had to chuckle, as she was still wearing the strap-on and dildo set, firmly filling Weston like a prize turkey, the strap-on in Weston's arse and the lube having dried out, his larger frame acting as the smaller spoon in their bed. Penny stifled a laugh as she shifted carefully, trying not to wake Weston. The events of the previous night felt like a fever dream—daring antics, emotional confessions, and the bizarre strap-on situation that had somehow led to this peculiar morning-after scene.

"Fuck, that hurts," she heard as she slowly extracted the strap-on from Weston's anal passage, its 14 inch length difficult to remove without eliciting groans of discomfort and the occasional muttered curse from Weston. Penny winced sympathetically, placing a reassuring hand on his back as she carefully removed the contraption.

"Sorry, O'Rourke," she murmured, setting the now infamous strap-on aside on the bedside table. "Next time, remind me not to accept Toni's dares—or at least not to take them this seriously."

Weston let out a tired laugh, though his voice was still groggy. "Remind me to check my arse for structural damage later," he quipped, rolling onto his side to face her. His eyes were half-lidded, his ginger curls a mess, but there was a faint smile playing on his lips. "Morning, by the way."

Penny couldn't help but smile back, brushing a stray curl from his forehead. "Morning? It's..." she said, looking at the clock, "half past 2 in the afternoon."

Weston groaned, flopping back onto the bed and covering his face with a pillow. "Half past 2? Christ, Carmichael, that's practically dinner time. How're we still alive after last night?"

Penny laughed, prodding him gently in the ribs. "Barely. But if you survive a night like that, you can survive anything—strap-ons and all." She smirked, tossing the pillow off his face. "Anyway, thank goodness its Sunday, so we're not at work. Fancy stopping here tonight and getting up early for your Western Ulster Vibes breakfast show tomorrow?"

Weston groaned theatrically but nodded, his voice muffled by the remaining pillow. "Aye, sounds like a plan. shit, I missed Mass."

Penny couldn't hold back her laugh. "You're worried about missing Mass after last night? Weston, I think you might've invalidated your confessional queue just by walking into Alma de Cuba."

Weston peeked out from under the pillow, his freckled face still flushed from the events of the past 24 hours. "Carmichael, faith isn't something you just switch off. Besides," he said, his voice softening, "it's not about the church so much as it is about feeling grounded. Even if the priest gives me the side-eye when I mention the strap-on situation."

Penny smirked, nudging him playfully. "You could always simplify it in confession: 'Bless me, Father, for I have sinned. I got a 14-inch plastic surprise from my girlfriend and joined a cocktail parade.' Think he'd buy it?"

Weston let out a laugh that melted some of the residual tension from the night before. "If he doesn't faint first, aye. But let's not push it. I'll try to sneak in an evening Mass later this week. Might even light a candle for Cillian."

Penny's smile softened at the mention of his cousin. She reached out, resting a hand on Weston's arm. "That sounds like a good idea. You've had a lot thrown at you this week. But you know, it's okay to take time to just... be. No dares, no chaos, no grandad-fuelled revenge plots. Just Weston O'Rourke."

"Grandad fuelled revenge plots?" Weston asked, confused, and Penny knew that Weston probably forgot what he had drunkenly said, just like he had forgotten, but she hadn't, that one of their Manchester colleagues had been ordained in the Universal Life Church and had married the two of them in a hilariously impromptu ceremony in the VIP lounge of Alma de Cuba.

"Never mind, husband," she said with a mischievous grin, climbing out of bed and stretching. "After all, you've-"

"Wait, husband?" Weston asked, confused as to what Penny meant by that.

Penny froze mid-stretch, her eyes darting toward Weston as her mischievous grin wavered. The look of confusion on his face was equal parts amusing and horrifying.

"Erm... about that," Penny began, running a hand through her tousled hair and trying to gauge how much Weston actually remembered from last night. She perched on the edge of the bed, biting her lip as she attempted to deliver the news gently. "You don't remember much from Alma de Cuba, do you?"

Weston frowned, his freckled face scrunching in concentration. "Bits and pieces. There was... dancing, shots, and... something about a flamingo? And... wait. Husband? Are you saying—"

Penny winced, cutting him off before his mind spiralled too far. "You, me, Fat Tony who does the Rochdale Breakfast on Manic Radio Rochdale officiating... he may of... well, married us. He's ordained through one of those online churches—Universal Life Church, or something. So, yeah. we might be married, even though we haven't signed the register at Liverpool Register Office..."

Penny noticed Weston laugh at how ridiculous the situation sounded. His laughter started as a low chuckle before erupting into a full-on, belly-shaking roar. He flopped back onto the bed, clutching his sides as tears pricked the corners of his eyes.

"Married?" he managed between gasps for air. "Carmichael, you mean to tell me that, in the middle of a Big Weekender, some bloke with an online certificate made us husband and wife in a VIP lounge... with a flamingo and a strap-on involved?"

Penny tried to keep a straight face, but Weston's reaction was infectious. She couldn't help but dissolve into laughter alongside him. "Well, yeah, and Toni may have got a photo of us and posted it on her Insta."

Weston groaned and grabbed his phone from the bedside table, scrolling quickly through social media. Sure enough, there it was—Toni Green's Instagram story: a grainy but unmistakable photo of him and Penny standing under a string of fairy lights in Alma de Cuba's VIP lounge, holding hands, with Fat Tony standing between them in a suit and an oversized novelty priest's collar.

@GreenieTonez: When the Manic crew go out on the lash and @PennyLaneManic & @WesRourkeWUV decide that tying the knot is the next logical step. 🍸 💍 #LoveAtManic

Penny watched as Weston cringe saw how drunk he was when Toni had took the photo and tagged them. He groaned, rubbing his temples as if trying to piece together the fragmented memories of the night.

"Well, I suppose this is one way to tell our grandkids how we got married," Weston muttered, his voice dripping with sarcasm. "In a nightclub, with a plastic flamingo and a dare involving a 14-inch strap-on. Proper love story, Carmichael."

Penny burst into laughter, unable to hold it in any longer. "Look on the bright side, O'Rourke—at least it's memorable. And hey, it's not legally binding unless we sign the register. So technically, we've got an out... although we did kind of consume it."

"You mean we consummated it," Weston said with a grin. "And technically we didn't, as you giving me anal sex isn't consummating it in the traditional sense. But," he added with a cheeky grin, "I'm pretty sure this whole situation still qualifies as 'living the Manic life' to the fullest. Only

at Manic could a drunken nightclub wedding with a strap-
on and a flamingo feel like just another Saturday night."

Penny rolled her eyes but couldn't help grinning. "Well,
Mr O'Rourke, shall we call this the most chaotic pre-
honeymoon ever, or just chalk it up to another Big
Weekender gone completely off the rails?"

Weston propped himself up on one elbow, his expression
softening as he looked at her. "Let's call it what it is,
Carmichael—a mad story we'll be laughing about for
years. And hey," he added, reaching out to tuck a strand
of hair behind her ear, "if I were to drunkenly marry
anyone, I'm glad it was you."

Penny felt a warmth spread through her chest despite the

absurdity of the situation. "Well, that's the sweetest thing
you've said all weekend. Although I'm not sure how
much of that is the hangover talking."

Weston chuckled, leaning back against the headboard.
"Maybe a bit of both. But seriously, Penny, thanks for
being... well, you. Strap-ons, flamingos, and all."

Penny smirked, leaning over to give him a playful nudge.
"And thank you for being the kind of guy who can laugh
through the madness. Now, let's get cleaned up, find some
greasy food, and figure out how we're going to explain
this to the rest of the Manic crew without becoming the
headline of tomorrow's breakfast shows."

****

# CHAPTER 13 – The Fallout
## Wednesday 25th September 2024

It had been three days since the 'marriage' of Penny and Weston, and the whirlwind of chaos that followed was far from subsiding. The photo that Toni Green had posted on her Instagram had gone viral within hours, not just across the Manic Radio network but among listeners and rival stations. The comments ranged from hysterical laughter to outright disbelief.

Of course, Weston's grandfather had something to say about the whole debacle and had, instead of leaving a Instagram post, a voicemail or an email, but had flew in from Ballymena by first class firebomb, literally throwing a Molotov cocktail at Penny's front door late Tuesday evening, burning the few plants that were lovingly maintained by her landlady, Mrs. Davies. Thankfully, the flames were extinguished before they could cause any serious damage, but the shock of the incident left Penny and Weston rattled. The police had been called, and while no one had been hurt, the charred remnants of the doorstep were a stark reminder of how far Michael O'Rourke's wrath could reach.

Sitting at her desk, Penny was reading the script for her next drivetime show when she felt a pair of hands on her shoulders, the soft hands that she knew that her 'husband' possessed.

Weston leaned down, his ginger curls brushing against her cheek as he planted a soft kiss on the top of her head. "Alright, Carmichael?" he murmured, his Northern Irish accent tinged with concern. "You look like you're ready to throttle someone."

Before she could say anything, a message on Teams came through from one of the front desk receptionists, saying that there was a Mick O'Rourke waiting at reception, asking to speak with her and Weston.

Penny froze, her stomach knotting instantly. She had the feeling that it was Weston's grandfather and that he'd be bringing more than just harsh words this time. Weston's hands tensed slightly on her shoulders, and she glanced up at him, her eyes reflecting the unease she felt.

"Weston," she whispered, her voice barely audible over the din of the office. "He's here. Your grandfather. Reception just messaged me."

Weston's expression hardened, his light-hearted demeanour evaporating in an instant. He straightened, his jaw tightening as he took a deep breath. "Of course he is," he muttered, running a hand through his dishevelled curls. "The man doesn't know when to quit."

Penny rose from her chair, smoothing down her skirt and steadying her nerves. "What do we do? We can't just leave him down there—it'll cause a scene."

Weston nodded, his face unreadable as he considered their options. "We'll talk to him. But we're not doing it here—not in the middle of the hub where everyone and their dog can eavesdrop. Let's take him to one of the meeting rooms. Neutral ground."

Penny hesitated before nodding. "Alright. But if he so much as raises his voice, I'm calling security."

Weston's lips quirked into a faint, humourless smile. "Don't worry, Carmichael. If it comes to that, I'll handle it."

he two of them made their way to reception, the buzz of the office fading into the background as they approached the front desk. Sure enough, Michael O'Rourke was standing there, his imposing frame somehow looking even larger in the sterile fluorescent light of the reception area. His sharp eyes narrowed as he caught sight of them, his lips curling into a sneer.

"There they are," Michael said, his voice low and cold. "The disgraceful grandson and his... English wife. Didn't even do it in the Church but in a fecking

nightclub, no less. A mockery of marriage and everything it stands for." His voice carried a sharp edge, and the receptionist glanced nervously between them.

Penny felt Weston stiffen beside her, his shoulders squaring as he stepped slightly in front of her, as if shielding her from the full force of his grandfather's wrath. "Granddad," Weston began, his tone measured but firm, "if you've come here to throw more accusations around, you might as well leave now. We've got nothing to say to you if that's your angle."

Michael's eyes burned with a mix of anger and disdain. "You think you can just sweep this under the rug, do you? Gallivanting around with this English lass, bringing shame to the family—marrying in sin. The family council has decided that you're no longer welcome in Ballymena or to hold the O'Rourke-"

Penny decided that hearing Michael run his mouth off and slapped Michael across the face, her palm connecting with a sharp crack. The room seemed to freeze for a moment, and the receptionist let out a soft gasp. Penny's hand tingled, but she held her ground, her eyes blazing with fury as she stepped forward, putting herself directly between Weston and his grandfather.

"That's enough," Penny said, her voice steady despite the adrenaline coursing through her veins. "You've already made your stance clear, Mr O'Rourke. But you don't get to march in here and spit venom at us like we're children who need your approval. Whatever issues you have with Weston, you leave me out of it. I'm not some pawn in your family drama."

Michael's face darkened, a flicker of shock crossing his features before he regained his composure. "You've got some nerve, girl," he said, his tone low and dangerous. "You don't know the first thing about our family, about what it means to bear the O'Rourke name. You better watch yourself as the lads-"

"Threatening me with an IRA crew, are we, Michael?" Penny interrupted, her voice laced with icy disdain. "Because that'll go down really well with the Police here in Merseyside. Even though there's an Irish community here in Liverpool, this isn't Ballymena. Threats like that don't carry the same weight when you're on British soil and dealing with the authorities here. So, unless you want to escalate this into a proper legal matter, I suggest you think twice before uttering another word."

Weston stepped beside her, his hand finding hers in a silent gesture of solidarity. "Granddad, you've already done more damage than you realise. You're stuck in a past that's long gone, clinging to bitterness and hatred while the rest of us are trying to move forward. You might be family by blood, but that doesn't mean we'll tolerate your toxic behaviour anymore."

Michael's lips tightened into a thin line, his piercing gaze shifting between the two of them. For a moment, it seemed as though he might launch another tirade, but something in Weston's resolute stance gave him pause. His eyes narrowed, the fire in them dimming slightly, replaced by a flicker of something almost resembling regret—or perhaps defeat.

"You're making a mistake, boy," Michael said finally, his voice quieter but no less cutting. "You think you're free of this, free of me, but you'll see. Blood doesn't just disappear because you want it to. And this..." He gestured to Penny with a dismissive wave. "This will only lead to more heartbreak."

Penny opened her mouth to respond, but Weston squeezed her hand gently, a silent plea for her to let it go. Instead, he stepped forward, his voice calm but unyielding. "This is the last time, Granddad. If you come near me or Penny again—if you so much as breath a threat—you'll have the police to deal with. Whatever hold you think you have over us, it ends here."

Michael stared at him for a long moment, the weight of unspoken words hanging heavy in the air. Finally, with a sharp exhale, he turned on his heel and strode out of the building without another word. The receptionist let out a small sigh of relief as the tension in the room eased.

Penny and Weston exchanged a glance, the unspoken understanding between them clear. This wasn't over—not entirely. But for now, they had faced the storm together, and that was enough.

"Fancy a cuppa?" Weston asked after a beat, his voice

lighter but still tinged with exhaustion.

Penny smiled faintly, her fingers brushing against his as they turned to head back to the office. "Only if you're making it."

* _ * _ * _ *

"It's 4pm, Liverpool, and Rory's off today, and so's producer Abby, so it's me, Penny Lane, and producer Weston here on Manic Radio Liverpool Drive. And, oh, what a day it's been! It seems like everyone's still talking about last weekend's chaos—and I've got to say, some of your messages have had us absolutely howling here in the studio. Keep them coming! We've got all your greatest hits coming right up, but first it's the news from Ally McKenzie."

Penny looked at Weston who was tinkering with the Zetta and GSelector interface, making sure that the playout of the different tracks that the network control in the building next door had setup for the national playlist, which would go out on the local stations. His earlier tension seemed to have melted away now that they were back in their element, the comforting rhythm of the show pulling them into the present.

As the news jingle faded and Ally McKenzie's voice filled the airwaves, Penny leaned back in her chair, taking a moment to catch her breath. She glanced at the messages pouring into the WhatsApp chats that listeners could send voice notes and texts into. The buzz of interaction lifted her spirits after the tense encounter with Michael earlier.

The first track, Carry You Home by Alex Warren played out straight after the news, and Penny knew, looking at the Zetta screen on her side of the desk that it would be a back to back quadruple header of Alex Warren, Be Alright by Joel Corry, Wake Me Up by Avicii, and Flowers by Miley Cyrus.

"15 minutes of bliss before we go back on air, eh, Wes?" she said with a grin, leaning back in her chair as the music filled the studio. "Fancy a quicky before we have to go back on air?"

Weston grinned with a mischievous twinkle in his eye, swivelling his chair to face her. "Carmichael, you never fail to surprise me. I'd be remiss if I didn't do my husbandly duties, but let's not give the listeners any unintended live content, eh?" he teased, leaning in just enough to make her blush.

"The buttons for the mics are your side, so if we fucked on my side of the desk, we'd be safe," Penny shot back with a smirk, her cheeks tinged pink but her tone playful. "After all, you did promise in our vows you'd give me 10 orgasms a day."

Weston looked at Penny confused, and Penny knew that he still had no memory of any of the events during their chaotic "wedding" at Alma de Cuba. She couldn't resist the urge to toy with him just a bit more.

"You don't remember that part either, do you?" Penny teased, crossing her arms and raising an eyebrow.

"Now hang on, Carmichael," Weston said, his confusion deepening as he leaned closer to her. "Are you telling me that I promised something that ridiculous in front of the whole Manic crew?"

Penny grinned, leaning forward as if to let him in on a secret. "Oh, you did. Danny can confirm that if you want. I'll open up the link to Studio 1 if you want to ask him while we're both playing out the same songs. Shall I?" Penny's grin widened, mischievously teasing Weston as she pressed the inter-studio private comms that allowed her to connect with Studio 1, where Danny O'Neil was doing his network drive for the Manic regions that didn't have their own local drive show.

As Penny leaned into the comms link to Studio 1, her grin grew wider. The playful tension between her and Weston was just what they needed to shake off the morning's heavy confrontation.

"Danny, you there, mate?" Penny's voice carried through to the other studio.

A moment later, Danny O'Neil's voice came crackling back through the speakers. "Oi, Penny Lane, what's up? Causing chaos as usual, I see."

"Always," Penny replied with a chuckle. "Quick question for you, Danny—do you remember Weston's... uh, vows from the weekend?"

Danny's laughter burst through the comms like a firecracker. "Oh, do I ever, Penny! Classic Big Weekender material. Weston, mate, you were promising the moon and the stars—ten orgasms a day, a lifetime supply of pints, and I think you threw in a free round of Guinness for the entire Speke hub at some point. Proper poetic, you were."

Penny shot Weston a triumphant smirk, folding her arms as if daring him to challenge the story. Weston groaned, running a hand down his face in mock despair. "Bloody hell, O'Neil. You couldn't have just told me I sang Wonderwall and passed out, could you?"

Danny chuckled, clearly enjoying Weston's predicament. "Nah, mate. This is too good not to remember. But hey, you're the talk of the network now. Strap-ons, flamingos, and vows worthy of Shakespeare—you're practically Manic royalty."

Penny leaned back in her chair, her grin stretching ear to ear. "See, Weston? I told you it wasn't just me. Your Big Weekender performance is the stuff of legends now."

Weston threw his hands up in defeat, a lopsided smile breaking through his faux exasperation. "Fine, fine. But you've got to admit, Lane, if we're Manic royalty, then you're the queen of chaos."

Penny raised an imaginary crown above her head and placed it dramatically. "Long may I reign," she declared with a wink before turning back to the controls and closing the link that connected them to Studio 1.

Weston shook his head, laughing under his breath as he adjusted his headphones. "Alright, Queen of Chaos, let's not forget we're on air in ten. We've got that link to get listeners to text in with their mid-week Liverpool game predictions, then ads, then Alfie's live from Anfield to get the atmosphere ahead of the match. No time for you to stage another revolution during the show."

Penny winked at him as the final bars of Flowers by Miley Cyrus played out. She quickly straightened her headphones and leaned into her mic as the studio countdown hit zero.

"And that was 15 minutes of pure CHR bliss," she began, her voice smooth and upbeat. "Welcome back to Manic Drive Liverpool! Penny Lane here, joined by the one and only Weston O'Rourke—yes, the same Weston who managed to make vows about pints and orgasms the talk of the nation. Isn't that right, Wes?"

Weston groaned theatrically, his voice laced with humour as he leaned into his mic. "Why do I feel like I'm going to regret that night for the rest of my life? You've got me cornered here, Penny."

Penny laughed, shaking her head. "It's all in good fun, Weston. Speaking of fun, let's get to tonight's big question: what's your prediction for Liverpool's game against West Ham. After all, we're not Liverpool FC's hottest station, Manic Radio, for nothing. Do you think Arne Slot's lads will beat West Ham, or do you think the

London squad will make van Dijk and the Reds work for it? Drop us a WhatsApp, 0151 496 0425, or tweet me, @PennyLaneManic, and I'll read out your best predictions live on air. Weston, what's your prediction for the... oh, yeah, you're a Ballymena United fan, and the only football predictions you're interested in involve the NIFL Premiership. How about you take a guess anyway—Liverpool or West Ham?"

Weston leaned back in his chair, the hint of a smirk on his face as he considered the question. "Well, Penny, my dear wife," and Penny laughed as he emphasised that word, "I may not be a dyed-in-the-wool Red, but I'll throw my hat in the ring. I reckon Liverpool will edge it 2-1. Arne Slot's got them playing well, and with the Anfield crowd behind them, they'll nick it late on. How's that for a neutral's prediction?"

Penny grinned, clearly amused by his attempt at diplomacy. "You heard it here first, folks—Weston O'Rourke, Manic's resident Ballymena boy, has officially backed the Reds for tonight. Well, let's see if you lot agree. Keep those predictions coming in!"

The buzz of incoming messages lit up their shared screen, and Penny dove straight into the interaction. "Alright, here's one from Sophie in Childwall—'3-0 to Liverpool, Darwin to get a brace and Trent with a free-kick banger.' Love the confidence, Sophie! Who else have we got? Oh, here's one from Gaz in Bootle—'1-1 draw, both teams to work for it."

Suddenly the WhatsApp screen logged itself out, and Penny had to chuckle, as it was normal for the WhatsApp system to occasionally glitch during busy moments. Penny glanced at Weston, who was already fiddling with the settings to try and reconnect. "Technical difficulties, folks," she said smoothly into the mic, her voice brimming with playful sarcasm. "Looks like WhatsApp couldn't manage the heat of your predictions! Anyway, in a few minutes we'll head over to Anfield for Alfie's live report to get a feel for the atmosphere as Liverpool prepares to take on West Ham. Stick with us—this is Manic Radio Liverpool, where the chaos is just part of the charm!"

Weston gave a thumbs-up as he managed to reconnect the WhatsApp system, a fresh wave of messages flooding the screen. He leaned into his mic, a cheeky grin spreading across his face. "Looks like we're back in business, Penny. Keep those predictions coming, folks—let's see if we can break WhatsApp again. Alfie, mate, you'd better be ready to carry the show while we wrangle the tech!"

As the next set of ads rolled, Penny took off her headphones and leaned back in her chair, letting out a deep breath. "What a day, Wes. Between your grandfather's theatrics and the strap-on saga still making the rounds, I'm starting to wonder if we should rebrand this show as a soap opera."

Weston chuckled, spinning his chair slightly to face her. "Soap opera or not, Carmichael, you've managed it like a pro. And hey, at least the listeners are loving it. You're basically the queen of Manic now."

* _ * _ * _ *

As Penny and Weston finished their show at 7pm, Penny knew that Toni Green's show would be airing across the network from Studio 1, where Danny had just finished his show, and therefore the chaos in Studio 1 would shift seamlessly to Toni Green's high-energy antics. Penny noticed an email in her inbox from an anonymous sender. The subject line read: "A Word of Warning About Michael O'Rourke."

Curiosity tinged with caution, Penny clicked it open. The message was short and to the point.

**Unknown Sender:** *Penny, Michael won't stop. He never does. Be careful who you trust—even within your circle. Not everyone is on your side. You and Weston need to watch your backs. He has allies everywhere.*

Her stomach dropped. The anonymity of the email only made it more unsettling. She glanced over at Weston, who was tidying up the playout system for Toni's transition, his face calm but clearly fatigued from the day's events.

"Wes," she said softly, her voice barely audible over the faint sound of Toni's intro jingle bleeding through the wall. He looked up, concern immediately flashing across his freckled features.

"What's up, Carmichael? You look like you've just seen a ghost."

Wordlessly, she turned the screen toward him. He scanned the email quickly and chuckled. "Really? Granddad had to send it to the work system, didn't he?" Weston muttered with a mix of exasperation and amusement, shaking his head as he leaned closer to the screen. "Classic Michael—always one step away from outright melodrama. But this? Sending cryptic warnings like he's in some kind of spy thriller? He's really lost the plot."

Penny frowned, tapping her fingers against the desk. "But what if it's not from him?" she countered. "The tone doesn't exactly scream 'angry grandfather.' It's... calculated. Almost like a warning from someone who knows what he's capable of but isn't willing to come forward directly."

Weston's expression shifted, the humour fading as he considered her words. "You think it could be one of his 'allies,' as the email says? Someone trying to warn us without putting themselves in the firing line?"

Penny shrugged, her eyes scanning the message again. "Could be. Or it could be a bluff to rattle us. Either way, it's unnerving. And if it's true that he has 'allies' here in Liverpool..."

Weston leaned back in his chair, rubbing a hand over his face. "Christ, Carmichael. Just when you think the man can't stoop any lower, he finds a way to pull another stunt. But listen," he added, his tone softening as he reached for her hand, "whatever this is, we'll deal with it. Together."

Penny managed a small smile, squeezing his hand in return. "You're right. We've faced worse, haven't we? I mean, there's only so much a Molotov cocktail and some cryptic emails can throw at us."

"Exactly," Weston said, his voice firmer now. "And if Granddad thinks he can scare us into backing down, he clearly doesn't know you as well as I do. You're the queen of chaos, remember? This is just another curveball for you to knock out of the park."

Penny laughed despite herself, the tension in her chest easing slightly. "Alright, Mr O'Rourke. Let's call it a draw for now. But if any more mysterious emails show up, we're taking them straight to the police."

Weston nodded, his expression serious. "Agreed. No more playing games. If Michael's trying to drag others into this, we'll make sure the authorities know exactly what he's up to."

With that, Penny closed the email and logged out of her account, determined to put the unsettling message out of her mind—at least for the evening. As she and Weston left the studio, the hum of Toni Green's network show filling the air behind them, Penny felt a renewed sense of resolve. Whatever Michael O'Rourke had planned, she wouldn't let it derail their lives any more than it already had.

****

# CHAPTER 14 – Visiting The Town Hall
## Thursday 26th September 2024

Penny how to chuckle at the plan that she and Weston had come up with. It had all been because of a WhatsApp from a listener on the previous night show, that message being from an official at Wirral Council talking about how, in fact, their wedding in Liverpool the weekend just gone was not actually legally valid and, to make it legal, the two would need to actually need to wed in front of a registrar, and that it would usually would need to be in either the residential area of one of the parties, or in a licensed venue, again in front of a registrar. The official had jokingly suggested that, given Penny was from the Wirral, they could make it official at Birkenhead Town Hall.

Penny on the Liverpool City Council website to find out that in fact where they had been wed, Alma de Cuba, was such a licensed venue by Liverpool City Council, however as Fat Tony was not a licensed registrar from the city Council, the impromptu ceremony was more of a theatrical performance than a legally binding marriage.

In addition, they had to supply notice of them being married to the council within a time frame of 29 days before the ceremony and have lived in the district for at least seven days prior to giving notice. None of these requirements had been met during their whirlwind Big Weekender antics. The discovery left Penny equal parts relieved and amused—relieved that they weren't legally bound just yet and amused at the absurdity of the situation.

Technically, as Weston lived in Garston, which was in the Liverpool city Council jurisdiction and Penny was a long term Wirral resident, having been born and bred in Hoylake, she knew that either Council would be able to do it, as long as a month passed before giving notice and the appropriate documentation was submitted. But the idea of going to Birkenhead Town Hall to give notice of their intention to marry was too tempting for the pair to pass up. It wasn't just about the legalities; it was about leaning into the absurdity of their situation and turning it into another adventure in the chaotic tapestry of their lives.

Waking up, Penny saw a text on her phone from Weston, asking if he could move in with her full time, as Toni wanted to move her boyfriend, Northern Vibes drivetime presenter, Al Crozier, in for weekends and the odd night home. Penny knew that Al was one of the Dudley hub presenters, and that Toni's flat in Garston had become a kind of unofficial crash pad for Manic's transient staff, often hosting visiting presenters from the wider Manic network. Weston's message didn't come as a total surprise, but it did prompt a thoughtful pause. Penny was used to the solo rhythms of her life in her Birkenhead flat, but Weston had become an increasingly central part of her world. Sharing her space full-time, though? That was another layer of chaos entirely.

As she stretched, scrolling through her texts, Penny fired off a reply to Weston.

**Penny Lane**: *Move in? Bold move, O'Rourke. Let's talk about it after we've sorted this 'marriage.' See you at mine in an hour?*

**Weston O'Rourke**: *Aye, Mrs. O'Rourke. I'll bring coffee. Flat whites, yeah?*

Penny chuckled at the message. She wasn't quite sure how serious Weston was about making their impromptu, not-quite-legal marriage a reality, but the thought of him referring to her as Mrs. O'Rourke was oddly endearing.

Looking around on Amazon, as she was bored, Penny noticed a book from 2003 that stood out to her that had the tagline "All chocolate will be illegal from 5pm today" and the title "Bootleg". The title alone piqued her curiosity. Penny added it to her basket on a whim, thinking it might be a good distraction from the whirlwind her life had become. After all, there was something about the ridiculousness of illegal chocolate that felt fitting given the absurdity of her current situation.

"The Good For You Party is running the country, and forcing everyone to lead healthier lives. Chocolate addicts Smudger and Huntly watch in horror as their favourite food is swept from the shops and Chocolate Trooper police arrest anyone caught with sweets. When the boys discover the recipe for making chocolate and a hidden store of the right ingredients, they fight back. Their secret bootleg operation is soon a brilliant success - but how long can they keep selling illegal chocolate before the Good For You thugs catch them?" the blurb of the book promised a quirky tale of rebellion. The irony that it had come out the same year she had been born, and so marked a piece of literary nostalgia from her birth year, wasn't lost on Penny. She figured the whimsical premise might offer a moment of levity in her increasingly bizarre life.

Taking a screenshot, she posted it on the 'Liverpool Hub Goss' chat on WhatsApp, adding that she'd never heard of it and if anyone remembered it from back in the day. Within minutes, Calvin, one of the older staff members and a 33 year old, responded with a laughing emoji.

**Calvin Foster**: *Bootleg? I remember when CBBC did a 3 part TV adaptation of it! Proper nostalgia, Penny. Reminds me of the days of Twister on CITV with Nigel Mitchell, Get Your Own Back on CBBC with Dave Benson Phillips, and rushing home from school to catch Raven as well. Blimey, I never thought I'd be brought back to the early '00s outside one of our throwback tracks like Busted or McFly.*

Penny knew that Calvin, one of the Manic Rock hosts who was based at Speke, would continue his nostalgic train of thought whenever given the chance. She smiled as more responses rolled in from the group chat.

**Toni Green**: *OMG, I lived for Raven! "Are you ready to face the Way of the Warrior?" Honestly, I was 12 when the original run ended and I kinda had a crush on him who played Raven, James Mackenzie. 😄 Bootleg, though—classic chaos. Penny, are you planning to set up your own chocolate empire? Manic-style black market KitKats? Count me in!*

**Abby Blue**: *I remember when Brookie ended, can't believe it's been 21 years (and I was only 8 when it* *ended). But yeah, Bootleg was pure nostalgia. Also, Penny, if you start a chocolate empire, can we call it 'Manic Munchies'? Anyway, does anyone apart from me remember Grange Hill?*

Having been 5 in 2008, when Grange Hill ended, Penny barely remembered it herself. But the chatter in the group chat soon turned into a whirlwind of nostalgic tangents, from Byker Grove to Tracy Beaker, as the Manic crew bonded over their shared childhood memories. Suddenly Rory posted a news article from a week and half ago which made Penny feel even more nostalgic.

***"'What's the new story in Balamory?' - kids' show gets a reboot***

*Children's television favourite Balamory is set to return two decades after it was last filmed, the BBC has announced.*

*The Bafta-winning pre-school programme about the fictional town of Balamory was originally set in Tobermory, the colourful harbour town on the Isle of Mull.*

*The shows centred around a nursery school and its teacher Miss Hoolie, attracting two million viewers a week in the UK at its peak and watched by millions more around the world.*

*Two new series of the show, commissioned for a reboot on CBeebies in 2026, are expected to include some of the original characters."*

Penny read the article and chuckled at the thought of Balamory making a comeback. The nostalgia in the group chat had evolved into full-blown excitement. Even those who hadn't been avid fans chimed in with memories of the iconic theme tune and the brightly coloured houses that had become synonymous with childhood mornings.

**Rory Carter**: *Can you imagine a Manic Radio version of Balamory? Each presenter would have a house colour. Penny, you'd obviously be green for your chaotic energy. Weston could be orange because... well, Northern Irish roots and all that. And Alan Hamilton would definitely be a moody grey.*

**Toni Green**: *OMG, we could rewrite the theme song: 'What's the story in Manicory? Wouldn't you like to know?'*

Penny laughed as she read the messages, imagining the absurdity of her colleagues in a Balamory-style setting.

**Penny Lane**: *Toni, if this becomes a thing, you'd better call dibs on Miss Hoolie. You've got the storytelling voice for it. And Calvin, you're the postman. No debate.*

**Abby Blue**: *Wait, who's PC Plum? We need someone who loves a bit of drama.*

**Rory Carter**: *Weston, obviously. He's got the accent for it. PC Plum's Irish cousin!*

Weston finally jumped into the chat, having stayed quiet during the earlier banter:

**Weston O'Rourke**: *Yous lot are off yer heads. I'm not dressing up as a cartoonish cop. Penny, tell them they're barred.*

**Penny Lane**: *Too late, PC Plum O'Rourke. It's already canon.*

**Abby Blue**: *We'll have to rewrite the scripts for this for drive, you know, as the listeners would probably love it. Weston as PC Plum O'Rourke solving petty Manic chaos? Penny, you'd better pitch this to Alan.* 😄

**Penny Lane**: *Can't do it til I get to the studio. Just waiting til Weston finishes his Western Ulster Vibes production meeting and then we're off to the Town Hall.*

The messages pinged through thick and fast as Penny read through the thread, shaking her head at the whirlwind of ideas. She glanced at her watch, realising she needed to get ready for the next step in her and Weston's impromptu marriage adventure, giving notice of their intended marriage at Birkenhead Town Hall.

**Rory Carter**: *Wait? You two're making your vows?*

**Penny Lane**: *Not yet, Rory. We're just filing the notice today. Official business, y'know, to make our Big Weekender antics legally binding. While you and Abby were off, Ro, we had a listener who works for Wirral Council WhatsApp in and say that our Alma de Cuba ceremony wasn't quite 'official.' Apparently, we need to give proper notice to the registrar, and since I'm a proud Wirralite, it's only fitting we do it at Birkenhead Town Hall.*

* _ * _ * _ *

Walking up the steps of Birkenhead Town Hall, Penny knew that this part was the formality needed to turn their chaotic pseudo-marriage into something legally binding. The grand Victorian architecture of the building stood proudly amidst the grey Wirral sky, its imposing façade a sharp contrast to the irreverent journey that had brought them here. Penny glanced at Weston, who was carrying two takeaway cups of coffee and looking surprisingly composed, considering the week they'd had.

"You ready for this, Mrs O'Rourke?" Weston teased, his Northern Irish lilt making her name sound both ridiculous and oddly comforting.

Penny rolled her eyes but couldn't suppress a grin. "As ready as I'll ever be, PC Plum. Let's get this done before someone from your family lobs another Molotov in our direction."

Weston chuckled, passing her one of the coffees. "Fair point. Though I reckon Granddad's all out of petrol bombs for the week. He'll have to stick to scathing voicemails and ominous emails."

Inside the Town Hall, Penny noticed that the official who was on the reception was busy on the telephone dealing with a caller, presumably about a bureaucratic issue, judging by the clipped tone and slight exasperation in their voice. Penny and Weston exchanged a glance, their shared smirk revealing their mutual amusement at the everyday chaos they seemed to stumble into, no matter where they went.

As they waited, Penny glanced around at the Town Hall's interior. The high ceilings and ornate plasterwork exuded an air of historic importance, though the slightly scuffed floor and outdated noticeboards reminded her that this was still very much a working council building. Weston leaned against the counter, sipping his coffee casually as if they were waiting for a train rather than filing notice of their intention to marry.

Eventually, the receptionist finished the call and turned to them with a professional smile. "Good morning. How can I help you?"

Penny stepped forward, trying to suppress her nerves, though she knew Weston's presence made her feel steadier. "Hi, we're here to file a notice of intention to marry."

"Ah, did you book an appointment?" the receptionist asked, glancing at a clipboard on the counter.

Penny hesitated, feeling a twinge of worry. "Erm, no. We weren't aware we needed one. We just thought we could, you know, walk in and sort it?"

The receptionist offered a polite but firm smile, clearly used to dealing with similar misunderstandings. "Unfortunately, appointments are usually required to file a notice, as we need to verify your documentation. You'll need to fill out the form on the Council's website, and then we'll contact you with an appointment date. Typically, it takes about a week to process the booking, and you'll need to bring proof of identity and residence for both of you, as well as evidence of your single status. If either of you were previously married, we'd also need to see the relevant decree absolute or death certificate. Furthermore, there's a fee of £42 per person. Now, do both of you live in the Wirral district?"

Penny exchanged a quick glance with Weston, already bracing herself for the bureaucratic hoops they'd have to jump through.

"Well, I live here in Birkenhead," Penny explained, her tone polite but tinged with the faintest hint of exasperation. "Used to live in Hoylake til I was 18 and then moved to Manchester, but then back here a few months ago."

The receptionist nodded, jotting something down on her clipboard. "And you, sir?" she asked Weston.

Weston smiled warmly, though Penny could sense he was already crafting a cheeky reply. "Ah, I live in Garston, just across the Mersey in Liverpool. Moved there a month ago. Before that Belfast, and before that Ballymena."

The receptionist's pen hovered mid-air as she processed Weston's convoluted explanation. Penny shot him a look that was equal parts amusement and warning, silently willing him not to go off on one of his infamous tangents.

The receptionist nodded slowly, clearly accustomed to dealing with all manner of characters. "Right, well, as you live here in Birkenhead, then you'd need to give notice here, as you're a Wirralite, but as for you Mr...?"

Weston leaned in with a charming smile. "O'Rourke. Weston O'Rourke."

The receptionist jotted down his name, glancing at him over her glasses. "Mr O'Rourke, since you live in Liverpool, you'll need to give notice to Liverpool City Council as well. Both notices must be filed in the districts where each of you resides, even though the marriage can take place in either jurisdiction."

Penny let out a small groan, rubbing her temples. "So, basically, we have to jump through hoops in two councils before we can officially make this madness legal?"

The receptionist offered a sympathetic smile. "I'm afraid so. It's standard procedure. You'll each need to submit your notice separately within the next 12 months, but remember, the notices are only valid for a specific period—usually 12 months—so you'll need to plan accordingly, and you'll need to book an appointment online for both here and Liverpool City Council."

Weston nodded, still smiling, though Penny could tell he was just as exasperated as she was. "Got it. Sounds like a lot of paperwork for something we already did in a nightclub, but rules are rules."

"Nightclub? Hang on, you're Penny Lane off Manic Radio Liverpool, aren't you?"

Penny felt her cheeks flush as the receptionist's eyes lit up with recognition. She offered a sheepish smile, the corners of her mouth twitching upwards in amusement. "Guilty as charged," she replied. "And yes, the nightclub thing was... well, let's just say it's a long story."

The receptionist chuckled, clearly delighted to have recognised her. "I knew it! My daughter listens to your drive show all the time. She's always going on about the chaos at Manic. And the wedding story—oh, we've all heard about that. Quite the headline-maker, wasn't it? Give me a second, I'll see if my colleague who deals with the notice forms is free for a quick word. She's a big fan of the show too—might be able to squeeze you in for some guidance today."

As the receptionist disappeared into the back office, Penny and Weston exchanged an incredulous glance. "I can't decide if this is a stroke of luck or just another layer of chaos," Penny muttered, sipping her coffee.

"Bit of both, I reckon," Weston replied with a grin. "Though I'm not sure if it's good or bad that even council staff are following the 'Penny and Weston Wedding Drama.' We're practically a soap opera."

Before Penny could respond, the receptionist returned with another woman in tow—a middle-aged lady with a warm smile and an air of efficiency. "This is Janet," the receptionist said. "She handles the marriage notices here at Birkenhead Town Hall."

Janet extended her hand to Penny and Weston, her expression friendly. "Lovely to meet you both. And I have to say, I've been following your story—it's been the talk of the Wirral!"

Penny shook her hand, laughing nervously. "I'm starting to feel like our lives are just one long Manic promo."

"Well, you've certainly brought a bit of excitement to the Town Hall," Janet replied, her tone light. "Now, I can't promise any shortcuts but let me see what I can do to help.

If you've got your IDs on you and proof of address, I can at least start the process for Penny's notice today. Weston, you'll still need to contact Liverpool City Council for yours, but we can get the ball rolling on one side."

Penny felt a surge of relief. "That would be amazing. Thank you."

Janet led them into a small office lined with filing cabinets and stacks of paperwork. She gestured for them to sit while she pulled up the necessary forms on her computer. "So, Penny, we'll need your passport or driver's licence, and something like a utility bill or bank statement as proof of address."

Penny rummaged through her bag, producing her passport and a recent utility bill. Janet took the documents, her fingers flying over the keyboard as she began entering the details.

"Penelope Euphemia Hortense Petunia Carmichael," Janet read aloud with a chuckle as she typed. "Well, now I see why you go by Penny Lane. Your parents had quite the flair for names, didn't they? Born 19th April 2003 in Arrowe Park Hospital to Linus Alan Carmichael and Morticia Felicity Carmichael, née Thornberry," Janet finished, clearly amused by the elaborately vintage names on Penny's birth certificate. "I can see why you call yourself Penny Lane on Manic Radio—rolls off the tongue much easier!"

Penny laughed nervously, brushing a strand of hair behind her ear. "Yeah, my parents really went for it with the name. You wouldn't believe how many times I've had to explain the Euphemia part. Safe to say, 'Penny Lane' is a lot easier for everyone involved."

Janet chuckled warmly as she entered the details into the system. "Well, it's a great on-air name. And Weston," she added, glancing at him with a raised brow, "any equally colourful middle names we should know about?"

Weston grinned, leaning back in his chair. "Nothing quite as grand as Penelope Euphemia Hortense Petunia, I'm afraid. Just Weston Patrick O'Rourke. Born and bred in Ballymena, though I've called a few places home since then."

Janet nodded, her fingers still flying over the keyboard. "Alright, Penny, we've got your details in. Now, as I mentioned, you'll need to wait the 28-day statutory period before the notice is validated. Once that's done, you can book your ceremony at any licensed venue or registrar's office within the Wirral or Liverpool district."

"And for Weston?" Penny asked, glancing at him. "What happens if he doesn't file his notice on the same day?"

"It's not an issue," Janet reassured her. "As long as both notices are submitted and validated before your intended wedding date, you're good to go. You'll just need to coordinate your timelines to make sure everything lines up."

Weston leaned forward, his grin playful. "So, technically, if I take my time filing in Liverpool, I could delay the whole thing for months?"

"Exactly. Now, before I press submit, we need to know a venue where you wish to be officially married," Janet continued, her smile softening. "Any ideas, or shall I just put Birkenhead Town Hall down for now?"

Penny glanced at Weston, her eyebrow raised. "Birkenhead Town Hall sounds a bit too... predictable, don't you think? After the chaos of Alma de Cuba, I feel like we need something equally memorable... unless..."

She noticed Weston grin and mouth 'Alma De Cuba', and Penny knew that Weston was all in for making the venue where their chaos began the site of their official vows. Penny felt a mix of amusement and trepidation at the thought. Alma de Cuba, with its stained glass windows and nightclub atmosphere, wasn't the most traditional of choices—but then again, neither were they.

"Alma de Cuba," Penny said finally, her lips curling into a mischievous grin. "Let's make it official where it all started."

Janet raised her eyebrows, clearly entertained by the idea. "Well, that's certainly unconventional—I believe that Liverpool have that as an approved venue on their list of licensed locations, but you'll need to check with them to see if it is or not."

Penny and Weston exchanged a quick glance, their mutual grins confirming that Alma de Cuba was indeed the perfect place to make their chaotic love story official. Janet, clearly amused by their unconventional choice, tapped a few more keys on her computer.

"Alright," she said with a smile, "we'll list it as a preliminary venue, pending confirmation from Liverpool City Council. Once Weston files his notice and you've got the date sorted with the venue, everything should fall into place." She handed Penny a printout. "This is your confirmation of notice submission. Keep it safe—you'll need it when the time comes."

Penny carefully tucked the paper into her bag, nodding her thanks. Weston leaned forward, his voice warm and teasing. "Thanks, Janet. You've made what I expected to be a bureaucratic nightmare surprisingly painless. I'll be sure to give Liverpool City Council a hard time in your honour."

Janet laughed, standing to shake their hands. "Well, if they're half as charmed by you two as I've been, you should be fine. Good luck with the rest of the process—and don't forget to send us an invite when it's all official!"

****

# CHAPTER 15 – News for Weston
## Thursday 4th October 2024

The autumn drizzle tapped against the windows of Penny's flat as she sat cross-legged on the sofa, her laptop balanced precariously on her knees. The day had been relatively calm—an unusual occurrence for someone whose life often resembled a reality show gone awry. She had spent most of it editing a new promo for her drive-time show, leaving Weston to prep for his Ulster Vibes Saturday Evening show remotely.

But now, as the evening settled in, as the two had had a day off, booked annual leave, Penny could feel the quiet tension simmering in the air. Weston had been uncharacteristically subdued all day, his usual banter replaced by moments of distracted silence. She could sense something was weighing on him, but Weston being Weston, he hadn't yet said a word about it.

"Alright, PC Plum," she teased, glancing over at him as he stood by the window, his phone in hand. "What's got you brooding like a soap opera heartthrob? Don't tell me Garston's run out of Guinness."

Weston turned, a small smile tugging at the corner of his lips. "Carmichael, you'd know better than anyone that Guinness is the least of my concerns. Besides, if Garston ever ran out, I'd just come to yours and raid your wine rack."

Penny snorted, setting her laptop aside. "You're avoiding the question. Come on, spill it. What's going on?"

He hesitated, running a hand through his curls, his usual easy confidence giving way to something more vulnerable. "I got a call earlier," he admitted, his voice low. "From Ballymena."

The mention of his hometown immediately set Penny on edge. She knew how much Weston's relationship with his family—and especially his grandfather, Michael—had affected him in recent weeks. She leaned forward, her expression softening. "What's happened? Is it your dad? Or—?"

"It's Granddad," Weston cut in, his tone a mix of frustration and resignation. "He's... well, he's dead. Seems me dad's decided to take things into his own hands and kill the bastard. Well, technically Dad's under arrest on suspicion of murder, but you know the PSNI from what I've told you before. They won't release him unless they're absolutely sure it was him. They're holding him until they figure it all out."

Penny stared at Weston, her mouth slightly open as she tried to process what he had just said. Michael O'Rourke—Weston's manipulative, deeply entrenched grandfather—was gone. And his father was now at the centre of what sounded like a brewing storm in Ballymena.

"Wait, Weston," she began carefully, "are you saying your dad… actually killed Michael? Or at least that's what they think?"

Weston sighed, rubbing the back of his neck. "That's the thing, Carmichael—I don't know for sure. Dad's always been adamant about staying above Granddad's twisted ways. But given how much tension there's been between them recently, and after what happened with Cillian…" He trailed off, his voice thick with emotion.

Penny stood and crossed the room, placing a comforting hand on his arm. "Hey," she said softly, "you don't have to figure this out all at once. What do you need to do? Do you need to go back to Ballymena?"

Weston met her gaze, his green eyes clouded with uncertainty. "I'm not sure," he admitted. "Part of me thinks I should go, you know? For Dad. For Mum. But another part of me…" He broke off, shaking his head.

"You're scared of getting pulled back into it," Penny

finished for him, her voice gentle.

He nodded. "Aye. The O'Rourke name's already a bloody curse. If I go back now, especially with Granddad's old crew still skulking about, it might drag me deeper into everything I've spent years trying to escape. Thing is, if I go, it'll be long term, not a quick visit, so..."

"So, you might miss our wedding date that we'd planned, and you'd miss everything we've been building here." Penny finished his thought, her voice steady despite the knot tightening in her stomach. She took a deep breath and squeezed his arm. "Weston, this is huge. You don't have to decide tonight, but whatever you choose, you're not doing it alone. We'll figure it out—together."

"No, Penny... I need to, as its it's my dad. No matter how much I've tried to keep distance, family's still family.

He's the one who stood up to Granddad when no one else would. If he's in trouble because of all this, I can't just leave him to face it alone." Weston's voice was resolute, but there was a flicker of doubt in his eyes that didn't escape Penny's notice.

Penny nodded slowly, her hand still resting on his arm. "Alright," she said, her voice calm but firm. "If you feel like you need to go, then you should. But you're not doing it without a plan—and without making sure you've got the support you need. The last thing you need is to walk into whatever mess is brewing in Ballymena and get caught up in something you can't control."

Weston let out a humourless laugh, his shoulders sagging slightly. "Carmichael, you sound like my mam when I first told her I was moving to England. 'Have a plan, Weston. Don't let the chaos win.'" He glanced at her, his lips quirking into a small smile. "You're right, though. I need to think this through."

Penny crossed her arms, tilting her head as she studied him. "Good. So, let's start with the basics. If you're going back to Ballymena, what's the first thing you need to do?"

Weston hesitated, his brow furrowing as he considered her question. "I suppose… contact a solicitor. If Dad's been arrested, he'll need proper representation. I don't trust Granddad's old connections not to muddy the waters."

"Okay," Penny said, nodding. "And what about you? Are you planning to stay with your mum while you're there?"

Weston shrugged, running a hand through his curls.

"Probably. Mam'll need the support, and I don't fancy staying in the old family house. Too many ghosts in those walls."

Penny couldn't help but reach out and brush a stray curl from his forehead, her touch light but grounding. "Alright, so you've got a starting point. But what about us? If you're going back long term, what does that mean for... this?"

Weston's expression softened, and he reached out to take her hands in his. "Carmichael, you've been my rock through all this madness. I don't want to lose what we've built here. But if I have to stay in Ballymena for a while, I'll do everything I can to make sure we don't lose each other in the process. I'll come back as soon as I can—once things are sorted."

Penny gave him a small smile, though her chest tightened at the thought of him leaving. "Just promise me one thing," she said, her voice steady despite the lump in her throat.

"Anything," Weston replied without hesitation.

"Promise me you won't let Ballymena pull you back into its darkness. You've worked so hard to move forward, Weston. Don't let this undo everything."

Weston's grip on her hands tightened slightly, his green eyes locking onto hers with an intensity that took her breath away. "I promise, Carmichael. No matter what happens, I won't let it take me back there. You've shown me there's more to life than what I left behind. I'm not losing that."

The weight of his words settled over them, a solemn yet comforting declaration that seemed to fill the room with a sense of quiet determination. Penny nodded, her fingers lacing through his as she pulled him into a hug.

"We'll figure it out," she whispered, her cheek resting against his shoulder. "Together."

*_*_*_*

A few hours later, Penny had decided to go out to collect some food that she and Weston had ordered, a pair of pizzas with stuffed crust, an Hawaiian for Penny and a Farmhouse for Weston and, for Penny a portion of cheesy chips, and for Weston a portion of Halloumi fries, when she had a realisation—Weston wasn't going to come back from Ballymena, that this was his farewell, whether he admitted it or not. As much as Penny wanted to believe in his promise, she couldn't shake the nagging feeling that Ballymena and its weighty legacy would pull Weston back in ways neither of them could predict.

By the time she returned to the flat, the comforting warmth of the pizza boxes in her hands did little to ease the chill that had settled in her chest. She found Weston sitting on the sofa, scrolling through his phone with a contemplative expression. He looked up as she entered, offering her a small smile.

"Dinner's here," Penny announced, forcing a cheerful tone as she set the boxes and sides on the coffee table. "Let's eat before the cheese turns into rubber."

Weston chuckled, reaching for the Farmhouse pizza. "Good shout, Mrs O'Rourke. Can't face Ballymena on an empty stomach."

Penny settled beside him, picking at her cheesy chips as Weston took a hearty bite of his pizza. The silence between them wasn't uncomfortable, but it was heavy with unspoken thoughts. Penny finally set her food down, her appetite dwindling under the weight of her concerns.

"Wes," she said softly, breaking the quiet. "Do you really think you'll come back? Or are you just telling me what you think I want to hear?"

Weston paused mid-bite, his expression caught between surprise and guilt. He set his pizza down carefully, wiping his hands on a napkin before turning to face her fully. "Carmichael," he began, his voice low but earnest, "I meant what I said. I don't want to lose this—you, us. But I'd be lying if I said I wasn't scared. Ballymena's got a way of dragging people back, even when they don't want to be there. Anyway, I've... well, I've booked my flight."

Penny's stomach dropped at Weston's words, though she tried to keep her expression neutral. She leaned back against the sofa, her cheesy chips forgotten. "When's the flight?" she asked, her voice steady despite the tremor in her chest.

"Tomorrow at 4 from John Lennon to Belfast International. EasyJet flight was the only one that I could book. Nearly £130 for it though!" Weston replied, his face shocked at the price.

Penny nodded, her mind racing. Tomorrow. That wasn't much time to process everything, let alone say goodbye. She looked at Weston, his freckled face softened with uncertainty, and the familiar spark in his green eyes dimmed by the weight of his decision.

"Tomorrow," she repeated, more to herself than to him.

"That's… soon."

Weston gave a small, apologetic smile. "Aye, it is. But if I delay any longer, it'll only make it harder for Dad—and for me."

Penny exhaled, her fingers playing with the hem of her jumper as she searched for the right words. "Do you want me to come with you? I could help, be there for your mum, keep you sane while you deal with… everything."

The offer hung in the air between them, and for a moment, Weston seemed tempted. But he shook his head, his curls bouncing with the movement. "No, Carmichael. This is something I need to handle on my own. You've already done more for me than I could ever ask. And… well, I need you to be here so my post can be forwarded… and… well, our wedding, if we… well, book it for New Years Eve, that way we can still stick to the Alma de Cuba plan. Plus, I don't want you getting tangled up in Ballymena's madness. It's bad enough for one O'Rourke to deal with."

Penny's heart twisted at his words, torn between understanding his need to face this alone and the growing ache of knowing she'd be left behind. She reached out, taking his hand in hers and squeezing it tightly.

"Alright," she said, her voice steady despite the lump in her throat. "But you have to promise me one more thing."

Weston tilted his head, a flicker of curiosity breaking through his sombre expression. "What's that, Mrs O'Rourke?"

Penny smiled faintly, her thumb brushing against his knuckles. "Promise me you'll call. Text. Whatever. Don't let me sit here wondering what's going on while you're knee-deep in family drama. I need to know you're okay—and that you haven't forgotten about New Year's Eve at Alma de Cuba."

Weston's lips curved into a small but genuine smile. "I promise, Carmichael. I'll call every chance I get. And I could never forget about our wedding. After all, who else could handle the chaos of being my wife?"

Penny laughed softly, her grip on his hand tightening for a moment before she released it. "No one, that's who. Now, eat your pizza before I change my mind and keep you here by force."

As the two ate their pizza, Penny turned the television over to Clubland TV, where they were showing 'Cascadia In The Mix', a show which featured back-to-back bangers from Cascadia, complete with music videos from the late 2000s and early 2010s. The high-energy beats of Everytime We Touch filled the flat, momentarily lightening the mood as Weston started bobbing his head to the rhythm.

"Ah, Cascadia," he said with a grin, picking up another slice of pizza. "Now this takes me back. Nights out in Belfast with the lads, giving it the full dad-dance routine."

Penny smirked, settling back into the sofa. "You're not old enough for dad dancing yet, O'Rourke. But I'm sure you gave it your best shot."

Weston chuckled, tossing a stray olive from his pizza onto Penny's plate. "Don't you dare mock my moves, Lane. They're a cultural treasure. Besides," he added with a cheeky glint in his eye, "I reckon my skills could rival your infamous Alma de Cuba shimmy."

Penny laughed, throwing the olive back at him. "You're right. The shimmy's unbeatable. But you're welcome to try at our New Year's wedding, Mr O'Rourke. If you're lucky, I might even let you lead."

Weston feigned shock, clutching his chest dramatically. "Let me lead? Be still my heart. Carmichael, you truly are the most generous of brides."

Their banter continued as the music videos played, the tension from earlier slowly melting away. But even as they joked and laughed, Penny couldn't ignore the weight of the coming day hanging in the background. Tomorrow, Weston would board that flight, and their lives would diverge—at least for a little while.

As Evacuate the Dancefloor transitioned into What Hurts the Most, Penny felt a pang of bittersweet emotion. She turned to Weston, who was air-drumming with a slice of pizza in hand and made a mental note to remember this moment. No matter what happened in Ballymena, she wanted to hold on to the lightness they shared tonight.

"Weston," she said suddenly, her voice cutting through the music. .

He looked over, his drumming stopping mid-beat.

"What's up, Carmichael?"

Penny hesitated for a moment before shaking her head with a small smile. "Nothing. Just... don't forget this, alright? Nights like this. The pizza, the Cascadia, the ridiculous banter. It's what makes everything worth it."

Weston's expression softened, and he leaned over to press a quick kiss to her forehead. "I won't forget, Penny. I promise."

* _ * _ * _ *

As the clock struck ten minutes to midnight, Penny looked at the lock screen of her mobile phone, a photo of her and Weston taken the previous week from Studio 2, when Weston was covering for Abby, and Rory was on leave, the two of them handling the Liverpool drive show together, their smiles wide and carefree as they posed in front of the mic. The memory felt distant now, but Penny clung to it as she turned to Weston, who was lying beside her on the sofa, scrolling idly through his phone.

"You know," she began, her voice soft, "this flat's going to feel a lot emptier without you here. It's funny, we've been dating nearly a month, you moved in only a week ago, and... well, I've got kinda used to your carcass on my sofa every evening."

Weston chuckled, setting his phone down and shifting to face her. "Carmichael, you'll have me blushing if you keep that up. But seriously, it's only temporary. As soon as I've sorted everything back home, I'll be right back here—annoying you on this very sofa, stealing your pizza toppings, and putting on dad-dancing masterclasses."

Penny gave him a small smile, though her heart wasn't entirely convinced. "I'll hold you to that, O'Rourke. And don't think I won't text you daily to remind you of all the chaos you're missing here."

Weston grinned, leaning forward to nudge her shoulder. "I'd expect nothing less. And hey, while I'm away, maybe you could start planning the wedding properly. Alma de Cuba isn't going to decorate itself, you know. And if I come back to find you've gone for some Pinterest-perfect nonsense, I'll be lodging a formal protest."

Penny rolled her eyes but couldn't suppress a laugh. "Oh, don't worry. I've already got a vision—neon lights, confetti cannons, and a first dance to Cha Cha Slide. The ultimate Manic wedding."

Weston groaned, throwing his head back dramatically. "Carmichael, you're going to be the death of me. But if that's the price for marrying the Queen of Chaos, then so be it."

For a while, they simply sat together, the room quiet save for the faint hum of the TV in the background. Penny rested her head on Weston's shoulder, her thoughts swirling with a mix of hope and trepidation. She didn't want to think about the distance that would soon separate them, or the challenges Weston would face in Ballymena.

For now, she focused on the warmth of his presence beside her and the way his arm draped protectively around her shoulders.

As midnight approached, Weston broke the comfortable silence. "You know, Carmichael, I never thought I'd end up here—on the Wirral, in this mad relationship, planning a wedding that started as a drunken dare. But for all its chaos, I wouldn't trade it for anything."

Penny tilted her head to look up at him, her eyes soft with affection. "Neither would I, O'Rourke. You might drive me mad half the time, but you're worth every second of it."

He smiled, leaning down to kiss her gently. "Don't go getting all soppy on me now, Mrs O'Rourke. I've got a reputation to uphold. Anyway, fancy a shag? A sort of last night before I have to go find me pot-o-gold shag?"

Penny let out a laugh, unable to keep a straight face. "You're incorrigible, O'Rourke. A pot-o-gold shag? That's a new one, even for you."

Weston grinned, the cheeky glint in his eye unmistakable. "Well, you've got to admit, it'd be a memorable send-off. Better than a handshake at the airport, anyway. Anyway, I've gotta be up in 4 hours for work, so we might as well make the most of the time we've got."

Penny smirked, shaking her head. "Alright, Mr O'Rourke. But just so you know, if you fall asleep mid-shag, I'm billing you for emotional damages. You've been warned."

Weston laughed, pulling her closer as he leaned in. "Carmichael, you've got a way of making even the end of the world feel like a comedy show. Let's make this night one to remember."

As the night deepened, the drizzle outside became a soft patter against the windows, the world beyond their little bubble fading away. For a moment, there was no Ballymena, no looming family drama, and no goodbye waiting on the horizon. It was just Penny and Weston, tangled in each other's laughter and warmth, holding onto the fleeting joy of a love that had somehow found them amidst the chaos.

The future could wait—just for now.

****

# CHAPTER 16 – Weston's Farewell
## Friday 5th October 2024

Penny knew it was coming. The first person she had truly fallen in love with since she was fifteen was about to leave, and no amount of cheeky banter or radio chaos could soften the blow. Weston O'Rourke had made his decision, and Penny respected it, even if her heart ached.

He was returning to Ballymena, as his grandfather, Michael, had died the previous day, in a suspicious manner, and his father had been arrested on suspicion of murder. Penny knew that Weston needed to step up and support his family through the turmoil. As much as she wanted to ask him to stay, she understood that this wasn't just about family—it was about loyalty, legacy, and facing the ghosts of his past.

He had wrapped up his final Western Ulster Vibes breakfast show earlier that morning, his final show producing for Manic, even though he had pre-recorded some stock programming that would be going out on Ulster Vibes and Western Ulster Vibes over the months ahead. The reality of his departure had hit her when she heard his sign-off, a bittersweet farewell that resonated across the airwaves.

Penny could almost hear the emotion in his voice, hidden beneath his usual cheeky charm. It wasn't just a goodbye to his listeners; it was a goodbye to a part of his life that he was leaving behind.

The irony in that Penny had walked into the hub early, as she had been asked to host the early-afternoon shift on

Manic Dance, the EDM/Club/House station that Manic owned, before her regular drive-time show on Manic Liverpool later in the day. The double shift had been a welcome distraction, a whirlwind of energy and thumping beats that kept her from dwelling too much on Weston's impending departure.

Looking at her watch, she saw it was nearly twelve, an hour until the show she was covering for Linus Poplar, the regular early-afternoon host on Manic Dance, was set to begin. She'd promised herself she'd spend that last hour with Weston before he left. Penny wasn't one for grand goodbyes or dramatic scenes, but this one felt different. It wasn't just a colleague leaving—it was someone who had managed to carve out a space in her chaotic, often guarded life.

As she walked into Studio 3, where Weston was finishing his last Ulster Vibes Saturday afternoon show, a pre-recorded show simulcast on both Ulster Vibes, the pan-regional Northern Ireland station, and Western Ulster Vibes, the Londonderry and Derry station, which focused on Irish CHR artists and local talent, Penny paused for a moment in the doorway. Weston was sat at the desk, headphones on, mic muted, as he queued up the final tracks for his show. His usual confident energy was tinged with a solemnity that she hadn't seen before.

"And that was Hozier's All Things End, here on Ulster Vibes and Western Ulster Vibes. We're going to be heading to Kaz Poynter in a bit with Manic's Urban takeover, but first, as it's my last show for a bit, here on Manic Radio across Ulster and the Republic of Ireland, I wanted to take a moment to say thank you. Do gach éisteoir aonair a bhí ag tiúnáil isteach, a sheol téacs, nó a ghlaoigh isteach chun gáire nó scéal a roinnt, rinne tú mo chuid ama anseo do-dhearmadta. Ba mhór an phribhléid na haerthonnta a roinnt libh go léir, agus cé go bhféadfadh sé seo a bheith slán go fóill, tá súil agam nach mbeidh go deo. Bí cúramach, coinnigh an ceol os ard, agus cuimhnigh - tá an saol ró-ghearr gan damhsa a dhéanamh ar an bhfonn is fearr leat. Seo chugaibh Westlife le ceann de na cúlchistí clasaiceacha a bhí agam riamh, Flying Without Wings."

Penny knew that she didn't understand a word of the Irish Weston had just spoken, but the emotion in his tone transcended any language barrier. It was heartfelt, a poignant goodbye not just to his listeners but to a chapter of his life. The familiar opening notes of Westlife's Flying Without Wings played, a fitting choice that made Penny's chest tighten.

Weston glanced up as Penny entered the studio, his green eyes softening as they met hers. He took off his headphones and muted the studio mic. "Carmichael," he greeted with a small smile, his Northern Irish lilt more subdued than usual. "Come to make sure I don't nick the equipment on my way out?"

Penny snorted, leaning against the doorframe with her arms crossed. "Nah, just here to make sure you don't turn Studio 3 into your personal stage for a Westlife tribute act. Though I've got to say, Flying Without Wings? Proper send-off material, O'Rourke."

Weston chuckled, running a hand through his curls.

"Figured I'd go out with a classic. Anyway, shouldn't you be prepping for your Manic Dance gig? Or are you here to nick my leftover coffee?"

"Cheeky sod," Penny shot back, stepping further into the room. "I've got an hour before I go on. Anyway, I'm in here for my show. Shouldn't you be at John Lennon by now? After all, it's only a five minute walk from here."

Weston glanced at the clock on the studio wall and chuckled. "Nah, I've got a couple of hours. I've paid for fast track security, and I've... well, kept most my stuff at yours. I'll be coming back and forth a few times to pick stuff up, so I don't have to pay the extortion that is baggage fees." Weston leaned back in his chair, his gaze lingering on Penny. "But if you're trying to kick me out early, Carmichael, just say the word. Can't have you getting too attached, now, can we?"

Penny rolled her eyes, but the smirk tugging at her lips betrayed her amusement. "As if you're that easy to get rid of, O'Rourke. You're like a particularly annoying song that gets stuck in your head—catchy, irritating, and impossible to forget."

Weston laughed, the sound lighter than it had been all day. "I'll take that as a compliment. Anyway, Carmichael, it's not like I'm going to Ballymena forever. I'll be back for Christmas, and then... well, we've got a wedding to plan, don't we?"

"Assuming you're not dragged into some dodgy O'Rourke family scheme while you're over there," Penny retorted, her tone teasing but her eyes betraying a flicker of genuine concern.

Weston's smile softened, and he stood, closing the distance between them. "Penny," he said, his voice quieter, "I meant what I said yesterday. I'll handle what I need to handle, but I'm coming back. I've got too much waiting for me here—too much worth fighting for."

Penny looked up at him, her arms still crossed but her stance less guarded. "You'd better, Weston. Because if you don't, I'll personally fly to Ballymena and drag you back myself. And trust me, you don't want to see me when I'm in full chaos mode."

Weston grinned, reaching out to tuck a strand of hair behind her ear. "I wouldn't expect anything less from the Queen of Chaos."

For a moment, the studio fell silent, save for the faint hum of the equipment and the muffled strains of Westlife's soaring chorus. Penny felt the weight of the moment settle over them, the reality of Weston's departure hitting her square in the chest.

"I'm going to miss you, you know," she admitted, her voice barely above a whisper.

Weston's hand lingered at her cheek for a moment before he dropped it, his smile tinged with melancholy. "I'm going to miss you too, Carmichael. But like I said, this isn't goodbye. It's just... see you later."

Penny nodded, blinking back the sting of tears. "Right. See you later."

* _ * _ * _ *

An hour later, as Penny sneaked out of the impromptu party that Kyle and Sue, the early-afternoon hosts of Manic's main CHR station, had organised for Weston in the Speke hub's communal kitchen, she knew that her show on Manic Dance, that would be at the same time as Kyle and Sue's one in Studio 1, was about to start, so she headed back to Studio 3. The energy in the communal kitchen had been high—laughter, heartfelt speeches, and a playlist of Weston's "greatest hits" filled the air. Kyle had even brought out his infamous 'Mersey Mix' cupcakes, decorated with miniature Guinness pint toppers in honour of Weston's roots. Yet, amidst the lively chatter, Penny had felt a pang of loneliness creep in, knowing that soon Weston wouldn't be part of this daily chaos.

As she settled into the studio, the familiar glow of the Zetta playout system on the monitors brought a sense of comfort. Her producer, Jean Noakes, for the show was sat on the opposite side of the mixing desk, cuing up the next set of tracks, a perfect blend of high-energy club bangers to kick off the early afternoon on Manic Dance. The studio countdown hit zero, and the opening strains of Joel Corry & Jax Jones feat. Fireboy DML - Me and My Guitar filled the airwaves. Penny slipped on her headphones, letting the pulsating beat steady her nerves.

"Alright, Britain, it's your gal, Penny C, her on Manic Dance, live and across the nation, bringing you the Friday energy you need to kickstart your weekend! We've got the hottest tracks lined up, so don't go anywhere. You've got two hours to get your entries in for the returning £500k

Money Drop, yes, the big £500k Money Drop is back, but I'll be telling you more, right after Joe Corry and Jax Jones featuring Fireboy DML with Me and My Guitar. Keep it locked on Manic Dance, where we keep the beats pumping and the vibes high!"

Penny leaned back in her chair, letting the music do its job as she took a moment to steady herself. The station's signature energy was infectious, and despite the ache in her chest, she felt herself falling into the rhythm of her show. The control room lights dimmed slightly, casting the studio in a cosy glow as Jean gave her a thumbs-up, ready with the next track.

As the song faded, Penny hit the mic button. "That was Me and My Guitar, and if you're just tuning in, welcome to Manic Dance! Penny C here, holding it down for Linus this afternoon, and boy, have I got a show lined up for you. We're talking back-to-back bangers, your shout-outs, and, of course, all the info you need for our £500k Money Drop. Imagine how many nights out you could fund with half a million quid—enough to keep the drinks flowing at Alma de Cuba for years! Now, to enter, just text us at 87106, with the word DROP, visit www.manicradioplays.co.uk or phone us on 0330 880 3601 for your free entry. Lines close at 3pm today, so get in quick if you fancy a chance at the jackpot. Winners are picked from an entry who's listening at any of the Manic Radio stations, Manic Dance, Manic Rock, Manic Goldies, Manic Soul and Manic Metal, as it's a network-wide competition. Calls are free, but texts and web entries are £3, and for today only, as a special offer, its double entry on texts! So, if you want that extra shot at half a million, now's the time to go for it! Up now its Slim Shady himself, Eminem, with his newest track, Houdini."

The opening bars of Eminem's Houdini filled the studio, and Penny leaned back into her chair, exhaling a deep breath as she briefly let the track carry the energy of the show. Her producer, Jean, gave her a knowing smile through the glass, sensing that Penny's usual cheeky bravado was laced with a tinge of melancholy today.

As the track played, Penny allowed herself a moment to reflect. Weston's departure hung over her like a cloud, but the controlled chaos of the Manic Dance studio was its own kind of therapy. Music had always been her escape, her way of channelling emotions she couldn't fully articulate. And now, it was her way of holding it together.

Jean's voice crackled in her headphones. "Great start, Penny. Keep the energy up. Text lines are buzzing already."

Penny grinned, adjusting her mic. "Cheers, Jean. Let's give them a Friday afternoon to remember."

As Houdini faded out, Penny's voice slid effortlessly into the mic. "That was Slim Shady himself, proving once again that magic isn't just for Hogwarts. Now, let's talk shout-outs! Get on the WhatsApp, send us a text or a voice note, our digits are 0330 880 3601, and I'll be reading them out all throughout the show. Up next, it's some Swedish House Mafia with Heaven Takes You Home, because let's face it, the weekend deserves nothing less than pure euphoric vibes to lift you up. This is Manic Dance, and I want to know what you're up to today. Are you stuck at work, bunking off early, or already getting the party started? Hit me up, 0330 880 3601 or find me on socials at @ManicDance. I'm here in for Linus Poplar, who'll be back next Friday with his usual chaos, but until then, let's keep this party going!"

The track transitioned seamlessly into the uplifting beats of Swedish House Mafia, and Penny let herself relax slightly. She knew that, unlike CHR, which was more focused on fast-paced listener interaction, her time on Manic Dance allowed her to let the music lead the energy while still weaving in her own cheeky charm. It was the perfect mix of distraction and focus.

Looking at the script and schedule, she noticed that the show went 'in-the-mix', where it would be mainly music with minimal presenter links, between 2 and 3, and another memo had been added saying that the studio would be used for the Manic Radio Liverpool drive show, which she and Rory normally presented, straight after her Manic Dance show ended at 4, so Rory and Abby would be coming in around half 3 and doing their setup while she continued with her final links for Manic Dance. She had a fleeting thought—would Weston's absence affect her on-air chemistry with Rory? Even though Penny had only been with Manic since the start of September, a month of time at the station, and she had already built strong dynamics with her colleagues, it was Weston who had been her anchor in the whirlwind of chaos that defined life at Manic Radio. She pushed the thought aside. This was the world of CHR and EDM radio—high energy, unrelenting beats, and an audience that lived for the now. Penny reminded herself she had a job to do, and her listeners were counting on her to deliver.

As Heaven Takes You Home reached its crescendo, Penny's voice filled the studio once more.

"That was Swedish House Mafia taking us straight to cloud nine! And if you're just tuning in, it's Penny C here on Manic Dance, keeping you company this Friday afternoon while Linus is off causing mayhem elsewhere. Don't forget, you've got just over an hour to enter the

£500k Money Drop. Who wouldn't want half a mil to spend on nights out, a new wardrobe, or maybe even booking Swedish House Mafia for your private party? Keep those texts and calls coming! Next up, we're taking things up a notch with a hot new remix of a classic Madonna track—Ray of Light, reimagined by David Guetta and Kygo. This one's guaranteed to have you turning the volume up wherever you are. Stay tuned to Manic Dance, where the only rule is the beats don't stop!"

The energetic intro to the remix filled the studio, and Penny leaned back, allowing herself a moment of reprieve as the track pulsed through the speakers.

"You're doing quite well, transitioning from regular CHR, Carmichael," Jean said with a grin from the opposite side of the desk where the usual third presenter slot sat on the Ulster Vibes breakfast show. "You've got the energy dialled up just right for Manic Dance. Normally CHR hosts struggle with the crossover with EDM formats, but you're managing it like a pro. Maybe Linus should watch his back."

Penny laughed, spinning her chair slightly to face Jean. "Don't tell Linus that, or he'll have me doing every cover shift on Dance. Besides, I'm just borrowing his decks for the day—no plans to dethrone the king. Yet."

"And good read on the £500K Money Drop," Jean added, glancing from her notes. "Anyway, remember we throw to Studio 1 at ten past 3 for the winning call."

Penny nodded, mentally bookmarking the reminder about the £500k Money Drop winner announcement. It was moments like these that kept the energy alive, even amidst personal turmoil. As the remix of Ray of Light reached its climax, she glanced at the clock, realising she still had some time before the in-the-mix segment began.

"Alright, Penny," she muttered to herself, straightening her posture. Looking at the clock, she noticed it was barely 20 past 1, and that there were 2 and half hours to go until the end of her first show, and then she'd be going straight onto her usual afternoon drivetime show on Manic Liverpool. The prospect of an intense double shift was daunting, but Penny welcomed the distraction—it was better than dwelling on Weston's departure. The energy of the studio, the beats reverberating through her headphones, and the thought of her loyal listeners kept her focused.

Looking at what was next, she saw that there were two more songs to go until her next link, Toca's Miracle by Fragma, and Pam Pam by Rudimental feat. Flowdan & Mystic Marley, two tracks that were regulars on the Manic Dance playlist. Penny smiled, knowing the audience would love this back-to-back duo. It was the perfect set to keep the momentum going.

As Toca's Miracle began, Penny took the brief downtime to glance at her phone. A message from Weston lit up the screen:

**Weston O'Rourke**: *Heading off soon, Carmichael. Don't let the studio fall apart without me. And don't miss me too much.* 😊

Penny smirked, typing back quickly:

**Penny Lane**: *Already planning to replace you with Jean. You're old news, O'Rourke. Safe flight. And remember— wedding planning doesn't stop just because you're gallivanting around Ballymena.*

She hit send and set her phone aside, forcing herself not to linger on the thought of him walking out of her life— even temporarily. The familiar opening notes of Pam Pam by Rudimental filled the studio, pulling her attention back to the desk.

Jean spoke up through the glass, her voice warm and encouraging. "You alright, Penny? You're smashing it today, by the way."

Penny glanced up, giving her a thumbs-up. "Cheers, Jean. Just keeping busy. No rest for the chaotic, eh?"

Jean chuckled. "That's the spirit. Anyway, we've got a load of texts coming in about the £500k Money Drop. Some people are already planning to spend it on Ibiza trips. Classic Manic audience."

Penny grinned, slipping her headphones back on as the track began to fade. She hit the mic button, her voice sliding seamlessly into the mix.

"That was Pam Pam by Rudimental, bringing all the Friday vibes you need! You're listening to Manic Dance with Penny C, holding down the fort while Linus takes a well-earned day off. Now, let's talk £500k Money Drop—because who doesn't want to kickstart their weekend with half a million quid? We've got entries flooding in, and I'm loving your ideas for how you'd spend the cash. Ibiza trips, new cars, someone even said they'd buy a hot tub for their dog. Absolute legends. Keep those texts and voice notes coming—0330 880 3601—and remember, double entries on texts for the £500k Money Drop for today only!"

As Penny wrapped up her link, she leaned back in her chair, the buzz of the live show pushing her lingering sadness to the background. The familiar beats of the next track—Sigala's remix of Dua Lipa's Dance the Night—filled the studio, lifting her spirits as she read through some of the listener texts that Jean had queued up.

"Hi Penny, its James in Wolvo here, any chance you could drop the newest KAAZE Remix of Never Going Home Tonight by David Guetta & Alesso?" one of the voice notes that was on WhatsApp caught Penny's attention. She grinned, hitting the mic button to acknowledge the request live as soon as the track ended.

"Alright, James in Wolverhampton, I see you! KAAZE Remix of Never Going Home Tonight by David Guetta & Alesso—absolute banger, and a top shout. Let me see what I can do for you, mate," she said, seeing that Jean had slotted that into the playlist for the top of the next hour. "First up, even though its 81 days until Christmas, someone here at Manic has decided that Whamageddon should start now, Last Christmas by Wham is up next, followed by a bit of your current Manic Dance Top40 number 1, BACKBONE by Chase & Status and Stormzy, and then some Supermen Lovers with Starlight. It's Manic Dance with me, Penny C, and it's half 1, and you're locked into the biggest beats to power your Friday afternoon. Don't go anywhere!"

The studio's energy was electric, fuelled by the pulsating rhythms and the texts flooding in. Penny felt a spark of gratitude for her listeners, whose enthusiasm made every second on air worth it. She glanced at the clock again—half an hour down, two more tracks until her next link.

As Wham's Last Christmas played out, Penny couldn't help but chuckle at the cheekiness of playing it this early. The irony wasn't lost on her—Christmas vibes in October matched the quirky chaos of Manic Dance's audience.

*_*_*_*

It was five minutes to three, and Penny could see that the 'in-the-mix' segment of the show was nearly ending, with a remix of Busted's Air Hostess, a classic track from what Penny described on air as being "the soundtrack of my early 2000s childhood," transitioning smoothly into the final minutes of the mix. The studio felt alive with the thrum of energy, the pounding beats vibrating through the air as Penny leaned back in her chair. This was the moment Manic Dance listeners lived for—the culmination of their Friday buzz, fuelled by high-octane tracks and the promise of the £500k Money Drop announcement.

"Alright Manic Dance, it's thirty seconds until the lines close, so get your last entries in now! Text DROP to 87106, visit manicradioplays.co.uk, or call 0330 880 3601 for your free entry. Remember, one lucky listener is about to win half a million pounds, and it could be you! Kyle and Sue will be phoning someone in the next 10 minutes and we'll be joining them for the live announcement."

Looking at her screen, Penny chuckled as she heard an audible comedic 10 second countdown which defined that there were only seconds left for entries to the £500k Money Drop competition. She leaned into her mic, her voice playful but tinged with the electric buzz that filled the studio.

"And that's it, folks! Lines are officially closed. If you got your entry in, good luck—this could be your moment to win big! Kyle and Sue are ready to make the call of a lifetime. Stay locked, because in just a few minutes, we'll be joining them live to hear who's taking home the £500k jackpot. This is Manic Dance, and the energy doesn't stop here! I've got the latest mixes of some Timbaland, some Dua Lipa and one that Linus has done of a classic Fatboy Slim track, Brimful of Asha, all before the all-important £500k Money Drop winner announcement live from Studio 1. Don't go anywhere—this is Manic Dance, where Fridays hit differently!"

As the track transitioned into Timbaland's Give It to Me (2024 Club Mix), Penny glanced over at Jean, who was busy coordinating with Studio 1 for the live crossover. The tension in the air was palpable, the kind of high-stakes energy that came with such a massive competition.

Penny took a sip of water, preparing herself for the handover.

As the remix of Brimful of Asha faded out, Penny leaned into her mic with her signature upbeat tone. "Alright, Manic Dance listeners, the moment we've all been waiting for is here! The £500k Money Drop winner announcement is about to go down live from Studio 1 with Kyle and Sue across the Manic network. Who's ready to find out who's taking home half a million quid? I know I am! Let's hand over to Kyle and Sue and find out who the luckiest listener in the UK is today! Kyle, how's London doing you?"

Penny had to admit, that line in the script, claiming that Kyle and Sue were in the London studios whereas they were instead just down the hallway in Studio 1, was a bit of harmless CHR theatre, but it always amused her to play along. What made it even more ironic is that Kyle's response to her was pre-recorded and so smoothly inserted into the live broadcast, creating the illusion of seamless interaction. The recorded line came through with Kyle's signature cheeky charm:

"Thanks, Penny! London is buzzing as always—though I'm not sure it compares to the energy you've got going on at Manic Dance! Let's get to it, shall we? One lucky listener is about to become half a million quid richer. Sue, are you ready to make the call?"

Penny knew the next bit was near live, with the phone calls being delayed by a minute to prevent profanity or unexpected chaos from hitting the airwaves. She listened intently, her headphones catching Sue's bubbly response:

"Absolutely, Kyle! This is the moment we've all been waiting for. Let's dial the number and see who's about to have their Friday made!"

The sound of a phone ringing filled the air, and Penny could almost feel the collective anticipation of listeners across the country. Her studio was quiet except for the faint hum of the equipment and Jean tapping away on her keyboard. Penny leaned closer to the monitor, her curiosity piqued as much as the audience's.

"Hello?" A hesitant voice answered the call, the kind of voice that didn't yet know it was about to receive life-changing news.

"Hi, you're live across the Manic network, and you've just won half a million pounds in the £500k Money Drop!" Kyle's voice boomed with infectious excitement, and Penny could almost hear the shock radiating through the phone line.

The silence that followed was brief but deafening. Then, a scream erupted on the other end of the line, the kind that could only come from someone whose life had just been turned upside down in the best possible way.

"Are you serious?!" the voice cried, breaking into laughter and what sounded like sobs. "Oh my God, I don't believe it! This is unreal!"

Sue's laughter bubbled through the speakers. "Believe it, love! You've just won £500,000! How does it feel to be half a million quid richer?"

The winner struggled to form words, their excitement tumbling out in incoherent bursts. "I can't—oh my God—thank you! This is going to change everything. I don't even know what to say!"

Kyle jumped back in with his usual cheeky banter. "You've said plenty! Now tell us—what's the first thing you're going to do with all that cash?"

There was a pause as the winner collected themselves. "Honestly? Probably cry some more! But after that… I think I'll book a holiday. Somewhere sunny, with a beach and no stress. This is incredible. Thank you so much!"

Penny noticed that there was a cue on her screen which was for her to speak up on the call, despite it being Kyle and Sue who were leading. "It's Penny C here from Manic Dance, now, what's your name, whereabouts you from and which station are you listening to right now?"

The voice on the other end of the call steadied a little as the winner responded, their excitement still bubbling over. "I'm Laura! I'm from Cardiff, and I've been listening to Sue and Kyle on Cardiff Vibes."

Penny knew that Cardiff Vibes was the local brand for that specific CHR station under the Manic network, but the branding was tailored to give listeners a sense of regional pride while still being part of the national platform. She smiled, jumping in with her response.

"Laura from Cardiff, massive congratulations! Half a million quid—how does it feel knowing your Friday afternoon just went from ordinary to legendary?"

Laura let out a breathless laugh, still clearly overwhelmed. "Honestly, Penny, I don't know whether to laugh, cry, or scream some more. I never thought I'd win anything like this. Thank you, Manic Radio!"

Kyle's voice came back with his usual playful tone. "Laura, you deserve it. Now, let's not forget—this isn't just a win for you. It's also a win for the listeners who'll now get to live vicariously through your holidays and hot tub purchases. Just don't spend it all in one place, alright?"

Sue chimed in warmly. "Laura, enjoy every penny of it! Stay on the line and we'll get your bank details so we can transfer the cash, because here at Manic, we pay out within 10 minutes of the winning call, unlike our friends at Hits who take an hour to process theirs!"

Penny chuckled at Sue's playful jab, knowing full well the rivalry between Manic and Hits Radio. It was part of the CHR game, and the listeners loved the banter.

"Well, Laura," Penny said, her voice brimming with genuine excitement, "you've set the bar for Fridays on Manic Radio. Have an incredible time planning how to spend your winnings—and maybe save a little for some Manic merch, yeah?"

Laura laughed again, this time more composed. "Definitely, Penny. Thanks again to all of you. You've just made my year!"

Penny smiled as the Dance feed returned to her and she could promote the next weeks £500k Money Drop, straight after Spiller's Groovejet (If This Ain't Love) started playing in the background.

"Alright, Manic Dance, there you have it! Massive congrats to Laura from Cardiff, who's just bagged herself half a million quid in the £500k Money Drop. And don't worry if you didn't win this time—our next £500k Money Drop is just one week away, so make sure you're locked into the Manic network to find out how to enter. Fancy being the next person screaming down the phone live on air? You know what to do. Keep it locked to Manic Dance—because we don't just play the hits, we make dreams come true!"

The studio filled with the iconic disco beats of Groovejet, and Penny allowed herself a moment to soak in the energy. Despite everything going on with Weston and the emotional rollercoaster of the day, the joy radiating from Laura's win gave her a fresh jolt of positivity. It was moments like these that reminded her why she loved radio—the ability to connect, excite, and bring unexpected happiness to someone's day.

Jean gave her a thumbs-up from across the desk, her grin wide. "Nice one, Penny. That was seamless."

****

# CHAPTER 17 – Radio Silence From Weston

Radio Silence From Weston

It had been four weeks since Weston decided to return to Ballymena, and Penny had been trying to keep herself busy in his absence. But the lack of communication was starting to take its toll. At first, there had been the occasional text—a quick update about his dad's legal situation, a photo of his mum's infamous soda bread, or a cheeky remark about how Ballymena's radio scene was "crying out for a Manic injection of chaos."

But in the last week? Nothing. No texts, no calls, not even a sarcastic WhatsApp reply to her updates about the latest dramas at Manic Radio.

Penny had tried not to overthink it. Weston was dealing with a lot: his dad still under arrest, his family pulling him in all directions, and the weight of Ballymena's complicated legacy pressing down on him. But the silence was deafening, and Penny couldn't help but feel like she was losing him.

Penny stared at her phone, the lock screen showing a photo of her and Weston taken during his last show at Manic Liverpool. His cheeky grin and her exaggerated eye roll captured the playful dynamic they'd shared—a dynamic that now felt like a distant memory.

The autumn drizzle outside her flat blurred the view of the Wirral skyline. Penny had spent the morning pacing, trying to summon the courage to call him again. Her last two calls had gone unanswered, and though she'd left a voicemail after the first, she hadn't dared to leave another.

Tuning into Chester & The Wirral Vibes, the Manic station which covered Birkenhead and Chester, Penny found herself listening to the familiar mix of CHR hits and local updates, hoping the background noise would distract her from the sinking feeling in her chest, however the track that they were playing only served to make her feel even more sad, Basshunter's Now You're Gone.

She knew that it'd be playing across the Manic network on the various CHR stations at the same time, as it was part of the day's syndicated playlist. The song's melancholic undertone struck a chord, and Penny found herself sinking deeper into her own thoughts. Turning the radio to Hits Radio Liverpool, the former Radio City, the irony of them playing Avril Lavigne's When You're Gone was too much for Penny, so, switching to Capital and hearing David Guetta's When Love Takes Over, Penny let out an exasperated sigh. It was as if every station conspired to soundtrack her emotional turmoil.

Even the usually upbeat vibe of CHR radio wasn't enough to lift her mood. She switched the radio to Manic Rock, which was playing Handbags and Gladrags by Stereophonics, then Absolute which had joined, it seems, in the theme of emotional turmoil with No Doubts version of Its My Life, Heat which was playing My Happy Ending by Avril Lavigne, and finally Smooth North West, where they were playing, unusually, White Flag by Dido, a track which only deepened Penny's feelings of uncertainty. With a frustrated groan, she turned the radio off altogether, flopping onto the sofa with her phone still clutched in her hand.

Loading Selector2GO on her mobile, one of the various apps that Manic were now using since they had moved from PlayoutONE to the RCS suite of products, Penny glanced at the schedule for Manic Liverpool for her show later on in the day at drive. It was nearing twenty past nine in the morning, so Penny knew that she had no need to arrive before 1, and that she still had hours to kill. Looking at the playlist, it seemed that the network syndicated playlist wasn't sparing her emotions for drivetime, with every emotional track that existed in CHR, from Avril Lavigne's My Happy Ending to Clean Bandit's Symphony, seemed to be stacked in the hour-by-hour rotation for the Liverpool hub's drivetime slot. It was as if the music gods were intent on rubbing salt in her emotional wounds. Penny groaned, closing the app and tossing her phone onto the coffee table.

"Get a grip, Lane," she muttered to herself, running a hand through her hair. "You're not a teenager wallowing over their first heartbreak. You're a professional. Get up, get on with it."

Hearing her phone buzz, she picked it up, thinking it was Weston finally contacting her, only to see that it was one of her fellow Bauer Academy friends who worked at Hits Radio Birmingham, the former Free Radio, talking about a book she was writing about a princess who was required to find true love before midnight or she'd turn into a commoner and have to work as a barmaid for the rest of her life. Penny smiled faintly at the absurd premise but didn't have the energy to reply. Instead, she swiped back to her notifications, willing something from Weston to appear. Nothing.

The nagging feeling in her chest deepened. The radio silence wasn't just uncharacteristic—it felt like a wall had gone up between them. Weston wasn't the type to ghost people, even under pressure. Something was wrong, and the thought gnawed at her relentlessly.

* _ * _ * _ *

"It's Friday here on Manic Radio Liverpool, and boy, do we have a show for you," Penny heard Rory say as their drivetime show began at 4pm later that day. She sat in the studio, headphones clamped over her ears as Rory Carter's boisterous energy filled the airwaves. Penny managed a small smile, flicking through the playlist on Zetta. She'd been quiet all day, distracted by the lingering radio silence from Weston, but she knew Rory had her back. His usual banter and unrelenting humour would keep the chaos flowing, even if her heart wasn't quite in it.

"And joining me today, as always, the Wirral Wonder herself—Penny Lane!" Rory declared theatrically, shooting her a wink from across the desk.

Penny leaned into the mic, forcing a cheerful tone. "Ah, Rory, you've finally accepted that I'm the brains behind this operation. Nice to hear you admit it on air."

"Brains, chaos—same thing, right?" Rory shot back, grinning. "Anyway, it's Friday, Liverpool, so let's get you ready for the weekend! We've got your requests, shout-outs, and, of course, the usual mayhem. Hit us up on the

WhatsApp, you know the number, 0151 496 0425, either a text or voice note, and we'll read and play them out live. Anyway, we've issued Penny a challenge, haven't we Abby?"

Abby Blue, their producer, piped up from the control room, her voice crackling through the studio monitors. "That's right, Rory! We've challenged Penny to not to squeal during the show."

Penny groaned, as the challenge was actually a not to orgasm challenge, and that she was wearing a vibriator which was being controlled by Abby, who would set it off at any moment throughout the show, whenever Abby deemed it the most chaotic. Penny shot Abby a glare through the glass, though it was tempered by a reluctant laugh.

"Oh, come on!" Penny protested, leaning into the mic. "First you make me listen to emotional bangers all day, and now you've decided to turn my professionalism into a live experiment? Have a word!"

Rory erupted into laughter, clearly relishing the challenge. "Look, Penny, if you're going to call yourself the Queen of Chaos, you've got to embrace it fully. It's what the listeners love!"

Abby chimed in with mock seriousness. "You know the rules, Penny—if you squeal, you lose, and the listeners get to decide your forfeit."

Wiggling slightly, Penny did have to admit that the remote control vibrator did fill her snugly, and that it was pressing both inside of her, as well as nicely resting against her sensitive areas. She shot a sharp look at Abby through the glass but tried to play it cool on air, gripping the edge of the desk to maintain her composure.

"Oh, I see how it is," Penny replied, forcing a grin as she spoke into the mic. "Abby, the evil puppet master, and Rory the hype man, all conspiring to ruin my already fragile reputation. You know I've got a professional name to uphold here."

Rory snorted, unable to keep a straight face. "Professional name? Penny, you've been the poster child for chaos since you walked into this hub. The listeners know what they're here for—and we're giving them premium Friday chaos."

The phone lines lit up, WhatsApp messages flooding in as their regular listeners caught wind of the ridiculous challenge. Penny could already see Abby cackling behind the glass, her hand hovering over the control app for the vibrator. Penny crossed her legs tightly, leaning forward to adjust her posture, as if it would help her resist.

"Right," Penny said firmly, biting back a smirk. "Liverpool, if you hear me start to lose it, just remember—I've been set up by my so-called 'friends' here. I'm the innocent victim in this plot."

Abby's voice crackled through again. "We'll let the listeners decide that. Anyway..."

As soon as Abby said that, Penny felt the vibrations, and not a low blast but on the highest settings, coming from the remote-control vibrator. It shot through her like an electric current, her breath catching in her throat. Penny's hands immediately gripped the edge of the desk, her eyes wide as she fought to maintain her composure. She bit down on the inside of her cheek, determined not to give Rory or Abby the satisfaction of hearing her falter.

Rory, oblivious to her internal struggle for the moment, carried on with his usual banter. "Now, Penny, let's read out some of the listeners' messages. Liverpool's lighting up today! We've got Laura in Aigburth saying she's on her way to Alma de Cuba tonight—proper throwback vibes, eh?"

"Ah... yeah," Penny managed, her voice slightly higher than usual as she fought to steady herself. "Alma de Cuba—always a good shout for a Friday night. Top tier place for... for a bit of fun. Fuuuuuu....nnnnn. Grrr, this... fuuuuuuuddddge."

Penny's attempt to finish the sentence smoothly was completely derailed as Abby cranked the settings higher. The sharp, deep vibrations hummed insistently against her most sensitive areas, and for a split second, Penny's voice faltered entirely. She clamped her mouth shut, sucking in a shaky breath through her nose while Rory turned to her, bemused.

"Fudge? Is that what we're going with?" Rory teased, raising an eyebrow and clearly unaware of the internal war raging inside Penny. "You alright there, Lane? You sound a bit... flustered."

"Flustered? Me? Nah," Penny shot back quickly, though her voice wobbled as she tried to play it off. Her hands remained white-knuckled on the edge of the desk as she shot a murderous glare at Abby through the glass. Abby, for her part, looked like she was on the verge of tears from laughing.

"Anyway, Liverpool, it's time to spin some tracks," Penny said, as the vibrations stopped, and she noticed that the playlist for the first hour had been unchanged from when she looked at GSelector, with it all being melodramatic and soppy CHR hits, from John Newman and Calvin Harris's Blame all the way through to Love Song by Sara Bareilles.

Barely suppressing a groan, Penny clung to her last shred of composure, glancing quickly at the Zetta countdown timer. The intro to Calvin Harris and John Newman's Blame was already ticking down, mercifully buying her a moment to recover as the track thundered into the airwaves.

She slid her chair back slightly, taking a deep breath and narrowing her eyes at Abby through the glass. Abby grinned like the Cheshire Cat, her finger hovering ominously over the app's control settings. Rory, oblivious as ever, leaned back in his seat, feet up on the desk, thoroughly enjoying the chaos he'd set into motion.

As the track faded into Busted's Sleeping with the Light On fading up into the monitors, Penny braced herself, knowing she wasn't going to get through this show unscathed. Abby had clearly decided to commit to the bit, and the vibrator wasn't going anywhere anytime soon.

"Alright, you two, I know I willingly put the vibrator on, but which idiot decided to create the challenge in the first place?" Penny shot at Rory with a mix of mock outrage and breathless laughter. "Because I swear, if I lose my sanity on air, I'm blaming both of you. This will go in the record books as the day Manic Liverpool pushed me over the edge!"

Rory cackled, utterly entertained. "Don't look at me, Penny! This was all Abby's genius—she's the true mastermind behind the madness. I'm just here for moral support and to read out the listeners' comments when you inevitably lose."

Abby's voice crackled back through the monitors, mischievous and unapologetic. "You said you wanted more 'buzz' in the show, Penny! I'm just delivering what the listeners expect. Anyway, blame Danny... he gave me the idea while we were shagging earlier."

Penny nearly choked on air, shooting a wide-eyed look at Rory, who burst out laughing so hard he nearly fell off his chair. "Danny gave you the idea? That's next-level collusion, Abby! I swear, this entire station is out to get me."

"Careful, Lane," Rory teased, wiping tears of laughter from his eyes. "The listeners are absolutely loving this. I'm seeing texts like 'Team Abby for President' and 'Penny, stay strong, Queen of Chaos!'"

Penny forced a smile, adjusting her headphones as she prepared for the next link. "Liverpool, this is what happens when you work with absolute reprobates. I'm being tormented live on air, and you lot are just egging them on! But fine—if it's chaos you want, it's chaos you'll get. Abby, crank it up if you dare—I'm winning this challenge, no matter what!"

Abby gave her a slow, sinister thumbs-up through the glass, clearly ready to escalate. Rory cackled like a man unhinged, and Penny leaned into the mic with newfound determination.

"Alright, Liverpool, we've got......aggghhhhh..." Penny said as the vibrator suddenly buzzed to life again, sending a wave of heat pulsing through her body. She barely managed to hold back a squeal, her voice catching mid-sentence before she quickly covered it with an exaggerated cough.

"Sorry... I, er, think I swallowed a bit of dust there," she improvised, shooting a murderous glare at Abby, who had now collapsed into a fit of silent laughter behind the glass. Rory, of course, was absolutely no help, leaning back in his chair with tears streaming down his face as he tried to regain composure.

"Dust? Is that what we're calling it now?" Rory teased, his grin widening. "Honestly, Penny, you're a pro for keeping it together. I reckon most of Liverpool's waiting for you to crack under pressure, though. We're getting messages like, 'Penny, if you make it through this, you deserve a medal.' Anyway, you can watch the live stream on Kick-"

"Wait!" Penny said, feeling annoyed that Rory and Abby hadn't told her that the show was being live streamed on Kick, a streaming platform with a focus on looser moderation and higher revenue shares for streamers, and featuring names like Fabrizio Romano, Tfue, xQc and Ilya Maddison, nor that listeners could watch and hear the entire behind the scenes happenings in Studio 2. "Since when did we have Kick streaming rights? You lot have been keeping this from me!" Penny blurted, spinning around in her chair to glare at Abby and Rory.

Rory shrugged nonchalantly, wiping his eyes as he fought back another laugh. "Management wanted a bit of 'behind the scenes Manic magic.' We're basically giving Liverpool a front-row seat to your downfall. So, smile for the camera, Lane—you're the star of the show."

Penny groaned, her cheeks flushing as she tried to process the added chaos. "You what? I thought this was just radio. Now half the internet is going to see me squirm—literally! I'm going to kill you both when we're off air."

Rory grinned, clearly loving every second. "All part of the challenge, Penny. What's chaos without a little live-streamed humiliation? Abby, how many viewers do we have on our Kick stream so far?"

Abby's voice crackled through, still breathless with laughter. "We're pushing 8,000 live viewers right now. Apparently, word's spreading fast—people love to watch a bit of carnage on a Friday afternoon. Someone just commented, 'Penny for the win—this is better than Netflix!'"

Penny buried her face in her hands for a moment, stifling a groan. "Great. Just great. I'm the Wirral Gal turned viral calamity. Remind me to change my name and move to a cave when this is over."

Rory, ever the instigator, leaned back in his chair, smirking as he spun towards his mic. "No chance, Lane. You're Liverpool's sweetheart now, the Queen of Chaos live and unfiltered. Anyway, Liverpool, don't go anywhere—up next we've got in our Friday Feelings playlist, dedicated to making Penny drown because she hasn't heard from her man in a week, a classic downer in..."

The sound of a drumroll sound effect interrupted Rory's announcement, the unmistakable cue for something dramatic. Penny tensed, narrowing her eyes at him while Abby's hand ominously hovered over the app when it smashed into Sara Bareilles's Love Song.

The gentle piano intro filled the studio, the perfect emotional gut-punch to complete Rory's theatrical tease. Penny let out an exasperated sigh, slumping slightly in her chair as the song played through the monitors.

"Oh, brilliant," she muttered under her breath, only just audible on her mic. "Because what I really needed right now was a passive-aggressive ballad. Cheers for that, Rory."

Rory, loving every second of her torment, spread his arms wide in mock innocence. "Hey, blame the playlist gods, not me! I'm just the humble deliverer of vibes."

"Vibes?" Penny shot back, narrowing her eyes as she adjusted her headphones. "This is emotional sabotage, and you know it. If I didn't know better, I'd say you and Abby were conspiring with Weston himself to completely ruin my Friday."

"Weston who?" Rory teased, pulling on his best innocent face. "Oh, you mean the Weston O'Rourke? Your Irish prince, currently lost in the Ballymena wilderness? Don't worry, Penny, he'll turn up eventually—probably riding a white horse with a tin of Guinness under his arm."

Abby's voice crackled in again, full of mischief. "Or maybe Weston's watching this Kick stream right now, laughing his head off at how rattled you look. Want me to check the viewer list, Penny?"

Penny's face turned crimson, her composure slipping further. "Don't you dare, Abby. Don't even put that thought out into the universe."

The trio dissolved into laughter, the kind of easy, chaotic humour that only came from years of working together— or in Penny's case, two months of being thrown headfirst into the Manic madness. Even though the vibrator had mercifully fallen silent, Penny still shifted uncomfortably in her seat, her pulse steadying as the final chorus of Love Song built toward its triumphant end.

As the last notes faded out, Penny groaned as U + Ur Hand by P!nk started, and every time P!nk hit a particularly sharp note, Abby mischievously ramped the vibrations again. Penny's eyes shot wide, her breath hitching as she scrambled for composure, gripping the edge of the desk like it might save her from total meltdown.

She also noticed that every time that happened, the microphone had been activated by Abby, so the whole of Liverpool could hear her orgasm as the same time as she desperately tried to maintain her composure.

"Abby!" Penny hissed, her voice half-laugh, half-genuine panic, as the buzz intensified, and P!nk hit another sharp crescendo. Her cheeks flushed deep crimson, and she bit down hard on her lip to stifle a squeal. But it was too late.

The microphone caught the sound of her sharp, breathy gasp. Rory's eyes snapped to her, and his face broke into a wicked grin as he realised what had just happened.

"Ohhh, we heard that!" Rory cackled, doubling over in his chair. "Liverpool, did you hear that? We might have just witnessed Penny Lane losing this challenge live on air!"

Abby's voice piped in from the control room, pure glee dripping from every word. "And there it is, folks! The Queen of Chaos has officially fallen. I'd like to thank P!nk, a perfectly-timed vibrator, and our Kick viewers for their unwavering support. Now, for the forfeit, and the winner is Adam in Southport, who says that Penny must perform a live rendition of... The Fresh Prince of Bel-Air theme song live on air... in acapella."

Penny's jaw dropped. "You what? I've just been publicly humiliated, and now you want me to rap? Are you actually trying to end my career?"

Rory couldn't catch his breath, still howling with laughter. "Penny, it's the price of losing a challenge on live radio. Fair's fair! Adam in Southport, you're a genius—this is going to be legendary."

Penny threw her hands up in surrender, glaring daggers at Abby through the glass, who simply shrugged with a wicked grin. "Fine," Penny said dramatically into the mic, feigning indignation. "But let it be known across

Liverpool and the whole Manic network that this is a violation of my basic human rights. I expect full reparations in the form of wine, cheesy chips, and extra time off."

Rory clapped his hands together, spinning to face the mic. "Ladies and gentlemen, you're about to witness Penny Lane's finest moment yet—her live rendition of The Fresh Prince of Bel-Air. Acapella. Strap in, Liverpool!"

The WhatsApp messages flooded in with laughing emojis, cheering Penny on as the instrumental intro to the classic track briefly played, giving her a beat to find her rhythm. Penny leaned into the mic, closed her eyes for dramatic effect, and launched into the opening verse with as much sass and theatrical flair as she could muster.

"Now this is a story all about how my life got flipped, turned upside down…"

The entire studio erupted. Rory was slapping the desk in hysterics, Abby was doubled over behind the glass, and Penny's attempts to stay serious while delivering Will Smith-level confidence made it all the funnier. She powered through the chorus, even throwing in an exaggerated "Smell ya later!" to finish it off with a flourish.

The studio's laughter peaked as Penny threw her hands in the air, grinning despite herself. "There! Are we satisfied, or do I have to mime the Carlton dance next?"

Rory wiped tears from his eyes, still gasping for air. "Penny, you absolute legend. I think Liverpool has just found its new anthem. Adam in Southport—top marks for that forfeit. Worth every second."

Abby's voice crackled through the monitors, her own laughter still audible. "Honestly, Penny, you nailed it. But don't think you're off the hook for the vibrator incident. That's already trending on Kick under 'Manic Radio Madness.' You're going viral, Queen of Chaos!"

Penny buried her face in her hands, equal parts mortified and entertained. "Fantastic. I always knew I'd go viral for something stupid—just didn't expect it to involve The Fresh Prince and… other equipment."

Rory chimed back in, voice bubbling with delight. "Liverpool, that's the kind of chaos we're bringing you on a Friday. Penny, you've cemented your place in Manic Radio history today."

As the next song kicked in—appropriately, Cascada's Everytime We Touch—Penny slumped back in her chair, shaking her head with a wry grin. "You lot are evil, you know that? Proper evil."

Abby waved back through the glass, grinning like a devil.

"We love you, Penny. Never change."

****

# CHAPTER 18 – Meeting Reevesy at a Big Weekender
### Saturday 2nd November 2024

The past week had been tense for Penny. Every Manic Radio show, from breakfast to late-night, seemed to be running promos for a new show launching on Manic Dance: Ibiza Weekender, hosted by the network's rising star, Jimmy Reeves. The jingles were loud, vibrant, and impossible to miss, with their slick voiceovers hyping Jimmy as "the freshest voice on Manic Dance." Penny, though, couldn't help but chuckle at how they were promoting it as the next big thing.

For Penny and Rory, the directive had been clear: weave the promo into their banter during their Manic Radio Liverpool Drive Show, on a par with how much they were to promote the £500k Money drop, constantly and with relentless enthusiasm. But while Rory embraced the challenge with his usual swagger, Penny found the whole thing mildly grating. After all, there was only so much you could say about a show that hadn't even aired yet, hosted by someone she hadn't met... but had followed for the past few days on Instagram.

She had to admit, for a newbie in the world of radio, Jimmy Reeves was a hunk, even though he was dating Kylie Morgan, a presenter of Warwickshire Stars Breakfast, the local station that covered Coventry and the surrounding areas. Kylie's polished glamour and Jimmy's cheeky, relatable charm made them a power couple in the eyes of their followers.

The fact he looked like a younger Matthew Lewis, the actor who played Neville Longbottom in the Harry Potter films, certainly didn't hurt either. Penny had scrolled through his Instagram, feigning casual disinterest but secretly analysing his every post. His effortless blend of humour, style, and flirtatious captions seemed to draw fans and colleagues alike into his orbit.

Of course, she knew that Toni knew more about him via her boyfriend of 4 months, Northern Vibes drivetime host Al Crozier, who's patch covered Stoke, Staffordshire and Cheshire, which was, like Reeves, based at the Dudley hub of Manic.

Penny knew that Dudley rarely contributed to the Network programmes—it was more a regional stronghold for Manic, one of the battleground areas where Bauer, through Hits Radio Birmingham and Global, through Capital Midlands, as well as Midlands Manic, the Manic CHR station in the Midlands, fought fiercely for dominance. The Dudley hub had a reputation for producing solid regional content, and had been the regional home for Kyle and Sue, the early afternoon duo who had joined Midlands Manic in 2014 and had got the Network slot in March 2020 when the Coronavirus pandemic forced a massive shake-up in how radio was produced. Even though their show was produced from Speke, and the Sunday evening show, Fed's Teatime, was a Dudley network show, the rest of the shows either came from Speke, Stratford or Exeter, three of the main hubs for Manic's network programming. The fact that Dudley still managed to make an impact spoke volumes about the talent it nurtured.

"Looking forward to meeting Reevesy?" Toni asked, her arms coming around Penny's chest, and Penny could feel a strap-on poking into her arse that Toni was wearing, hidden beneath her dress. Penny's cheeks flushed, a mix of embarrassment and amusement bubbling up inside her. Toni's unfiltered humour had become a staple of their banter off-air, and while Penny had grown accustomed to it, moments like this still caught her off guard.

"Erm, yes... but maybe not that much," Penny replied, stepping forward to escape Toni's playful grasp. "Reevesy seems like a good laugh on socials, but I'm not sure how much of it is for show. You know how these big Manic personalities can be—'relatable' on air, but divas behind the scenes."

They were at Toni's flat in Garston, not far from Garston's centre, and so the pre-drinks for the Big Weekender had already begun. Toni, ever the life of the party, had set the mood with a playlist of classic Manic anthems from the past decade, tracks that Penny remembered blasting in her student days. The atmosphere was electric, with a mix of excitement and nerves in the air as they prepared for the chaos that the Big Weekender promised.

"Don't worry, love," Toni said with a cheeky grin, handing Penny a cocktail that was a lurid shade of pink. "Anyway, Reevesy isn't his actual name."

"Wait, what?" Penny looked up, intrigued. "His name's not Reevesy? What is it then?"

Toni smirked, clearly relishing the moment. "James Smith. Can you get more basic than that? Reeves is his mum's maiden name. His dad's that Pete Smith from the Dudley hub," Toni said, taking a swig of her own drink.

"And get this, he's not even a full-time presenter."

"Wait, he's not full-time?" Penny asked, incredulous. "But they're hyping him like he's the next big thing!"

Toni shrugged, her grin widening. "Welcome to the Manic hype machine, babe. Reevesy—or James, if you want to strip away the mystique—is a final year uni student. Only signed his contract Monday. Al had him co-hosting with him on the Stoke Drive Tuesday, and he sounded like he'd come out the CHR Clone Factory that we, Bauer and Global seem to all have. Smooth, cheeky, relatable—but polished to within an inch of his life. You know the type."

Penny nodded, sipping her cocktail as she processed this new information. It was hardly unusual for CHR stations to market their rising stars aggressively, even if they were still finding their feet. Still, the idea of someone juggling university and such a high-profile launch felt surreal.

"Guess it's easier to build the myth when you've got a fresh face and a good social media game," Penny said with a shrug. "And a famous dad doesn't hurt either."

Toni cackled, nearly spilling her drink. "Exactly! And don't get me started on Kylie Morgan. She's been with the company a year, started on the Warwickshire Breakfast back in July, before that had been in her final year at Uni. It's how they recruit half of us, fresh out of Uni or while we're in our final year. They get us while we're still green enough to mould but ambitious enough
278

to burn ourselves out chasing the dream. Kylie was one of the lucky ones—she nailed her first few shows, got big on socials, and boom, now she's the face of Warwickshire Stars. And of course, being attached to Reevesy doesn't hurt her image either. Anyway, babe, it's your eighth Big Weekender since you started.

Penny laughed, swirling the pink cocktail in her glass as she sat on Toni's sofa. The flat was already buzzing with energy as more of the Manic crew trickled in, their laughter and chatter mixing with the pulsating beat of the playlist. Big Weekenders were becoming a regular feature of her life since joining Manic Radio Liverpool, and she had learned to navigate the chaos with a mix of excitement and caution.

"Eight Big Weekenders, and they still don't get old," Penny said, raising her glass. "Though I'm not sure if that's a good thing or a sign that I'm becoming one of you lot."

Toni grinned, raising her own glass in a mock toast. "Darling, if you've survived eight of these, you're one of us now. No going back to 'normal radio.' Once you go Manic, you're in it for life—or at least until the burnout hits."

Penny smirked, but she couldn't deny there was truth to Toni's words. The high-energy culture of Manic was addictive, and even though it was exhausting at times, it was also exhilarating. The endless promos, the relentless push for social media engagement, the wild nights that blurred into early mornings—it was all part of the job, and she'd thrown herself into it with everything she had.

The doorbell rang, cutting through the music. Toni bounded to answer it, her sequined top catching the light as she moved. Penny took another sip of her drink, bracing herself for the arrival of more colleagues.

"Oh, here he is!" Toni's voice rang out, dripping with exaggerated enthusiasm. "The man of the hour, Jimmy Reeves himself!"

Penny's heart skipped a beat as the tall figure stepped into the flat, dressed in a Manic Dance hoodie and skinny jeans, his beanie slightly askew in a way that somehow added to his charm. His smile was easy, his demeanour casual but confident. He looked every bit the polished presenter the promos had hyped, but there was something disarmingly boyish about him in person.

Seeing him with Kylie Morgan, Al Crozier and Liam Price made Penny feel like she had just stepped into the middle of a celebrity entourage. Kylie, radiant in a sequined top and leather hotpants, flashed a perfect smile as she greeted Toni with a hug, her presence effortlessly commanding the room. Al Crozier, with his gruff charm and mischievous grin, followed close behind, already cracking jokes with the ease of someone who owned every room he entered. Liam Price, the smooth-talking presenter of Mid Wales Manic Breakfast, the Shrewsbury and Powys station within the Manic network, rounded out the group, his sharp suit and slicked-back hair giving him an almost managerial air. Together, they exuded an aura of effortless charisma, and Penny couldn't help but feel a twinge of awe—and a bit of nervousness.

Penny watched as Toni all but dragged James into her bedroom and chuckled as Rory headed over to Kylie and started kissing her as if the party weren't in full swing. It was the kind of dynamic Penny had grown to expect at Manic: blurred lines, a mix of professional and personal, and a constant undercurrent of cheeky banter. But tonight, the energy was electric, even by Manic standards.

Kylie pulled away from Rory's kiss with a teasing laugh, smoothing her hair and giving Penny a quick wink. "Looks like you're next for the Reevesy charm offensive," she said, motioning toward the hallway where Toni and James had disappeared.

Penny raised her eyebrows, feigning indifference. "I think I'll wait my turn. He seems busy getting inducted into the Toni Green experience."

Kylie laughed, her voice lilting over the music. "Oh, you have no idea. She's a handful, that one. But don't let her scare you—Reevesy's alright. Just a bit green still."

Penny nodded, taking another sip of her drink as she tried to steady her nerves. It wasn't like she was meeting a celebrity, but something about James Reeves—or rather, James Smith—carried a weight of expectation. The promos had built him up as the next big thing, and now here he was, in the flesh, navigating the same chaotic world she was.

"Have you ever had lezza sex?" Kylie then asked to which Penny grinned, having had several female presenters both eat her out, use strap-ons and even share intimate moments in the chaotic whirlwind of the Manic culture.

Penny leaned back with a playful smirk, deciding to tease Kylie back. "You could say I've explored the 'Manic extracurriculars' a bit," she quipped, raising her glass. "But it's all part of the experience, isn't it?"

Kylie burst into laughter, clearly enjoying Penny's cheeky response. "That's the spirit, love! Manic life is about diving in headfirst—sometimes literally," she joked, giving Penny a nudge. "Mind if I go muff diving on you?"

Penny choked on her drink, both amused and startled by Kylie's cheeky comment. She had quickly learned that no topic was off-limits in Manic's irreverent culture, but Kylie's boldness still managed to catch her off guard. "Well, Kylie," Penny replied, her voice dripping with playful sarcasm, "that's certainly one way to break the ice."

Kylie grinned, clearly enjoying Penny's reaction. "Oh, come on, babe, it's all in good fun. You're one of us now, remember? Gotta keep the banter alive!"

Penny raised her glass in mock agreement. "To Manic life," she said with a smirk, taking another sip as the room buzzed with energy.

The flat had filled out by now, with more presenters and producers from the Manic family arriving. The air was thick with a heady mix of anticipation, music, and the unmistakable scent of mischief. Penny felt a sense of belonging she hadn't expected when she first joined Manic. It wasn't just a workplace; it was a lifestyle, chaotic and relentless but undeniably addictive.

* _ * _ * _ *

It was half hour after Toni and James had headed to the master bedroom and Penny noticed that some of the Hits, Heart and Capital crew that was joining them for the evening had been in and out as if it were a revolving door, each one leaving the room with flushed cheeks and conspiratorial grins. The infamous Big Weekenders had a reputation for pushing boundaries, and it seemed tonight was no exception.

Penny sat on the sofa, chatting with Rory and a producer from Manic Radio South Coast while keeping an eye on the growing crowd. She'd heard whispers about these legendary gatherings before she'd even joined Manic, but experiencing one firsthand was something else entirely. It was the kind of environment where professional facades slipped, and everyone revealed their true colours—raw, unfiltered, and unapologetically wild.

The door to Toni's bedroom opened, and James stepped out, looking a mix of exhilarated and slightly dazed. His beanie was askew, and his hoodie was unzipped, revealing a Gorillaz t-shirt underneath. She noticed that he had, like most of the other crew present, that faint white powder of cocaine on his upper lip. He headed to grab a bottle of scotch and then headed back to the bedroom.

"Oi, Penny, get your pussy in here," Toni shouted from her bedroom. "Reevesy wants to fuck you."

Penny froze for a split second, feeling a surge of heat flood her cheeks as the room erupted into laughter. The Big Weekender vibe was always charged with irreverence and chaos, but Toni's blunt proclamation took things to another level entirely. Penny glanced around, catching

Kylie, who had Danny deep within her while sucking Al off, smile as she locked eyes with Penny, mouthing a teasing, "Go on!" while giving her an encouraging nod.

Penny stood, trying to play it cool as she made her way toward the door of Toni's bedroom, her heart pounding in her chest. The music seemed to fade into the background as she entered, the chaos of the party momentarily forgotten. Inside, the room was lit softly, its atmosphere a stark contrast to the thumping energy outside.

Toni was perched on the bed, grinning like the Cheshire Cat. James, now minus his beanie, leaned casually against the wall, his charm dialled up to eleven. He looked at Penny with that easy confidence she'd seen plastered all over his social media. There was a bag of cocaine that was nearly empty, and Penny knew that it was her time to enjoy the white powder-fuelled energy that seemed to define the night's escapades. Penny felt the electric charge of the moment as Toni motioned her over with a playful smirk, holding out a rolled-up £50 note like it was an invitation to dive headfirst into the madness.

"Don't be shy, love," Toni teased, her tone dripping with mischief. "It's not every day you get inducted into the Reevesy experience. You know it's his first time shagging more than 1 woman at a time today."

Penny looked at James with a mix of curiosity and amusement. His slightly dishevelled appearance and the lingering buzz of the night gave him an air of youthful exuberance that was hard to ignore. She raised an eyebrow, deciding to match the playful energy that seemed to charge the room.

"First time, Reevesy?" Penny teased, taking the rolled-up note from Toni. "Well, don't worry, love. We'll make it memorable for you."

James laughed, the sound light and boyish. "Go easy on me, Penny. Don't want to ruin the brand on my first proper night out with the crew."

Toni burst into laughter, pouring another round of drinks from the bottle James had brought in. "Oh, love, you're at a Big Weekender. The brand thrives on chaos. Now, let's get this party properly started."

Penny bent over the table, inhaling a quick line of the remaining coke, feeling the immediate rush as the sharp sting hit her senses. The room seemed to brighten, the music from outside a distant pulse as her nerves melted away. Straightening up, she flashed a grin at James, who looked equal parts nervous and excited.

Toni leaned back on the bed, clearly enjoying her role as the orchestrator of the night's antics. "Alright, Reevesy, time to see if you're really cut out for the Manic life. Penny here's one of the best—you're in good hands."

Penny smirked, feeling the playful camaraderie of the moment. She knew the night was teetering on the edge of madness, but that was the thrill of being part of Manic. It wasn't just a radio station; it was a lifestyle, a world where the lines between personal and professional blurred in ways that defied convention.

"Alright, Reevesy," she said, stepping closer to him, her voice low and teasing. "Let's see if you're as good at keeping up off-air as you are on it."

James grinned, his confidence growing as he matched her energy. "You're on, Penny. But fair warning—I don't go down without a fight."

* _ * _ * _ *

"Right, folks," Penny heard Toni say. It was quarter to nine, and the taxis that would take the 30 strong Manic, Hits, Heart and Capital crew from the Speke flat to the city centre were lined up outside. Toni had just shouted the rallying cry, and the room buzzed with anticipation.

"Alright, Liverpool!" Toni said, her voice echoing over the excited chatter, "tonight we're hitting the town, so let's get in those cabs before they leave us behind!" She pulled James and Kylie aside, her smile a mixture of encouragement and warning. "Remember, tonight isn't just about blowing off steam. Manic's watching, and you two are the faces of the new vibe we're selling. Keep it wild, but keep it memorable, alright?"

Penny noticed James nodding at Toni's words and felt, in a way, sorry for him, as it was his first time at a Manic Big Weekender, and the expectations placed on him were immense. Yet, as he adjusted his hoodie and flashed that boyish grin at Kylie, it was clear he was determined to live up to the hype.

Penny watched as the crowd began to file out of Toni's flat, the energy palpable. The taxis idled outside, their engines purring against the cool night air. Penny caught a glimpse of James and Kylie slipping into one cab, their laughter trailing behind them. She smiled to herself, shaking her head at the whirlwind dynamic they exuded—young, ambitious, and seemingly untouchable.

Rory sauntered over, his arm slung casually around her shoulder. "You ready for this, Pen? I had to admit, hearing you and Reevesy going at it in Toni's room made me stiff as a board."

Penny smirked, rolling her eyes at Rory's unfiltered comment, but the teasing camaraderie brought a certain levity to the moment. She elbowed him lightly in the ribs. "Oh, shut it, Rory. Save the stiff jokes for the morning show."

Rory laughed, his easy charm diffusing any awkwardness. "Fair enough, but you've got to admit, these Big Weekenders are something else. If this is Reevesy's induction, he's in for one hell of a baptism."

As they headed for the taxis, Penny felt the familiar mix of excitement and trepidation that always came with these nights. Liverpool's city centre would be buzzing, and with the Manic crew—and their competitors from Hits, Heart, and Capital—in the mix, it promised to be a night of high-energy antics and memorable chaos.

Sliding into the cab with Rory and a couple of producers, Penny caught a glimpse of Toni holding court in the front seat of another taxi, already animatedly chatting with Kylie and James. Her energy was infectious, and even from a distance, Penny could see how easily she drew people into her web.

As they pulled up outside the first bar, Penny noticed Hits Radio's Hattie Pearson, one of the network presenters, leaving with some of the other Hits crew, her sequined dress catching the light as she laughed and linked arms with her friends.

"Hey, Hattie, fancy meeting you here!" Penny heard Toni say as the Mancunian hugged Bauer's star presenter. Hattie grinned, clearly unfazed by the rival Manic crew rolling in like they owned the night.

"Toni! Well, look who decided to take Liverpool by storm tonight!" Hattie called back, striding over to give Toni a hug, the two networks' presenters sharing an easy camaraderie. Despite being competitors, Manic and Hits both shared a certain kinship, knowing they each fed into the same electrified, fast-paced culture of CHR radio. "Me and some of the Hits gang are going down the Cavern Club. I see you've got some of the Manic lot here. You're not gonna cause too much trouble, are you?" she teased, casting a playful glance at James and Kylie.

Toni laughed, pulling James and Kylie into the exchange. "Oh, you know us! Just a bit of innocent fun, showing the Scousers what a proper Manic night looks like!"

Hattie smirked, crossing her arms. "I'll believe that when I see it! Enjoy, and try not to get yourselves banned from anywhere. Oh, and Toni, you owe Hirsty a fiver when you're next in Manc. She said that Reevesy was probably pre-recording his Headbangers while she does Belters live as the real deal!"

Toni rolled her eyes, chuckling. "Tell Hirsty she'll get her fiver when she manages to get through a whole Belters set without playing 'Rhythm is a Dancer'!"

The two women laughed at that, as Rhythm is a Dancer was a regular on the Stephanie Hirst's Bangers show, the 90s classic having become a running joke among the stations. Hattie gave them a final wave before disappearing down the street with her crew, and Toni led the Manic group towards their first stop for the night—a high-energy, neon-lit bar known for its wild atmosphere called Crystal.

"Right guys," Toni said to the assembled crew from the various CHR stations. "We've got the VIP section reserved at Crystal, so let's make it a night to remember! Drinks are on Manic's tab until midnight, so get stuck in!"

The energy was electric as the Manic crew surged into Crystal, a kaleidoscope of sequins, neon, and the unmistakable thrum of CHR hits reverberating through the air. The VIP section, roped off with velvet cordons, provided a prime view of the dance floor below, where Liverpool's nightlife pulsed in technicolour chaos.

* _ * _ * _ *

The VIP section buzzed with energy as the Manic crew settled in, their presence impossible to ignore. Penny leaned against the bar, nursing a cocktail as she watched the group loosen up. Kylie and James were the centre of attention, as expected, with Toni perched on a nearby table, laughing uproariously at a joke Rory had just told.

The drink flowed freely, and the DJs from Manic, Hits, and Capital began to mix more easily, their rivalries temporarily forgotten in the shared haze of a Big Weekender. Penny found herself drawn into a conversation with Liam Price, the Mid Wales Breakfast presenter, who was regaling her with tales of on-air blunders and late-night escapades from the Shrewsbury station.

"...and then," Liam said, barely able to contain his laughter, "the producer panicked and cut to the wrong regional ad break. So instead of hearing about the new Tesco opening in Powys, listeners got two minutes of silence followed by a rogue ad for a funeral parlour in Birmingham!"

Penny burst out laughing, shaking her head. "Sounds like something that would happen at Manic. Though I reckon we'd have turned it into a viral TikTok by the end of the day."

Liam grinned. "That's the difference, isn't it? Manic leans into the chaos. At Hits, they pretend it never happened."

As they talked, Penny noticed James standing on the edge of the VIP area, his hoodie swapped for a leather jacket he must have grabbed from the cab. He was chatting animatedly with Al Crozier and Rory, but every so often, his eyes flicked towards her. She felt a flicker of amusement. Was Reevesy nervous about her?

Toni's voice rang out over the music, cutting through the chatter. "Alright, listen up, you lot! We've got a tradition for first-time Weekenders. Reevesy, this one's for you!"

The room erupted into cheers and whistles as James was dragged to the centre of the VIP section, his boyish grin slipping into an expression of mock horror.

"What's this, then?" he asked, raising his hands in surrender. "Go easy on me, yeah? I'm still the new guy!"

Toni smirked, holding up a tray of brightly coloured shots.

"Oh, don't worry, love. Just a little initiation. One shot for each Big Weekender host here tonight. Think of it as a toast to your future in CHR!"

James groaned but didn't resist, dutifully lining up the shots. The crowd counted down with each one, cheering louder as his confidence grew. By the time he downed the final shot, his grin was back in full force, and he threw his arms in the air like a victorious footballer.

"Ladies and gentlemen," Toni declared, raising her own glass, "welcome Jimmy Reeves to the madness of Manic!"

The room erupted into applause, and Penny found herself clapping along, caught up in the energy. For all her scepticism about Reevesy, she had to admit he had a certain charm.

****

# CHAPTER 19 – Notices
## Tuesday 5th November 2024

The internal noticeboard, Penny noticed, was full of various staff memos, schedules, and promotions, all tacked haphazardly as if they were competing for attention. Some of them were shift swap requests, that presenters could opt for to get their existing shifts covered by another colleague, while others were announcements from management about upcoming events or programming changes. Penny's eyes landed on a bold new notice pinned right in the middle, printed on bright yellow paper:

**MANIC RADIO CHRISTMAS LAUNCHES 1ST DECEMBER 2024!**

**DURING CHRISTMAS PERIOD - PRESENTERS NEEDED FOR NATIONAL SCHEDULE**

**LITE GROUP AQUIRES ST JOHNS BEACON AND ONE SNOW HILL LEASES**

The latter line made Penny chuckle. Bauer Media had recently announced that its Hits Radio Liverpool station would be vacating the iconic St John's Beacon—home to the station for decades, and that Manic's owners, Lite Group, had acquired the lease. The thought of Manic moving into such a landmark building brought a mixture of amusement and trepidation as it meant that Manic Radio Liverpool would soon occupy one of the most iconic symbols of the city. St John's Beacon wasn't just a building; it was a part of Liverpool's skyline and radio history. Penny couldn't help but imagine the chaos that would ensue once the Manic team moved in. The polished professional legacy of Radio City would be replaced by the wild, irreverent energy of Manic.

"Only the local breakfast and drivetime shows will be produced from St John's Beacon for the Liverpool, Cheshire and Wirral regions," Penny muttered as she scanned the notice. "All other Speke produced local and regional shows will remain at the Speke hub until further notice." Penny raised an eyebrow, her mind racing with the implications. The idea of broadcasting from such an iconic location was thrilling, but it also marked yet another shift in the station's identity. The Speke hub had its own charm—if you could call barely contained chaos "charm"—and Penny wondered how the team would adapt to the grandeur and symbolism of the new location.

She glanced at the other memos pinned nearby. One caught her eye:

## ALL LOCAL STATIONS TO GAIN NEW 'MANIC VIBES' IDENTITY FROM APRIL 2025 - SOME STATIONS TO BE FOLDED INTO NEIGHBOURING STATIONS

Penny looked at the table which showed which stations were being converted to what brand, and had to chuckle at the fact that Drill FM, a national Urban and Grime station that Manic was in the process of purchasing, was set to become part of the newly launched Manic Urban UK network. The table was an odd mixture of nostalgia and corporate pragmatism, reflecting a radio industry grappling with modernisation while clinging to the past. Penny scanned further down the list.

- *Chester & The Wirral Vibes → Manic Goldies Chester & Merseyside*

- *Northern Vibes (Staffordshire & Cheshire) → Manic Vibes Stoke & Cheshire*

- *Cumbria Vibes → Manic Vibes Carlisle*

- *Manic Radio Liverpool → Manic Vibes Chester & Merseyside*

She had to chuckle, as Manic were finally embracing what Capital had done years ago and what Bauer had done back in April, scrapping the legacy names of stations in favour of a streamlined national brand. Having grown up with Juice FM and Capital Liverpool as her childhood and teen soundtracks, Penny was glad that Manic had finally embraced the modern trend of networked branding, even if it meant some stations would lose their unique local identities.

"Finally," a voice from behind her muttered and she recognised it as Dr Manic, or Troy Barrett, the Manic Dance evening presenter. "They're killing off the legacy station names. About bloody time, if you ask me. I've been saying for years we need to streamline everything under one identity, make it easier for the listeners and the advertisers. None of this Chester & The Wirral Vibes nonsense—sounds like a pirate station that's been running out of someone's garage since the '90s. Anyway, have you seen my stethoscope?"

Looking at the 34-year-old, Penny was confused, until she turned round and noticed he was wearing scrubs and a Royal Liverpool University Hospital badge. His outfit made no sense in the context of a radio station, but then again, this was Manic, where chaos was part of the brand. Penny raised an eyebrow.

"Your stethoscope?" she echoed, suppressing a laugh. "Troy, why are you dressed like that?"

"I've just come off shift at A&E and my clothes got vomited all over by a patient, so I came straight here in scrubs," Troy replied with a shrug. "I've got the evening show to prep for, and besides, it's Manic. You think anyone's gonna bat an eyelid at me walking around like I'm about to do a bypass?"

Penny laughed, shaking her head. "Fair point. But seriously, you work in A&E and host a national radio show? How do you even have the energy?"

"Simple," Troy said, grinning as he mimed taking a swig of coffee. "Endless caffeine, a love for chaos, and no social life. By day I prescribe morphine and do emergency surgery as a registrar, and by evening I'm prescribing beats, bass and banter to the nation. It's the best of both worlds, really. Although," he added with a smirk, "it does mean I've had to ban myself from saying 'clear!' when I drop the bass."

Penny chuckled, trying to imagine Troy switching from saving lives in a hospital to hyping up a national audience. It was peak Manic Radio—a bizarre cocktail of personalities that somehow worked. "Well, at least you're consistent in keeping people's hearts racing, one way or another."

Troy winked, adjusting the ID badge clipped to his scrubs.

"Exactly. And speaking of keeping the pulse alive, you ready for this new St John's Beacon move? Bit of an own goal by Bauer to sack off the lease and go for a regular city centre studio. Can't imagine Radio City in anything but the Beacon. But hey, their loss is our gain. You know the cheekiest thing is that Bauer still have the lease on the signage though."

"Wait, what?"

"Yeah," Troy said, smirking. "They've got the lease for their new Hits Radio signage to be up there for another few years, so technically, Manic Radio Liverpool might be broadcasting from a building with Hits Radio plastered all over it. Imagine the confusion. Proper Scouse comedy, that."

Penny laughed, shaking her head. "That is peak Manic chaos. I can already picture the social media posts—listeners tagging us with photos of the wrong logo and asking if we're having an identity crisis. Hang on, noticed this one?"

## AL CROZIER RESIGNATION - EFFECTIVE IMMEDIATLY.

Penny knew that, two days earlier, Toni and Al had been covering Smitty's absence on the Sunday evening show on the Manic Radio network and Al had swore live on air, causing him and Toni to be suspended from their roles pending an internal investigation. Penny scanned the notice further, noting the slightly formal language typical of corporate memos:

Penny raised an eyebrow and turned to Troy, who had leaned against the wall, reading the same notice.

"Well, that's abrupt," she said, keeping her tone neutral. Troy smirked, his arms crossed. "Abrupt? Penny, this is

Manic. You know how it goes—one day you're the star of the show, the next you're an entry in the 'former staff' section of the Wikipedia page."

Penny chuckled, but her mind was already racing. She hadn't worked with Al directly, but she'd heard about the on-air slip-up from the station grapevine. "Do you think Toni's in trouble too?" she asked.

"Nah," Troy replied, shaking his head. "Toni's got nine lives, and she's already on her fifth or sixth. Besides, she's got that whole 'chaotic but lovable' thing going for her. Listeners adore her, and the bosses know she brings in the numbers. Al, though… not so much. OFCOM will no doubt be investigating it as it was just after 7 when the watershed kicked in, and swearing isn't exactly what you'd expect from a CHR presenter in that slot. Toni will get a slap on the wrist, maybe a week off to cool down, but she'll bounce back. She always does."

Penny nodded thoughtfully. "Still, it's a reminder that even in all this chaos, the rules still matter. I mean, the right kind of chaos is what makes Manic what it is, but slip up too far and—"

"—you're history," Troy finished for her, nodding sagely. "Exactly. Controlled chaos, Lane. That's the game we're playing. You push the boundaries, but you don't cross the line. And if you do, you'd better make sure it's for the right reasons and worth the fallout."

Penny leaned against the wall, her eyes drifting back to the noticeboard. The mixture of light-hearted and serious memos encapsulated Manic's identity perfectly—a blend of irreverence and professional intensity that somehow kept the wheels turning.

Her gaze returned to the bold Manic Radio Christmas announcement. "So," she said, glancing at Troy, "are you signing up for the national Christmas schedule?"

Troy grinned. "Of course. Time and half for Christmas Eve, double time for Christmas Day and Boxing Day, same with New Years Day, so it's a no-brainer. Only about a dozen people are exempt from that kind of slot - the cover/fill-in crew. They're paid hourly so they don't have to do the holiday shifts unless they want the extra cash. Anyway, I've gotta go find my stethoscope and then I've got a meeting with Alan about my contract as it's my annual renewal."

Penny watched Troy stride off in his scrubs, shaking her head at the absurdity of a man who balanced life-saving surgeries with hosting a national evening dance show. It was quintessentially Manic, she thought, where personalities this unique weren't just tolerated—they were celebrated.

Turning back to the noticeboard, Penny's mind lingered on Al Crozier's resignation. The ripple effects were already being felt across the station. Al's departure would leave a gap in the Dudley hub's line-up, one that would no doubt require a rapid reshuffling. Manic wasn't the kind of place to leave dead air for long; new talent, or familiar faces, would inevitably step in.

"Hey, Lane!"

Penny turned to see Rory Carter, her ever-energetic co-host, bounding down the hallway towards her, a half-empty Red Bull in hand. His hair looked like he'd just been dragged through a hedge backwards—typical for a Tuesday morning at Manic Liverpool.

"Did you see Al's notice?" Rory asked, though he clearly knew the answer. "Mate, they don't mess about here, do they?"

"Swift and brutal," Penny agreed, folding her arms. "Toni's probably counting her blessings that she got off with a suspension. Out of curiosity, how long has Al been at Manic?"

"Well, a year and half. He works with Lyra Nott on the Northern Vibes drive show – or did work, I should say. He was only covering for Smitty with Toni as Alan needed someone quick. People thought he might be next in line for something big, but… well, live swearing on a national slot? That's curtains. It's proper amateur hour, isn't it?" Rory's grin was half amused, half incredulous.

Penny shrugged, a small smirk tugging at her lips. "It's a tough gig, Rory. All it takes is one slip, and you're out.

The thing is, people forget we're human. There's only so much adrenaline and coffee can do to keep you sharp. It's no excuse, but Al's not the first, and he won't be the last."

Rory nodded in agreement, taking a swig of his Red Bull. "True. Anyway, Toni will be fine—probably already planning her triumphant return like the rockstar she is. Alan's got a soft spot for her, you know. Plus, she pulls numbers as she's one of the faces of Manic, doing the network evening show. Anyway, I'm not going to be on Drive today, or for the foreseeable."

Penny frowned at Rory, his casual tone not quite masking the significance of his words. "Hang on—what do you mean you're not on Drive for the foreseeable? What's going on?"

Rory shrugged, though his exaggerated nonchalance told Penny there was more to it. "I've been shifted onto Toni's show while she's under suspension, meaning, Penny, that you and Abby are flying solo."

Penny blinked, the news landing like a drumbeat in her head. "You're joking. They've pulled you off Drive to cover for Toni? What about our show, Rory? And don't tell me they're leaving me to carry the chaos by myself."

Rory grinned, though there was a flicker of sympathy in his eyes. "Look, Lane, you've got this. Alan says it's temporary—just until Toni's back, which knowing her, will be quicker than anyone expects. Plus, Abby's got your back, doesn't she? You're not totally alone."

Penny groaned, running a hand through her hair. "Abby? You mean the producer who sets me up for vibrator challenges live on air? Oh yeah, I feel so reassured."

Rory laughed, clapping her on the shoulder as he leaned in conspiratorially. "You'll smash it, Pen. Think of it as your chance to show the bosses what you can do. If you can survive me and Abby, you can survive anything."

Penny rolled her eyes but couldn't stop the smile tugging at her lips. "Fine. But when you're back, I expect you to treat me like the radio queen I clearly am."

"Deal," Rory said, flashing her a wink. "Now, I've got to go brief with Alan about Toni's show. You'd best start prepping for Drive—solo or not, Liverpool still expects the chaos."

As Rory disappeared down the corridor, Penny sighed, her mind already whirring. Taking on the Manic Liverpool Drive show solo was no small feat, and while she trusted Abby to keep things (somewhat) under control, it still felt like she'd been handed a grenade with the pin halfway out.

"Solo Drive," she muttered under her breath as she pulled out her phone and opened the playlist app. "I've officially been promoted to Chief Chaos Officer."

Suddenly a text came through which made her feel guilty about what happened at the Big Weekender, as the name "Galway Guy" on the chat, what she had jokingly renamed Weston on her contacts list as a nod to the track "Galway Girl" by Ed Sheeran, flashed up. The message was brief but stopped Penny in her tracks:

**Weston O'Rourke**: *Hey Pen, been meaning to call. Sorry for being MIA. Things at home are... complicated. Will explain soon. Hope you're good. Miss you x*

Penny stared at her phone, the rush of emotions catching her off guard. Four weeks of sporadic messages and two weeks of radio silence had left her feeling a strange mix of anger, sadness, and longing. Seeing his message—simple, apologetic, and affectionate—unlocked all the feelings she'd tried to bury under work, banter, and chaos.

Her thumb hovered over the reply button. She wanted to fire something witty back—something light-hearted to show she was fine, to hide just how much his absence had bothered her. But as she re-read the words "Miss you x," her resolve softened. Weston wasn't one for empty sentiment, and she knew it.

Penny: Glad to hear from you, Galway Guy. Complicated sounds about right for us both at the minute. Call me when you can. Miss you too x.

She hit send before she could second-guess herself, shoving her phone back into her pocket. Her brain was already back to spinning with everything she needed to handle—Rory covering for Toni, Al's abrupt exit, the looming St John's Beacon move, and now flying solo on Liverpool Drive. There wasn't time to let Weston's message derail her, though the ache in her chest said otherwise.

Turning, she saw Alan sitting on a desk, with Abby's lips around his quivering member, her nipples as hard as diamonds poking through her blouse. Penny let out a sharp breath and quickly looked away, the chaotic reality of working at Manic hitting her like a freight train yet again.

"Seriously?" she muttered under her breath, grabbing her notebook and heading down the corridor toward the breakroom. There were some sights that not even years of CHR radio madness could prepare you for, and Abby providing additional 'support' to Alan in broad daylight was one of them.

The hallways of the Speke hub were buzzing as always—producers darting between studios, presenters shouting last-minute script edits, and interns trying to balance trays of coffee without spilling them. It was classic Manic chaos, the kind of energy Penny had grown to thrive on, even if it did occasionally make her want to bash her head against a wall.

As she settled into the break room, she noticed Danny O'Neil sitting on one of the sofas, a Pornhub branded pair of jogging bottoms and hoodie on him, a parcel in his hand.

"Hey, Lane, got ya something for the next Big Weekender. We're doing it at Toni's place, and we're being sponsored for it."

Penny raised an eyebrow, eyeing the package warily. "Sponsored? Let me guess—some booze brand or another dodgy tech company?"

Danny smirked, shaking his head as he tossed the parcel onto the table in front of her. "Nope. Think bigger, Lane. Proper Manic chaos material, this. Pornhub's signed on for some 'adult-themed' sponsorship bits. It's all very cheeky, very on-brand for us."

Penny blinked, equal parts incredulous and amused. "Hang on. Pornhub is sponsoring the next Big Weekender? Are you lot serious?"

Danny grinned, settling back into the sofa with an air of smug satisfaction. "Dead serious. Management approved it yesterday. Look, it's a win-win. They get viral social media posts and a bit of cheeky press coverage; we get free merch and a brand that matches our 'edgy, irreverent' vibe. And you…" He gestured toward the parcel. "…get a Pornhub branded top, bottoms, thong, swimsuit, bra, some crop tops and... some dolphin shorts."

Penny stared at the parcel as if it might bite her. "Danny, I don't know whether to laugh, cry, or throw this out of the nearest window. Anyway, I notice you have a stiffy? Want me to soften it for you? Or are you waiting for the Hub Cum Dump to sort it out. Who is it nowadays, as I've forgot?"

"Nah, Alfie's being fucked six ways to Sunday by Mags and her clique, the little cum slut that he is, so if you're up for a shag then so am I."

Penny grinned, putting the guilty thoughts out of her mind as she unzipped her skirt, the dildo in her pussy poking free. "Alright then, Danny, I guess this makes us even after that prank last week," she teased, kicking off her heels and climbing onto the sofa beside him. Danny's grin widened as he pulled her onto his lap, his hands resting firmly on her hips as their lips met in a heated kiss. The chaos of the Manic hub seemed to fade for a moment as Penny lost herself in the moment, their banter giving way to something far more primal.

Penny's head spun as Danny's hands roamed with teasing confidence. For all his ridiculous banter and cheeky antics, there was something oddly comforting about moments like this—where chaos gave way to connection, however fleeting or impulsive it might be. It wasn't love or even proper romance, but in a world like Manic, where boundaries blurred and relationships tangled like headphones in your pocket, it was enough.

Danny broke the kiss, a lazy grin on his lips. "You know, Lane, if HR ever decided to set up cameras in this place, we'd all be done for."

"HR don't give a fuck," Penny said, knowing that in her two months at Manic, the Human Resources team were just as bad as the presenters, and that even Lucy Love, one of the newest HR officers, who had in her first week been an idealistic stickler for the rules had become a cock hungry fixture in the chaos. "They'd probably be the first ones uploading the footage to Pornhub for some extra sponsorship cash."

Danny chuckled, brushing a strand of hair away from her face as his hands wandered to her thighs. "Fair point, Lane. I think HR stopped pretending to be professional the minute they signed off on the Pornhub sponsorship."

Penny laughed, her earlier guilt and stress momentarily melting away as Danny's lips grazed her neck. It was just another day at Manic—a whirlwind of chaos, inappropriate banter, and moments that defied any traditional workplace standards.

Stroking his trousers, Penny noticed that he was as erect as a flagpole during a military parade. She smirked at him, her fingers deftly teasing the waistband of his Pornhub-branded joggers. "Danny," she whispered, "you better not disappoint, or I'm writing a full exposé on your skills for the Manic blog"

Danny chuckled, his hands firm on her hips as he guided her into a straddling position. "Lane, if you're going to write anything, it'll be a rave review. But let's not get ahead of ourselves—actions speak louder than words."

Before Penny could respond, the breakroom door creaked open, and Abby Blue peeked in, her face splitting into a mischievous grin when she caught sight of the pair.

"Am I interrupting, or is this an open invitation?" Abby teased, leaning against the doorframe with an air of faux innocence.

Penny rolled her eyes, though she couldn't help but laugh. "What do you think, Blue? If there's one thing I've learnt working here two months, it's that if there's a cock or pussy here, then as long as all parties are willing, then it's fair game. But since you're already here, you might as well join the chaos."

Abby smirked, stepping into the room and letting the door swing shut behind her. "Good, the baby is kicking so I need fucking. Two weeks until my maternity leave, and I might as well make the most of it," she quipped, shrugging off her jacket and kicking off her shoes as she made her way toward the sofa.

Penny shot Danny a mock exasperated look, but she couldn't help the grin tugging at the corners of her lips. "Guess it's a party now, Danny. Hope you're up for the challenge."

Danny laughed, his cocky grin never wavering as he leaned back, his hands resting on Penny's thighs. "Lane, Blue, you two are making this the best Tuesday in Manic history. Let's just say, I'll be putting this down as 'team building.'"

Abby joined them on the sofa, her bump barely slowing her down as she leaned in to kiss Penny, her lips soft yet commanding. Penny melted into the kiss, the surreal absurdity of the situation overshadowed by the heat of the moment. Danny watched, clearly enjoying the show, before Abby pulled back and turned her attention to him.

"Don't think you're getting off easy," Abby teased, her hands trailing up Danny's chest as she gave him a wicked smile. "You've got two of us now—better make it count."

The chaos of the Speke hub might have been raging just outside the door, but inside the breakroom, the world narrowed down to the three of them. It was messy, it was wild, and it was quintessentially Manic.

****

# CHAPTER 20 – Hits v Manic
## Friday 22nd November 2024

The irony that today was Hits Live, the seasonal showpiece event for Bauer's Hits Radio Network, wasn't lost on Penny. As a former Bauer Academy graduate, she had once dreamed of presenting for Hits Radio Liverpool, basking in the polished, glitzy world of CHR radio. Yet here she was, entrenched in the unapologetic chaos of Manic Radio Liverpool—a station known for veering wildly off the script, much to the delight of its equally unpredictable audience.

It was the first of a double header for both, and tonight it was Birmingham that was the two giants to have battle, with Manic sending Ali Hussain and Tom Lode, their network presenters from Manic Dance, to present the CHR network's Drive coverage live from the Utilita Arena, with them hosting the show on stage, Danny O'Neil presenting the evening show live from backstage instead of his usual slot of drivetime for the network coverage, and Warwickshire Stars's Breakfast host Kylie Morgan and her boyfriend, Manic Dance's Ibiza Weekender host, Jimmy Reeves, or James Smith as she knew him, acting as roving reporters to capture the behind-the-scenes madness. Penny, meanwhile, was tasked with keeping things steady back in Liverpool alongside Rory Carter, maintaining the regional drivetime which would occasionally cut to the generic network coverage from Birmingham.

The fact that House of Manic had been heavily promoting their presence at the event added to the pressure. With the stakes high and an audience eager to see which network would steal the show, Manic was banking on its signature unpredictability and raw energy to outshine the polished perfection of Hits Live, who were at the bp pulse Live, the former Resorts World Arena.

As Penny sipped her lukewarm coffee, perched precariously on the edge of her chair in the chaos of Manic's Speke hub, the buzz in the room was palpable. It was 2pm, two hours until the network coverage, as well as the various local opt-outs, kicked off. What made it worse was that the regular local management, Alan and his colleagues, were present in Liverpool, while the senior executives of the network level were also split between Liverpool and Birmingham, keeping order at what was a major event for the network. Alan, the Regional Head of Programming, was pacing the room like a general preparing for battle, his Bluetooth headset blinking as he barked orders at someone in Birmingham. The stakes were clear: Manic couldn't just keep up with Hits Radio tonight—they had to dominate.

Penny glanced over at Rory, who was back on the Liverpool drive as Danny O'Neil, the network drive host, was covering the 7pm to 10pm slot, going up against Hits Radio's Tom Green, who was broadcasting from the bp pulse Arena in Birmingham, the former Resorts World Arena, for Hits Live's own evening coverage. Rory, ever the joker, was leaning back in his chair, juggling a stress ball in one hand and scrolling through WhatsApp messages in the other.

"Great, Hits have picked Gemma Atkinson & Mike Toolan for their build-up coverage," Rory said, rolling his eyes as he tossed the stress ball into the air. "Toolan's got that smooth charm, and Gemma's likeable as hell. They're going to be a tough act to follow. Guess who they've got doing backstage interviews? Hattie Pearson."

Alan chuckled and Penny knew why - Hattie Pearson was one of Hits Radio's heavyweights, and if they were putting her into the backstage role, it meant Hits Radio were either scared that Manic was going to be a serious contender tonight, or they were doubling down on their polished image to make sure Manic's chaotic vibe didn't overshadow them. Either way, it was clear Hits Radio wasn't taking any chances.

"Ah, Hattie," Penny said, smirking. "She did a training session when I was part of the Bauer Academy, showing us how to handle live backstage interviews without breaking a sweat. Polished as they come. Bet she's got a fresh blow-dry and a script tight enough to survive a hurricane."

"Polished to the point of being predictable," Rory quipped, leaning back in his chair with a grin. "Meanwhile, we've got Danny broadcasting from behind a stack of speakers and Kylie probably getting lost in the crowd trying to find someone with a Manic-branded T-shirt."

"Don't forget Jimmy," Penny added, rolling her eyes. "He'll probably be too busy flirting with the audience to get any usable content. He's like a puppy—adorable but impossible to keep focused."

Alan glanced over, his face breaking into a wry smile.

"That's exactly why people love us, though, isn't it? Hits Live will have their glossy red carpet interviews, and we'll have Tom Lode and Ali Hussain hyping the crowd until they're screaming louder than the music. Raw energy beats rehearsed every time."

"Unless the mics cut out," Penny muttered under her breath, earning a laugh from Rory. "At least we've got Charli XCX, Ellie Goulding, Billie Eilish, Ella Henderson, The Weeknd, Sophie Ellis-Bextor and Dua Lipa. What have Hits got? Joel Corry, Leigh-Anne, Olly Alexander, Pixie Lott, Sigala, Sugababes, Tom Grennan and Tom Walker."

"Don't forget our surprise act," Benny Young, one of the senior production executives for Manic's CHR network, interjected as he entered the room, his clipboard stacked with notes. "We've got Calvin Harris making an unannounced appearance. That's going to blow Hits out of the water. Joel Corry and Sigala might be big names, but Calvin? He's in a league of his own. Just wait until those first beats drop. Anyway, today's the opening salvo, as we've got tomorrows Hits Live v House of Manic in Manchester, and we've got Ed Sheeran for tomorrow's surprise act. They've got some big hitters, sure, but let's see how they handle it when Ed starts belting out Shape of You or Bad Habits. That's when the game changes."

The room buzzed with excitement. Penny exchanged a look with Rory, both grinning like schoolkids about to pull off the prank of the century. Calvin Harris and Ed Sheeran? Manic wasn't just playing to compete—they were out to dominate.

"Right," Alan said, clapping his hands to bring everyone's attention back. "Tonight is all about energy. We know Hits will stick to their polished scripts and their perfectly curated vibe, but we thrive on chaos. I want raw, unscripted magic. Make Liverpool proud."

Penny nodded, feeling a surge of adrenaline. While she knew Hits would put on a flawless show, she also knew that the beauty of Manic was in its unpredictability. The audience didn't tune in for perfection—they tuned in for moments that felt alive, real, and messy in the best way.

"Penny, Rory," Alan said, pointing at them, "you're holding down the Liverpool fort. I want you to keep it local, relatable, and loud. Feed off the energy from Birmingham, but don't lose that Scouse charm. And no stunts—"

Rory raised an eyebrow. "No stunts? Us? Never."

Alan sighed, clearly unconvinced. "You know what I mean. Controlled chaos, okay? No vibrator challenges, no calling out Hits directly—just do what you do best and keep the listeners engaged."

"Got it," Penny said, though she shared a knowing smirk with Rory. Controlled chaos might be the official directive, but chaos without the "controlled" was what they excelled at.

* - * - * - *

"Good evening, Liverpool, it's time to finish work for the weekend as we've got..." Penny said, reading from the script as the clock struck 4pm, and the Manic Radio

Liverpool feed switched to Studio 2 and the local drive show, leading into an automated sweeper that announced that it was 3 hours until House of Manic Live.

"Yes, we've got a packed show tonight, including the terrible duo, Ali and Tom, as well as Manic Dance's Ibiza Headbangers duo, Morgz and Reevesy, live at the Utilita Arena for House of

Manic Live, and if you're not there yet, what are you waiting for?" Rory said, and Penny could see that he was really hyped up for the event, even though they were in Speke and the Utilita Arena was in Birmingham. "Tickets are flying out the door—join us as we bring you everything you need to know about tonight's biggest event. First, though, its Alfie Harrison with the news at 4."

Penny watched as Zetta transitioned smoothly into the news jingle, and Alfie Harrison's polished voice filled the air. She took the brief pause to sip her Red Bull, glance at the running order, and make sure everything was lined up for the next segment.

Rory leaned back in his chair, scrolling through social media feeds. "Looks like Hits are already posting backstage selfies with Pixie Lott and Joel Corry. Very on-brand. Meanwhile, Ali and Tom have just gone live on Instagram from outside the Utilita Arena. They've already roped some fans into singing Dua Lipa songs."

"Classic Manic," Penny replied with a smirk. "We don't do 'polished'—we do 'ridiculously relatable.' And sometimes just ridiculous."

The news segment wrapped up, and a final mention of the Manic £100K Daily Drop, which was a replacement for the £500k Money Drop that was a weekly competition, segued into the next part of the show. Penny adjusted her mic and glanced at Rory, who gave her a thumbs-up.

"Alright, Liverpool," Penny said, leaning into the energy she could feel buzzing from the control room, "Before we go straight to the tracks and the live updates from Brum, we've got a new producer here. As you guys know, Abby's last show was yesterday as she's gone off on maternity leave. Stepping into her chaotic shoes is none other than Luke 'The Lad' Fisher! Luke, say hi to Liverpool!"

Luke's voice came over the mic, full of nervous energy. "Hiya, Liverpool! Cheers for having me. Big boots to fill after Abby, but I'm ready for the madness."

Rory grinned, leaning into his mic. "Big boots? Mate, you've walked into a hurricane wearing flip-flops, but welcome to Manic. Let's see how you handle tonight."

Penny chuckled. "Luke, if you survive tonight, you'll be a legend. No pressure, though. Just remember—controlled chaos."

"Controlled chaos," Luke repeated with mock seriousness. "Got it. Totally in control. Nothing will go wrong. Probably."

Rory laughed. "That's the spirit! Now, Liverpool, don't forget to hit us up on WhatsApp—0151 496 0425. Send us your shoutouts, your tunes, and your House of Manic prep photos. We're live and loving it!"

"Anyway, we've got, for one day only, exclusive, behind the scenes, interviews with Charli XCX, Billie Eilish, Ella Henderson, The Weeknd, Sophie Ellis Bextor, Dua Lipa and the Midlands's own... Ellie Goulding, all who'll be performing live at House of Manic Live tonight! I'm telling you, folks, this is going to be one for the history books. We've got the stars, the music, and all the backstage drama you won't get anywhere else," Penny said, as the first track of the day, Charli XCX's Beg for You playing out, not just in Liverpool but across the Manic network. Penny knew that the energy would build from here, especially with the dual competition of Hits Live happening at the same time.

As Charli XCX's track played, Rory gestured at his phone. "Check this out—Hits just posted a teaser for their opening act. Looks like they've got Joel Corry kicking things off. Classic safe choice. Slick, but not exactly unpredictable."

Penny leaned over to glance at the screen, her grin widening. "They're playing it cool, but they're going to regret it when Calvin Harris steps out later. The crowd will lose their minds. That's our trump card, right there."

Luke, now stationed in the producer's booth, chimed in through the intercom. "Speaking of Calvin, we've got confirmation he's arriving backstage in about an hour. Danny's been tasked with keeping it under wraps, but knowing him, he'll probably hint at it on air before the big reveal."

The track faded out, and Penny hit the button for the next link. "Right, coming up, we've got a throwback from the queen of pop herself, Dua Lipa, and some fresh hits from Olivia Rodrigo. But first, let's head over to the Utilita Arena, where our very own Jimmy Reeves and Kylie Morgan are giving us the inside scoop on all things House of Manic Live. What's the vibe like over there, guys?"

Penny knew that the response would be generic as the same clip was going out across all Manic stations. Kylie's voice carried a perfect mix of energy and charm, lighting up the airwaves.

"We're here at the Utilita Arena in Birmingham, where the excitement is absolutely electric for House of Manic Live! "The stars are arriving, the fans are buzzing, and this is shaping up to be the event of the year!"

James stepped in seamlessly, his nerves masked by the upbeat tone he'd honed during his short but intense tenure at Manic. "That's right, Kylie! We've got an incredible lineup tonight—Dua Lipa, Billie Eilish, Ellie Goulding, and so many more. Plus, we'll be bringing you exclusive interviews with the artists, live reactions from the crowd, and all the behind-the-scenes action you can't miss. Now, we're out here in the car park of the Utilita Arena, and we'll be roaming round the crowds and backstage areas to give you an exclusive peek at all the buzz building up to showtime! The energy here is absolutely unreal—let's just say, if you're not here, you're missing out! We've actually got a group of early comers gathered outside the arena, braving the chilly Birmingham evening to get the best spots when the doors open."

Penny looked at Rory, chuckling at how the link was going, knowing their microphones were off so they could chat privately.

"Do you think there's actually anyone there or do you think Jimmy and Kylie are just hyping up a car park with three people and a dog?" Rory quipped, leaning back in his chair with a grin.

Penny laughed, shaking her head. "Honestly, wouldn't put it past them. The Manic hype machine is strong. They could probably sell a crowd of pigeons as an exclusive pre-show audience."

As the feed cut back to the studio, Penny leaned into her mic, her tone effortlessly upbeat. "Thanks, Jimmy and Kylie! It sounds like things are heating up in Birmingham already. We'll keep checking in with you throughout the night for all the updates. Liverpool, don't worry—we've got your back here with all the hits, shoutouts, and maybe a few surprises of our own."

Rory jumped in, his voice brimming with mischief. "Speaking of surprises, Penny, do you reckon Jimmy will last the night without tripping over a microphone cable or accidentally wandering into Hits Live?"

"Well, considering the other lot are at the bp pulse, which is the other side of Birmingham, I'd say Jimmy has a fighting chance," Penny quipped. "But knowing him, he'd probably end up giving a shoutout to Hits Live on our feed just to stir the pot."

Rory laughed, leaning into his mic. "Classic Reevesy. Meanwhile, we'll be here holding down the fort in

Liverpool, making sure you lot don't miss a second of the action. Whether you're stuck in traffic or getting ready for a night out, we've got you covered."

Penny glanced at the playlist countdown. "Alright, Liverpool, next up we've got an absolute banger, Calvin Harris and John Newman, we've got Ed Sheeran, a bit of Sophie Ellis-Bextor, and a throwback to Ellie Goulding's Anything Could Happen. Keep those texts and WhatsApps coming—0151 496 0425. Whether you're Team House of Manic or just here for the tunes, we want to hear from you!"

The Calvin Harris track thundered through the speakers, and Penny took a moment to check her messages. The studio was bustling, with Luke navigating the controls like he'd been born for it, and Alan occasionally popping his head in with updates from Birmingham.

By quarter to 5, Dua Lipa's Houdini was thundering through the speakers, perfectly encapsulating the high-energy chaos that was building across both Manic Liverpool and the Utilita Arena. Penny glanced at Rory, who was already prepping for their next live segment with a mix of uncontainable enthusiasm and cheeky mischief. The text line was lighting up with messages from listeners, many of them taking sides in the unofficial Manic versus Hits battle.

"Alright, Liverpool!" Penny announced as the track faded out. "We've got your messages coming in thick and fast. Sophie in Allerton says she's got her House of Manic t-shirt ready and is pre-drinking with her mates. Meanwhile, Paul in Widnes wants to know who would win in a dance-off—Ali and Tom from Manic Dance, or Toolan and Gemma from Hits?"

Rory burst out laughing. "No contest, mate. Ali and Tom would wipe the floor with them. They've probably got glow sticks in their back pockets right now."

"Let's be real," Penny added with a smirk, "Toolan would throw in the towel as soon as Ali started breaking out the worm. Classic Hits—polished but predictable. Anyway, it's time for the traffic and Rory, how chaotic is Merseyside today?"

"Chaotic enough to make you wish for a hoverboard," Rory quipped as he leaned into the mic, scanning the live traffic updates. "Alright, Liverpool, here's the latest: if you're heading out for pre-drinks or making your way to tonight's shenanigans, we've got a pile-up on Edge Lane—you'll want to avoid that unless you fancy using Calvin Harris as your personal playlist for the next hour. Queens Drive is looking like a car park, and, oh, joy, someone's stalled their car on the Rocket. Classic Friday chaos."

Penny chimed in with mock exasperation. "Honestly, Liverpool, can we have one Friday without someone causing gridlock on the Rocket? Anyway, if you're stuck, roll down your windows, crank up the volume, and let us be your soundtrack to not losing your mind. And if you're listening to us on the Manic Prime app while heading to House of Manic Live, the A38(M) Aston Expressway heading into Birmingham is crawling, maybe consider public transport—it's looking like the easier option tonight. Anyway, we're off to Jimmy and Kylie at the Utilita Arena, who are talking to Ellie Goulding."

Penny knew that this segment was timed for **8** minutes, as Goulding was scheduled to do a live song in the 'green room' for the radio listeners, a feature being live-streamed on Manic's social media, so they had to stick to the timings to avoid clashing with other elements of the show. As the link to Jimmy and Kylie began, Penny leaned back in her chair, taking a moment to glance at the live comments streaming in on the Manic app. Liverpool was buzzing with excitement, and the constant stream of shoutouts, cheeky messages, and playful digs at Hits Radio kept her smiling.

Jimmy's voice came through loud and clear, the crowd noise in the background adding an extra layer of energy. "Thanks, we're here in the green room at the Utilita Arena, and the atmosphere is absolutely electric. I'm joined by someone who needs no introduction—Ellie Goulding!"

Kylie chimed in, her voice smooth and enthusiastic. "Ellie, welcome to House of Manic Live! How are you feeling about tonight's performance?"

Ellie's laughter echoed through the speakers. "I'm feeling amazing! The energy here is just unreal. The crowd is already so hyped, and I can't wait to get on that stage. House of Manic always brings something special, and I'm just thrilled to be a part of it."

Jimmy jumped in, his boyish charm in full force. "Ellie, we've got to ask—any surprises for the audience tonight? A sneak peek, maybe?"

Ellie teased them with a coy smile in her voice. "You'll have to wait and see! But I will say this: tonight's setlist is all about bringing the party. We're going to have some fun, and I've got a few tricks up my sleeve."

Penny and Rory exchanged a look as the green room interview continued, their mics muted so they could chat.

"She's such a pro," Rory remarked, scrolling through the WhatsApp messages pouring in. "Hits will probably have Pixie Lott saying something similar right now, but there's just something about Ellie that feels more real, you know? Anyway, have you heard from Weston since the other week?"

"No, he's gone radio silent again," Penny said, her tone slightly clipped as she focused on the screen in front of her. "That text he sent a couple of weeks ago was the last I heard. It's just... complicated. I... I've got the feeling that he's slowly going to ditch me."

Rory raised an eyebrow, setting his phone down as he studied Penny's expression. "Ditch you? Nah, Lane. Weston doesn't strike me as the ghosting type. Complicated or not, he'll come back around. Probably just neck-deep in whatever madness is happening in Ballymena."

Penny forced a smile, grateful for Rory's optimism but unable to shake the nagging feeling in her chest. "Maybe.

But it's been weeks now. You'd think he could manage a
quick call or at least reply to my messages properly."

****

323

# CHAPTER 21 – A Surprise Test
## Wednesday 18th December 2024

Throwing up into a toilet, Penny decided, was not exactly the plan she had, especially as she was in work early, as she had offered to do the early afternoon on Manic Christmas, followed by her regular Manic Radio Liverpool drivetime show that she and her new producer, Luke Fisher were assigned to do.

Having arrived at 8am, Penny knew that this was the fifth time this week that she had vomited, and that she was also really late with her period, it coming as clockwork as anything, which meant possibly only one thing...

...and if it was true, then she was eligible for a £32,000 bonus just for being pregnant, a policy Manic put in place to encourage their female staff to remain with the company despite the chaotic demands of CHR radio. The policy was a rare corporate perk, albeit one wrapped in the peculiar Manic culture that turned everything into a competitive spectacle. The idea of a bonus for pregnancy was both generous and hilariously on-brand for a station where chaos reigned supreme.

The irony that Manic claimed it helped in their gender pay gap reporting wasn't lost on Penny either. After all, what other company would monetise maternity with a cash incentive and then act like it was an HR masterstroke? Still, £32,000 was £32,000, and if she was pregnant, it would definitely take the edge off the chaos her life had become since joining Manic.

Wiping her mouth with a damp paper towel, Penny leaned against the sink, her reflection staring back at her in the mirror. Her cheeks were paler than usual, her eyes slightly bloodshot from lack of sleep.

"Get it together, Lane," she muttered under her breath. "It's just a bug. Or nerves. Or… maybe not."

The thought of Weston crept into her mind, his absence a constant undercurrent of her daily chaos. If this was real, if she really was pregnant, she couldn't ignore the fact that he'd need to know. Not that it was an easy conversation to have when he'd been so silent for weeks.

And then there was a case of who was the father? Penny knew she had slept with not just Weston but three others without protection, as well as 34 other men with protection, so trying to figure out who the father might be was like trying to crack a code without the cipher. The last few months at Manic had been a whirlwind of parties, chaos, and moments of impulsive decisions that now seemed to loom over her like a storm cloud.

"Right," she muttered, splashing cold water on her face. "Step one: figure out if you're actually pregnant. Step two: deal with the rest."

Heading to the medical room, an irony in itself as Manic had quite a few female presenters in similar conditions to her, and so a permanent GP, as well as abilities to do a non-invasive prenatal test (NIPT) and basic pregnancy check-ups, were all standard facilities. Penny found herself walking into the small clinic-like space that seemed almost too polished for the rest of the chaotic Speke hub.

Dr Megan Taylor, the on-site GP who had become something of a confidante for many of Manic's staff, glanced up from her tablet and smiled warmly. Penny had to chuckle as she saw that Megan was herself pregnant, a significant baby bump on her lap as she adjusted her chair.

"Morning, Penny," Megan said, her tone cheerful despite the early hour. "You're in bright and early. What brings you to my domain today? Feeling un-Manic?"

Penny managed a small laugh as she closed the door behind her. "Something like that. I think I might be pregnant, but I need to know for sure. And… well, it's a bit complicated."

Megan nodded, gesturing for Penny to take a seat. "Complicated is my bread and butter around here. Let's start with the basics. How late are you?"

"About two weeks," Penny admitted, her voice barely above a whisper. "And I've been throwing up a lot. But it could just be stress—or the leftover vodka from the Big Weekender."

Megan raised an eyebrow, her expression both amused and understanding. "Let's not rule anything out just yet. We'll do a quick test to see what's going on, and if it's positive, we can talk next steps."

Penny nodded, her heart pounding as Megan handed her a small cup and pointed her towards the adjoining bathroom. The reality of the situation hit her harder with every step, the possibility of pregnancy now feeling more tangible than ever.

When she returned a few minutes later, Megan took the cup with the professionalism Penny had come to appreciate. "Give me a moment, and we'll know soon enough."

The wait felt eternal, each second stretching into what felt like hours. Penny tapped her foot nervously, her mind racing through every possible scenario—how she'd tell Weston, how she'd navigate the chaos of Manic while dealing with this, and most of all, how she'd handle the uncertainty of who the father might be.

Megan returned with a small smile on her face, holding

up the test. "Congratulations, Penny. It's positive."

Penny's breath hitched, her stomach flipping in a way that had nothing to do with morning sickness. "Oh. Wow. Okay. That's… that's big."

"It is," Megan said gently, sitting down across from her. "But you're not alone in this. Manic has a surprisingly robust support system for situations like this, as bizarre as that might sound coming from a place like this."

Penny laughed weakly, wiping a stray tear from her cheek. "Yeah, I've noticed. £32,000 isn't exactly a standard HR perk."

Megan chuckled. "No, it's not. But it's there to make sure people like you feel supported. Now, we have a way to find out the father, if you're interested, and to work out how far gone you are."

Penny took a deep breath, her fingers fidgeting with the hem of her jumper as she considered Megan's words. The thought of finding out who the father was sent a jolt of anxiety through her, but it was a step she knew she'd have to take. The mystery of paternity wasn't just personal; it could become a very public storm in the chaotic world of Manic if it ever leaked.

"How soon can we do the test?" Penny asked, her voice trembling slightly.

Megan gave her a reassuring smile. "We can do a non-invasive prenatal test (NIPT) as early as now, given you're far enough along. It'll analyse the baby's DNA from your blood and compare it to any potential fathers. Now, you may not know, but Manic routinely obtain DNA samples from each new male hire when they join, mostly to help settle these kinds of matters discreetly. It's all done confidentially, of course."

Penny's eyes widened. "Wait, you mean... Manic has a database of DNA?"

Megan nodded, her tone calm but slightly amused. "It's one of those peculiar policies they don't exactly advertise but exists to avoid HR nightmares. Given the... let's say unique culture here, it's proven to be useful more than once. If any of the potential fathers work here, we can match the DNA quickly. If they don't, you'll have to involve them yourself."

Penny exhaled deeply, her mind spinning at the layers of absurdity and practicality wrapped in Manic's approach. "Alright, let's do it. The sooner I know, the better."

Megan nodded and began preparing the necessary materials for the test. "We'll draw a small blood sample, and the results should take a few days. In the meantime, I recommend taking some time for yourself, Penny. This is a lot to process."

"Tell me about it," Penny muttered, rolling up her sleeve. The prick of the needle felt insignificant compared to the emotional whirlwind she was navigating. "Do I… do I tell management about this now, or wait until I know more?"

Megan chuckled. "Well, it depends on which payday you want your £32k bonus to land. Now, do you have any suspects so we can narrow down who might be the father? The fewer samples we have to compare, the quicker we can get an answer."

Penny let out a nervous laugh, leaning back in her chair. "Well, if I'm being honest, the shortlist isn't exactly short. Weston's the obvious one, but… there's also Danny, Kyle from production, and... okay, maybe one of the Capital crew after that Big Weekender. Oh, and I did use protection with most of them, so that's got to count for something, right? Hang on... there's that Reevesy... I mean James Smith, the one who's dating Kylie Morgan down at the Dudley hub."

Dr Megan raised her eyebrows, a mixture of professionalism and mild amusement dancing across her features. "Alright, Penny, that's quite the lineup. But hey, at least you're honest about it. We can narrow it down based on what you know about timing and work through the database from there."

Penny sighed, pinching the bridge of her nose as the weight of the situation sank in. "So, Weston, Danny, Kyle… and potentially James Smith. Oh, and I guess there's a small chance it could be that bloke from Capital, but I don't even remember his name."

Megan chuckled softly as she jotted down notes. "That's what the database is for. We'll start with the in-house options—Weston, Danny, Kyle, and James—and go from there. I'll get this sent off today, and we'll aim to have answers by the end of the week. In the meantime, Penny, take it one step at a time. You're handling this better than most people would."

Penny gave a dry laugh, shaking her head. "Better? Megan, I'm holding it together with caffeine, sarcasm, and sheer force of will. But thanks for saying that."

Megan smiled warmly, standing up and placing a reassuring hand on Penny's shoulder. "Well, you're in the right place for chaos. Manic's got your back, as strange as that sounds. And remember—whatever happens, you're not alone in this. Now, I do have a couple of questions. Do you drink, do coke or smoke?"

"Erm, I'm fully Manic, if you know what I mean," Penny replied, a sheepish smile playing on her lips.

Megan laughed, and Penny knew that not many of the staff at Manic smoked, but cocaine and booze was the most popular recreational mix at the station, with infamous tales of parties that turned into full-blown after-hours chaos. "Alright, Penny, let's address that. For now, cut out the coke entirely and minimise the booze. You're in the early stages, so there's time to make adjustments, but let's keep things as healthy as we can, yeah?"

Penny nodded, the reality settling further into her chest. "Got it. Clean living starts now. Well, as clean as you can get in a place like this."

Megan smiled, finishing up the paperwork for the test. "Good. Now, if you need any support—emotional or practical—you know where to find me. And hey, £32,000 could make 'clean living' a bit more bearable, right?"

Penny laughed weakly, standing up and adjusting her jumper. "True. Though knowing Manic, they'll probably make me do a maternity diary for social media or host a 'Manic Mums-to-Be' segment on air."

Megan chuckled. "Wouldn't put it past them. Now go, conquer Drive, and try not to let the chaos swallow you whole."

Leaving the medical room, Penny felt the familiar buzz of the Speke hub wash over her. The office was alive with activity—producers darting between studios, presenters shouting over playlists, and interns fumbling with coffee trays. It was chaos, but it was her chaos.

As she made her way to Studio 2, where she'd be hosting her Manic Christmas slot, Penny bumped into Luke Fisher, her new producer. He was juggling a clipboard, a tablet, and what looked like a half-eaten sausage roll.

"Morning, Lane!" Luke greeted her with his usual chipper energy. "Ready for the Christmas madness? We've got Mariah, Wham!, and Bublé on repeat, plus some cheeky shoutouts from Santa himself. And I've got the sleigh bell sound effects prepped for every link."

Penny smirked, rolling her eyes affectionately. "Luke, if I hear 'All I Want for Christmas Is You' one more time, I might shove those sleigh bells where the sun doesn't shine."

Luke laughed, clearly unfazed. "Fair enough. But hey, the listeners love it, and you know we've got to hit those festive vibes hard. Speaking of vibes, Alan's been in a mood all morning—something about Hits Liverpool beating us in the listener polls last week. Just a heads-up."

Penny groaned, rubbing her temples. "Brilliant. Nothing like management breathing down your neck to really get you in the Christmas spirit."

Studio 2 was already prepped for the show, with a festive backdrop plastered across the social media cameras and an overly enthusiastic automated sweeper declaring, "Manic Christmas—where the madness meets the magic!" Penny settled into her chair, slipping on her headphones as Luke ran through the schedule.

"Alright," Luke said, his tone professional despite the chaos around him. "An hour until kick-off, so if you want to grab a quick coffee or prep anything, now's the time. But don't take too long—I've got Santa lined up to call in at 1:15, and we can't keep the big man waiting."

Penny laughed, shaking her head. "Santa, eh? I'll try not to let him down. Just make sure the sleigh bells aren't overkill, alright?"

Luke winked. "Overkill is the Manic way, Lane. You should know that by now."

As she grabbed a coffee from the break room, Penny's thoughts drifted back to the test. The knowledge that she was pregnant was settling in, but the uncertainty of the father's identity gnawed at her. Weston's silence wasn't helping, and she had no idea how Danny, Kyle, or even Jimmy Reeves would react if it turned out to be one of them.

The chaos of the Speke hub buzzed around her, an odd comfort amidst the uncertainty. She knew she couldn't let this consume her—not today, not during a double shift. The listeners needed their Christmas cheer, and if anyone could balance impending motherhood with CHR madness, it was Penny Lane.

Looking at the clock, Penny noticed it was only quarter past 12, and that she had three quarters of an hour before she had to be live on air for Manic Christmas. The thought of navigating the festive chaos of her show while grappling with the knowledge of her pregnancy felt surreal, but she pushed it to the back of her mind. The audience didn't tune in for uncertainty—they tuned in for the unfiltered energy and irreverence that defined her presence on the airwaves.

Penny's phone buzzed with a text, snapping her out of her thoughts. She glanced down and saw it was from Rory

Carter, her usual co-host on Manic Liverpool Drivetime, who was back on the show with her now Toni Green's suspension had been lifted, even though OFCOM had yet to report on the incident.

**Rory Carter**: *Oi, Lane, I've just been told by Abby that she's given birth to a baby girl, 8 lb 3 oz, and guess who the daddy is? It's me! Baby number 4 of mine with the Manic crew!*

Penny's jaw dropped as she read Rory's text, her mind reeling at the revelation. Rory, the father of four Manic offspring? It was almost too on-brand for the chaos of Manic Radio. She quickly typed back, her fingers flying across the screen.

**Penny Lane**: *Bloody hell, Rory! Congratulations... I think? You've got your own Manic mini-network going on now. What's the little one's name? And don't tell me you're planning to call her Mariah after hearing her song 500 times this week.*

Rory replied almost instantly, his tone as cheeky as ever.

**Rory Carter**: *Cheers, Lane! Her name's Holly—festive but classy. And nah, Mariah's not happening unless I want Abby to kill me. Anyway, I'm going on paternity, so I won't be back until after Christmas.*

Penny smirked at Rory's reply, shaking her head at the sheer absurdity of the Manic Radio family dynamic.

**Penny Lane**: *Holly's perfect—festive without the karaoke nightmares. Congrats again, mate. You're single-handedly building Manic's future audience. Enjoy the* *paternity leave—although knowing you, you'll probably pop up on air from the nursery.*

**Rory**: *You know it! Don't let Luke throw you off too much—he's got that newbie energy. And try not to scare Santa away today. Merry chaos, Lane!*

Penny pocketed her phone, feeling a flicker of lightness amidst the swirling uncertainties. Rory's news was a reminder that, amidst the madness of Manic, life found a way to keep moving forward, messy and unpredictable as it was.

As the studio clock ticked closer to 1pm, Penny prepped for the show, her headphones snug over her ears as Luke buzzed around the control room. The playlist was stacked with festive hits, and Penny could already feel the sugar-rush energy of Mariah and Bublé about to invade the airwaves.

"Right, Manic Christmas Nation!" Penny declared as the clock hit the hour. "It's Penny Lane here, your naughty elf who's got Santa tied up in... elf and safety protocols, of course! We're here to bring you all the festive tunes, shoutouts, and chaos you could possibly need to get through this chilly December afternoon."

The Manic Christmas sweeper played, its over-the-top jingle bells and whooshes setting the tone for the next few hours. Penny felt the familiar adrenaline kick in as her voice filled the studio. This was her stage, her space, where the madness of her life melted into the vibrant energy of live radio.

"And let's not forget," Penny continued, "we've got Santa himself calling in at 1:15—so if you've got any last-minute Christmas requests or just want to prove you've been nice this year, fire us a WhatsApp, send us a text or a voice note, our digits are 0330 880 3601. Are you stuck at work, bunking off early, or already getting the party started? Hit me up, 0330 880 3601, or find me on socials at @ManicCrimbo, and get set for 100% Christmas tunes, as we start with the most annoying thing in the world at Christmas, it's a 2006 hit for a frog which still haunts us to this day. Yes, it's Crazy Frog's Last Christmas! Sorry, not sorry, Britain, we're live across the UK and Ireland, and on the Manic Prime app, your smart speakers and ad free when you subscribe for the Prime features on the app. Let's get festive and mildly annoyed together!"

Penny had to chuckle as the opening notes of Crazy Frog's Last Christmas blasted through the speakers, earning a groan and a laugh from Luke in the booth. Unlike the CHR side which was timed to the minute and had a centralised playlist, the Manic Christmas station allowed for the hosts to choose the tracks they played, as long as they didn't interfere with the ads, sweepers or sponsored segments. It was one of the rare times Penny felt like she could indulge in her love for throwing curveballs into the mix, and nothing screamed chaotic Christmas more than the infamously divisive Crazy Frog.

As the track played out, Penny adjusted her headphones, scanning the incoming messages. The WhatsApp line was already lighting up with a mix of festive cheer, groans about her song choice, and the occasional cheeky comment.

Luke's voice buzzed through the intercom. "You've officially ruined Christmas for at least ten people, Lane. Congrats! Also, Alan just walked past and gave me the thumbs-up, so I think you're safe—for now."

Penny laughed, her mood lifting as she leaned into the mic for the next link. "Alright, Britain, love it or hate it, Crazy Frog has officially kickstarted our Manic Christmas madness! Let's cleanse our musical palates with a classic. Coming up, it's All I Need is Love from CeeLo

Green featuring the Muppets. Yes, you heard me right—because nothing says festive chaos like a bit of soulful singing from CeeLo and a cameo from Kermit himself. Stick around for the feels, the laughs, and maybe a cheeky shoutout or two."

The transition to the next track gave Penny a moment to breathe, letting the festive vibe wash over her. Luke gave her a thumbs-up through the booth glass, mouthing something about a big incoming listener message. She flicked the studio chat screen open and laughed out loud at a voice note from a listener who had sent in their rendition of Crazy Frog's "ding ding ding" as their office Christmas party warmed up, knowing the show was only getting started.

****

# CHAPTER 22 – Some Shocking Results

## Monday 23rd December 2024

The news had come through - the baby was a boy, and it wasn't Weston's.

Penny sat in the medical room, staring at Dr Megan Taylor, her heart racing and her palms slick with sweat. The news had hit her like a freight train, leaving her reeling.

"It's not Weston's?" Penny asked, her voice barely a whisper. She gripped the edge of the chair, her knuckles white as her mind raced through the implications.

Weston's radio silence had been hard enough, but this revelation added a whole new layer of complexity.

Megan shook her head, her expression calm but sympathetic. "No, Penny. The DNA doesn't match Weston's. We did confirm paternity, though."

Penny's stomach churned as she held her breath, waiting for Megan to say the name. She had joked about the long list of possibilities, but now that the truth was about to be laid bare, it felt like the ground was shifting beneath her feet.

"It's James Smith's," Megan said, her tone measured.

*Reevesy?* Penny thought, her mind racing back to the weekend that he had first joined Manic, back at the start of November and those fleeting moments of chaos at the

Big Weekender. She remembered the whirlwind energy of that night, the electric atmosphere, and James's boyish charm that had made him impossible to ignore. But she hadn't seriously considered him as a possibility—not until now.

Penny blinked, trying to process the news. James Smith, or "Reevesy" as everyone called him, was still fresh on the Manic scene. He was young, still in university, and riding the wave of his sudden popularity with an ease that made her both envious and wary. And now… he was the father of her child.

"James Smith?" Penny repeated, her voice tinged with disbelief. "Are you sure?"

Megan nodded, sliding a printed report across the desk. "Absolutely sure. The DNA matches, Penny. He's the father. You're not the only one of his conquests... one of the Dudley hub girls is. I can't name who it is, for GDPR reasons, but you're not alone in this situation," Megan finished gently. "You do know who his dad is, right?"

Penny blinked, the weight of Megan's words sinking in. Of course, she knew who James's dad was—Pete Smith, the legendary radio presenter who had made a name for himself at Dudley FM before it turned into Midlands Manic when Breeze Media took it over in 2010. It had been announced recently that the veteran presenter would be moving to the new regional Manic Goldies West Midlands from April, when the changes to the Manic network would take place, renaming the stations into key brands. Penny knew her own Manic Radio Liverpool was being rebranded Manic Vibes, the new brand for the CHR stations, but the idea that her baby would be part of a family with such a storied radio legacy felt surreal.

"Well, that's… something," Penny finally said, her voice barely steady. She could feel the storm of emotions swirling inside her—shock, fear, and the faintest hint of relief. At least she had an answer. But the reality of navigating this with James, of all people, was daunting.

*Ping*

Penny looked at her phone to see a WhatsApp from Weston, who had got in contact with her for the first time in nearly a month.

**Weston O'Rourke**: *Hey, Mrs O'Rourke. I've got a flight back to JLA tonight, so I can see you tonight if you're free. Missed you x.*

Penny stared at the message, her emotions a tangled knot. The news about James was still fresh in her mind, but Weston's text reopened old wounds she hadn't had time to properly examine. His radio silence had hurt, and now, with this bombshell about the baby, she didn't know how to respond.

She glanced at Megan, who was watching her carefully.

"Weston just messaged me. Says he's coming back tonight."

Megan gave her a knowing look. "Do you want to tell him about the baby now, or wait until you've spoken to James?"

Penny bit her lip, unsure. "I don't even know where to

start. Weston's been MIA for weeks, and now this? And James… He's practically a kid himself, Megan. How do I even begin to explain this to him?"

Megan leaned forward, her tone firm but kind. "One step at a time, Penny. First, decide who you want to tell and when. You don't have to figure everything out today."

Penny nodded, clutching her phone like it was a lifeline. "Thanks, Megan. I think I need some time to process all this."

Megan smiled. "Take it slow. You're not alone in this, Penny. And remember—if you need someone to talk to, I'm here."

* _ * _ * _ *

Later that evening, after she had finished her single shift, local programming having been suspended over the Christmas period meaning that she was only doing a Manic Christmas show, Penny walked into her flat to see Weston standing there, his face featuring cuts, bruises and a noticeable weariness. He was leaning against the kitchen counter, his arms crossed as though he had been waiting for her.

"Hey, Penny," Weston said softly, his Irish accent carrying a hint of hesitation. His eyes scanned her face, searching for something—maybe an explanation for her silence, or a hint of how she felt about his sudden return. "I know I've been a ghost lately. Things back home have been... complicated."

Penny dropped her bag by the door, her heart racing. Seeing Weston in her flat after weeks of no communication was surreal, and she wasn't sure whether to hug him or demand answers. But the bombshell she'd received earlier loomed large, making it hard to focus on anything else.

"You think?" Penny replied, her voice sharper than she intended. "Complicated doesn't even begin to cover it, Weston. You disappeared without so much as a proper explanation. And now you just show up like nothing happened?"

Weston sighed, running a hand through his messy hair. "I'm sorry, Pen. Really, I am. I've been in a coma for a month, then when I was released from hospital, I got beaten up again by some of Granddad's IRA friends."

Penny froze, Weston's words hanging heavy in the air. *A month in a coma? Beaten up again?* Her initial anger gave way to concern, but the whirlwind of emotions she was already processing made it hard to fully grasp the weight of his confession.

"A coma?" she echoed, her voice softening. "Weston, what… what happened?"

Weston shifted uncomfortably, leaning back against the counter. "It's complicated, Pen. The fallout from my family back in Ballymena has been worse than I ever expected. First my dad's PSNI pals beat me up for digging into Dad's arrest, something about IRA connections. Then Granddad's old mates decided to 'send a message' because I was poking around where they didn't want me.

They left me for dead in an alley. Next thing I know, I'm waking up in hospital a month later, and everything's a bloody mess."

Penny stared at him, the mix of guilt, worry, and frustration bubbling up inside her. "You could have told me, Weston. I could have been there for you."

Weston shook his head. "How? I didn't even know what was happening most of the time. And after I got out, I didn't want to drag you into my family's chaos. You've got your own life here, your own stuff to deal with."

Penny crossed her arms, leaning back against the wall. She wanted to be angry, but the exhaustion in Weston's voice made it hard. Still, the revelation about James burned in the back of her mind, and she didn't know how to bring it up.

"Well, now you're here," Penny said after a moment. "But a lot has happened while you were gone, Weston. And you might want to sit down for this."

Weston raised an eyebrow, his expression shifting from apologetic to cautious. "What's going on, Pen?"

Penny took a deep breath, the words sticking in her throat. She had no idea how to say it, how to explain the situation without it sounding like a soap opera. But this was Manic—chaos was the norm, and she had to own it.

"I'm pregnant," she blurted out, watching as Weston's eyes widened. She knew that he knew about Manic's penchant for having presenters get impregnated by different men, not necessarily their partners that they may be in a relationship with, and so she hoped he'd understand that this situation wasn't as straightforward as it seemed.

Weston blinked, the weight of her words sinking in. "Pregnant," he repeated slowly, his voice barely above a whisper. His gaze darted to her stomach before returning to her face, a mixture of shock and uncertainty flickering in his eyes. "Pen… is it… mine?"

Penny hesitated, the moment stretching into an eternity. "No," she finally said, her voice steady but tinged with regret. "It's not."

Weston chuckled, and then smiled. "Ah, thought so. Doc said when they tested me, I had a low sperm count and might struggle to have kids naturally," Weston finished, his tone laced with a mix of resignation and humour. "So, who's the lucky dad, then? Don't tell me it's Rory—that lad's already got half the Manic staff calling him 'Daddy.'"

Penny couldn't help but laugh, the tension in the room easing slightly. Weston's ability to inject humour into even the most awkward situations was one of the things she admired about him. But the reality of her answer was far from light-hearted.

"It's… well, someone who started at Manic last month. He's based at the Dudley hub, and he does Manic Dance and Manic Rock, and he's dating one of the Dudley hub's breakfast hosts," Penny said, rushing as she saw Weston's expression shift from amused curiosity to cautious understanding.

"It's James Smith," she finished, her voice soft but firm. "Reevesy."

Weston blinked, the name hanging in the air like a balloon waiting to pop. Then, as if the absurdity of the situation hit him all at once, he let out a low whistle and rubbed his face.

"Wow. Is... is his cock big?"

Penny nearly choked at Weston's question, a sharp burst of laughter escaping her before she could stop it. "Weston!" she exclaimed, half-scandalised, half-amused. "That's not exactly the first thing I expected you to say."

Weston shrugged, a cheeky grin spreading across his bruised face. "Well, what do you expect, Pen? We work for Manic. Sex and cocaine are our bread and butter. I may be Irish and Catholic but shagging and doing coke is practically a job requirement at this point," Weston finished with a smirk, his humour a welcome relief from the tension in the room. "Alright, jokes aside. Reevesy, eh? That's a bit of a twist, even for Manic."

Penny couldn't help but smile despite the weight of the situation. Weston's ability to roll with the punches—even punches this unexpected—was part of what had drawn her to him in the first place. But she knew this wasn't a situation she could laugh her way out of entirely.

"Yeah, Reevesy," Penny said, running a hand through her hair. "And apparently, I'm not the only one. Megan said there's someone else at Dudley he's in the same situation with."

Weston raised an eyebrow, his grin fading slightly as he processed this. "Wow. Kid's been busy, hasn't he? You gonna tell him?"

Penny sighed, leaning against the counter. "I have to. He's the father, Weston. He deserves to know. But… he's so young. I don't even know how he'll handle it. He's barely out of uni, and now he's about to have a kid with me."

Weston nodded, his expression thoughtful. "True, but you know what, Pen? It's made my mind up… I can't wait for our wedding day. I mean, shagging you while someone's already impregnated you… it's kind of a kink. I can't wait to fuck your pregnant belly and make you feel special every step of the way." Weston's cheeky grin returned, but there was a flicker of sincerity behind his words that made Penny's chest tighten. His ability to navigate the chaos of their lives with humour and acceptance was a comfort she hadn't realised she needed.

Penny rolled her eyes, playfully shoving his arm. "You're impossible, you know that? But… thanks, Weston. For not freaking out. For just… being here."

Weston smiled, his expression softening as he reached for her hand. "Pen, we've both got messy lives. If there's one thing I've learned from everything that's happened back home, it's that we can either let the chaos drown us or we can ride the wave and make it work. And if Reevesy's part of this, then so be it. We'll figure it out."

Penny nodded, a small smile tugging at her lips. "Yeah. One step at a time, right?"

Weston squeezed her hand. "Exactly. And hey, who knows? Maybe little Reevesy Jr. will grow up to be the next big thing in radio. We can call him the 'Manic Mascot.'"

Penny laughed, the tension in her shoulders easing for the first time all day. Weston's presence, his ability to meet the chaos head-on, gave her the strength to face the road ahead. She didn't know how things would play out with James, or with Weston, or even with her career at Manic, but for the first time in weeks, she felt like she wasn't navigating it all alone.

As the evening wore on, they sat together, talking through the whirlwind of events that had brought them to this moment. Weston shared more about his time in Ballymena, the struggles he'd faced and the decisions he'd made to protect her from his family's mess. Penny, in turn, opened up about the chaos of her pregnancy revelation and the unexpected twists her life had taken since joining Manic.

By the time the clock struck midnight, Penny felt a sense of clarity she hadn't felt in weeks. The journey ahead was uncertain, but with Weston by her side, she was ready to face whatever came next. And as she drifted off to sleep that night, a tiny flicker of hope warmed her heart—hope that amidst the chaos, she could find a way to make it all work.

****